THE
**PHOENIX
COURT**
SERIES

"Magrs celebrates the things of this world with a vigilant prose that habitually disciplines the extravagant baroque flourishes of the story's fantasy."

TOM DEVESON IN
THE SUNDAY TIMES

"His is a world where a bus driver can reveal himself to be a great romantic, escaping up the motorway with the solitary passenger of his dreams, where a grimy wood full of old stuffed animals can seem, if only for a moment, to be Narnia. Magrs's characters have the courage to make themselves over to believe that there is still magic in the world. In a place like Phoenix Court, that is no small feat."

ERICA WAGNER IN *THE TIMES*

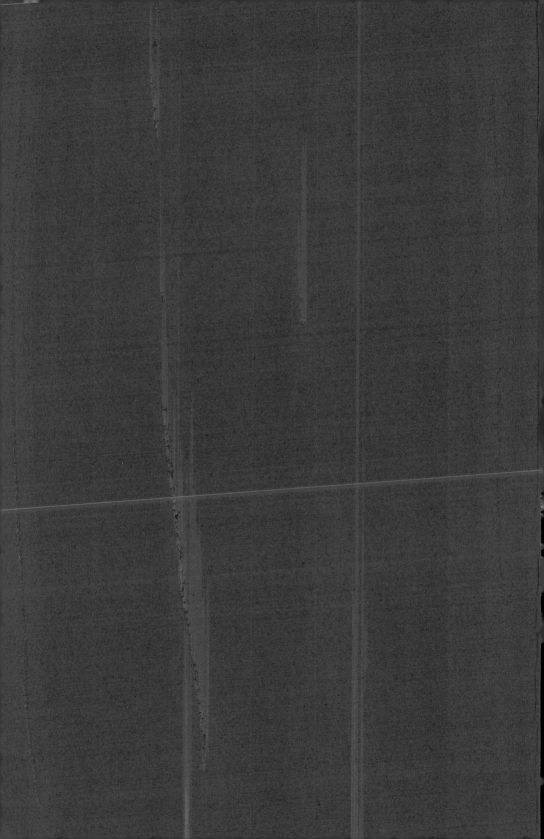

DOES IT SHOW?

PAUL MAGRS

LETHE PRESS

Published by LETHE PRESS
lethepressbooks.com

Originally published by Vintage in 1997

'Nude on the Moon' first published in *Crossing The Border:
Tales of Erotic Ambiguity* (edited by Lisa Tuttle)
'Bargains For Charlotte' first published in *Playing Out*

ISBN: 978-1-59021-648-4

Author photo by
CLAIR MACNAMEE

Cover and interior design
by INKSPIRAL DESIGN

i

Introduction

1

Does It Show?

221

Nude on the Moon

241

Bargains for Charlotte

INTRODUCTION

I BEGAN WRITING THIS NOVEL IN THE SUMMER OF 1991, WHEN I WAS preparing to return to college to start my MA in Creative Writing. It's quite common for people to do those courses now, but not so much back then. I could hardly believe that such a thing was allowed: that I could get a bursary to spend a further year at university, writing my novel.

That summer I was back at our family's house in Newton Aycliffe, on an estate where everything was built of black brick and which I call, in these early books, Phoenix Court. I hadn't been back for a while and that summer it was good to absorb the sights and sounds of the place again.

There was hardly any room in that house. Certainly not to work and write. I ended up more often than not perching on the back doorstep, reading library books and watching the world go by.

Our house in Guthrum Place was by the main road connecting all the estates. You could watch the minibuses running up down, doing circuits of all the streets and ferrying everyone to the town precinct and back. The precinct looked like *Logan's Run* or *Conquest of the Planet of the Apes*, but with pensioners in anoraks, pulling shopping trolleys.

I watched all our neighbours and the way they went from one house to the another. The women would drink tea in each other's kitchens and when the sun came out they would drag their chairs into their front yards and sit smoking and gossiping, their voices drifting over the dark, creosoted fences.

All the kids in our street were little that year. My sister was four and playing out with a whole gang of small kids who would go haring around, holding hands, in the wind and rain and some gloriously hot days.

There was so much going on to keep up with. There was the mother and daughter who were dragged out of their house by the police in the middle of the night, and everyone hurried outside to watch. It was well-known they were running a kind of brothel in their two-up two-down. Then there was talk of someone being held hostage. And there was the gang of rough lads across the main road in the Yellow Houses, who set their pit bull terrier onto the old man who lived next door to them. It was supposed to be a joke, but he fell down dead of shock on the hottest day in August. Everyone was out watching this happen: I remember the dog barking and the appalled silence.

I kept taking notes all summer. I kept writing down the dialogue. I was keeping tabs on everything, just as I always had, since I was a kid.

Gradually I formed a story to do with a woman who once lived in these streets in the Seventies and who was moving back in the Nineties, having reinvented herself out of all recognition. She had a daughter who was starting at the local Comprehensive School. Both women find themselves drawn into new friendships and relationships and the book would be all about huge human emotions and life-changing moments being played out on a seemingly tiny scale. It was going to be a Magical Realist epic on a council estate in the North-East. A phantasmagorical opera set in the midst of concrete brutalism.

Lancaster University was similarly concretized and minimalist. Soon I was back among its dreaming spires of poured cement. I had intended to use my MA year writing a gay bildungsroman, telling the tale of my childhood, my parents' divorce, my artistic and sexual awakening and all that jazz. Then the course began and I found I was writing about Phoenix Court.

The workshop group was composed mostly of well-to-do lady poets in their forties, returning to education. Some were friendly, some were not. It was all very middle class and polite, with the snarkiness dialed down for the few hours we spent in class each week, then unleashed full force in the vegetarian cafes and coffee bars where we wasted our afternoons. Again, I was agog – watching how all these characters behaved.

For my first submission to this class in the autumn of 1991 I found myself handing in a chapter about Fran and Frank on a hot summer's day in their yard. I loved the dialogue, that's why I chose to show it to the workshop, rather than writing a chapter of that Queer Autobiography I'd been planning. It made me laugh. It made some of them laugh, too. Others, though, were mystified.

One of the poets said, 'Forgive me, but can we really call this literary fiction? And isn't literary fiction what this course is about? I don't know what you would call this, actually. These are hardly the kind of characters one would expect to find in a literary novel.'

Someone shot back with an example or two of working class characters in literary fiction. They mentioned Faulkner. 'But that's in America. That's different.'

"And besides... this is much too like a... soap opera, isn't it? People talking like this in the North?"

"It's just fiction," I kept saying, all that term. "I don't believe in genres. There are two types of fiction. There's the good type, that you want to read and there's the bad type, that you don't want to read. There are books that are crap and sound bogus. And there are books that ring true. Books that are about something. Books where the voices are alive."

Maybe I didn't put it as concisely as that at the time. But that's the position I was trying to articulate, all that year, as I wrote my way into the story. Mostly I just kept quiet and smiled at their comments and wrote my weekly chapter.

As later submissions went in and were photocopied and disseminated I gave them episodes of gay sex and tales of Goths and taxidermists and pensioners finding love late in life. I delighted in mixing and stirring up my characters and having their stories overlap as the weeks went by. I loved revealing the secret of the novel's 'star', Liz. The class was shocked by the big reveal. They were disgusted. Some of them refused to believe it.

I tossed in surreal moments of Magical Realism. I let my narrator wander between points of view, moving stealthily from house to house, all over Phoenix Court.

"It's a kind of Magical Realist Queer Working Class Heterotopia," I told them. "Not a Soap Opera."

For me, it was about how people can live on a grand scale, even in reduced circumstances. A woman can be a queen in her own council house and in the midst of her own community. And so can a man.

Anyone in the books I write is capable of finding love, and sometimes they find that the things they're really looking for are quite surprising.

I was working all this out when I was twenty-two and doing my MA. And twenty-four years later I look back and see that I was learning to be my own kind of novelist. I was discovering that dark comedy was my thing. Also, that ensemble casts were my thing. I was finding that I love lots of dialogue and for description to be pared back, and I love flicking swiftly from scene to scene, moving as swiftly as TV movies do. I enjoy swimming from mind to mind and getting my readers to eavesdrop on fascinating characters as we witness them at their very best and their very worst moments.

My basic thesis was – and still is – that everyone has a fascinating life, whoever they are. It just depends on how much of it we are allowed to see, and how much they are willing to let it show.

Paul Magrs
Manchester
April 2017

DOES IT
SHOW?

PROLOGUE

PENNY HAD ALWAYS BEEN A BRIGHT KID. SHE WAS BORN ON THE NINTH anniversary of the first moon landing. Her father wrenched her from the incubator and ran to the steps outside, by the car park. It was a warm summer's night.

He held her out to the moon, swaddling clothes draped down to his elbows. "You're going there, Penny," he said, face shining. "You're going to the moon, you are."

And as the nurses came bustling through Reception to retrieve her, Penny glanced up at the moon, then witheringly at her father.

"Fat chance," she said. "I know where I'm going."

ONE

YOU'RE TOO GOOD TO BE TRUE, SHE THOUGHT.

He winked at her in the rear-view mirror again.

Jane smiled back. Oh, Christ! It can't be happening to me. Not on a bus. Not on a Road Ranger.

I think I've been reading too many of those books, she thought, straightening her skirt. Those £4.99 romances with the gold foil titles. They were to blame for this. All that passion in the past.

She could read a whole book in a night. Jane read fast. Now that Peter had his regular seven-o'clock bedtime, he could put her feet up with a cup of tea after *Coronation Street* and read straight through to the early hours. She couldn't sleep. She was becoming a romantic.

Into the slightest, shiftiest smile from a bus driver's mirror she could read an entire, torrid romance. It was a good job she'd finished with Jackie Collins. Because the sexy bits in books like those got her going.

Not, she grimaced, that there was anywhere for her to go.

Reading the sexy bits nowadays was like putting warm water into an old vase. Swirl it around to get the bits of dried mould out. It's still an old vase. And she squirmed at the memory of her husband. He revolted her in retrospect. Words on the page would fade back to being just that: a routine set of instructions, a black and white description of what someone else once got up to.

Those moments at night took her to the bedroom window to watch all the houses. The squat cubes, mustard under the sulphur lights; a cool silence with the occasional insomniac car passing by making the sound of ripping silk. Jane watched and protected the estate from fire, burglary, disaster. Until dawn came, touching the upturned faces of satellite dishes. If she kept still, the morning calm would draw the warmth out of her. Until last night's romance drained out of her memory.

"Had a nice day?"

The bus driver's half-reflection was looking at her. She took him in. Part of a head of soft dark hair. Smiling as if he really wanted to be talking to her. She was the only passenger. His question sounded too familiar for public transport. Jane was more used to the mute conversations held with her own hollowed-out face in the window.

At first she was content to let the question sink in, then stirred herself to answer. Over the sewing machine rattle of the engine she said, 'Not really. I went to the car-boot sale over at the Equestrian Centre. Six cars and a couple of wallpapering tables. Not many bargains.'

He nodded and grinned. She wondered if he thought she sounded cynical. Surely she never came across as hard like some the women round here? He must get them all coming on his bus, sitting in their ski pants and anoraks.

Jane concentrated on the real him, the back towards her, steering the vehicle. Did it cost him any effort, guiding this snub-nosed minibus through the estates. She didn't think so. He seemed ever so relaxed. They should keep the older drivers, the sour old men with their Woodbines and Brylcreem, for these endless roundabout runs. Surely her young driver, arm lolling easily out of his window, felt too confined here? Wouldn't he prefer the more taxing stretches? Up the scalding motorways in an Express Coach, to Newcastle or Middlesbrough on a limited stop.

"Are you working all day?"

She thought she better ask him one back, to show interest and keep the conversation running smoothly through the plotted terraces and crescents.

"I finish at half past two." He reached to rub the back of his neck. "Then I'm done for the day. After that I'll be out sitting in the sun."

"Lovely. It's a lovely day."

He could get out of that uniform. It must be stuffy on a day like this, all that nylon. A day when the colours were vivid: the houses orange, the newly planted trees a squeaky-clean green.

Driving must pay well, she thought, and he'd have a large garden at the posh end of town, sloping down to the building site beyond his fence. He'd be lying on a blanket on a freshly laid lawn. He'd lock that uniform away as though it was a snarling beast, to be held at bay till Monday. And his body would be lean and tanned, bristling with the dark, oily hair he was scratching now at the back of his neck. Lying senseless, sun-soaked in white shorts, no longer at the service of the public.

He was too good to be true. Friendly to all and sundry. There was a meaty, solid look about him. The reddish tan set off a white grin he would flash at anyone. But Jane was sure he never smiled at the other women the way he smiled at her.

This morning she had seen him leave his post to run after some woman who'd left her shopping on his back seat. He left the bus unattended to catch up with her. Climbing back aboard, he had caught Jane's glance. He smiled as if they both knew a secret. Her secret had been that she was watching his too-tight transport-issue trousers.

She wanted to kick the double seat in front in frustration. Even then he'd only look at her with a baffled smile.

She wanted to tell him to keep driving, to go right past her home stop. Take her miles and miles around the winding estates, no matter how mundane the journey, no matter how well routed. She wanted him to drive her to his garden, sit her on his lawn and ply her with soft drinks, wearing his white shorts.

"You'll think I'm mad," she said. "Because I've been on your bus four times today."

She watched his reflection. "It's the only way to travel in a town like this, isn't it?" he said. "And a day like today, well, it's too hot to walk."

He was right. It was an Indian summer.

A breeze whistled under the hydraulic doors, cooling her. Her damp palms were dirtying the paper bag around her newest paperback.

FRAN SAT DOWN ON THE KITCHEN DOORSTEP. SHE GAVE FRANK A WAN smile.

He was stripped to the waist in the back yard, teasing the kids in the paddling pool. They were screaming and floundering around under the slender ribbons of tap water from the hose pipe he trained on them. They were glad of an afternoon with their father in a playful mood. It was almost a shock to them to see him like this. Only yesterday he'd had one of his off days. He hadn't gone to work in the converted garage over the road, he couldn't face it; instead he sat in their darkened living room until bedtime. All day he had stared murderously at the kids' gerbils. The kids had kept right out of his way.

Jane's little Peter was there too, clambering up the side of the plastic pool to fling himself back into the soap-frothed water. Fran was surprised he wasn't missing his mum. She never thought Jane would leave him, even for an afternoon. Peter was growing up alone under her fierce protection and it wasn't often she let him out of her sight. She'd be back from the car-bootie soon, though, and Fran just knew she wouldn't take Peter straight home. As usual Fran would have to entertain the pair of them.

She hated asking Jane if she would have another cup of tea, knowing Jane would pretend to think about it and reply, 'Go on then.' As if she was doing Fran a favour. That riled Fran, but she would smile as the water drummed heavily in the kettle.

Jane was off looking for the Real Ghostbusters toys for Peter's Christmas. Fancy planning Christmas in September! Jane said she was almost ready for it; she could wait to get her turkey. Fran didn't dare think about Christmas yet, aside from getting the cleaning job at Fujitsu, five till ten of an evening, for a bit extra. She needed it, with the four kids and Frank. Jane only had Peter to think about.

She had so little else to consider, she had managed to learn everything there was to know about the Real Ghostbusters. She knew exactly what her son needed to complete his set. Today she was on the hunt for a plastic toilet that filled up with ectoplasm, but she wasn't sure she would find one. Fran had no idea what her kids' fads were. They seemed to change so much. The last she remembered was East 17 and Take That. Were they still trendy? Compared with Fran's kids Peter was a slow, resolute child, at least when he was with Jane.

"Dad!" Kerry was Fran's eldest, nearly ten and looking clumsy in her bathing costume. She submitted to this afternoon in the garden as a kind of ritual humiliation. But Fran could also see that Kerry was playing outside because she was pleased her dad was back to normal. "You'll have someone's eye out with that hose. Calm down, Dad!"

Laughing, Frank turned up the force. The jet thrashed the water into foam. The younger kids straggled, waving their arms, to the buckling sides.

"Frank!" Fran warned from the doorstep. He glanced down, readjusted the nozzle and looked suitably chastened.

At least he wasn't drunk. Fran just wished he would put a shirt on. He must be feeling happier about the situation at work. Most blokes would be happy, she thought, being self-employed, working just across the road from home. "What's the matter with you?" she'd asked more than once. "You're your own boss." Yet he reckoned that self-employment wasn't all it was cracked up to be. He didn't like the responsibility. At the moment he reckoned there was a terrible atmosphere between him and his apprentice, Gary. "I'm responsible for that little bastard and I really just want to deck him." Fran thought he took it too much to heart. She couldn't imagine her husband being anybody's boss, though. Somehow she never fancied going over the road to where he worked to check it out.

She was seven years older than Frank. He was twenty-four when they married and hardly drank at all. Their wedding reception was held in Fran's mother's front parlour, where Frank was told he was bringing Fran down in the world. "But she loves me," he protested. Fran's mother sneered. He was drinking Babycham at his own wedding and he had a whiny, womanish voice. He went on, "So there's nothing you can do about it."

He turned to play the one-armed bandit Fran's family kept in the parlour, at the end of the white leather bar. These were both from the dump. Fran's family had made a little money in 'antiques.' When he was plastered Frank would rail that what that really meant was that they were hawkers.

They toured the town dumps and flogged whatever they could find and clean up. Fran's mother could have her bandit, her bar, her archways and extensions all installed because she owned her own house and didn't need to ask the council for permission. She owned her own house because once, when her two sons were hauling a battered wardrobe across the council tip in Ferryhill, they pushed it too hard down a slope into a rusted truck. The wardrobe smashed and a hundred thousand concealed pound notes flew into the grey wind. The brothers ran about clutching them all from the air. They hushed it up and bought their own home. Frank had got to hear about it and sneered. "She's as common as shit, like the rest of us, your mother," he would tell Fran. "She got her money off a tip."

Fran kept quiet. There was no point bringing class into it.

Her mother still despised Frank. Right at the start she had said, "He's a little ginger bloke! How can you go knocking about with a little ginger bloke?" Fran's two brothers were strapping lads. They kept fit hauling rubbish off tips and working with horses. They laughed at Frank too.

"Taking you to live in a council house!" her mother spat, into a dry Martini. "And your family keeps horses!"

They never let him forget the horses. On their two most gleaming mounts Fran's two strapping brothers would pass by the council house. Just to piss Frank off. And it worked. It always reminded him that he was a mere upholsterer, stuffing settees for other people's fat arses, working in a converted garage, sharing his job with an apprentice.

"But they're not your real aristocracy, your lot," Frank would rail. "They aren't proper horsy people."

Fran said nothing. It was true. Her mother and her brothers simply liked horses and knew how to make money from them on the broad swathes of countryside all around Aycliffe and Ferryhill.

Now in her forties, Fran was becoming fleshy and thickset. I'm looking like a farmer's wife, she thought. She wore hard-wearing clothes picked up in charity shops. She would scrub tweedy skirts in the tub until her hands were red raw. Her hair was cut neatly and scraped back off her face for the day's work.

Frank was slipping into a life of slipshod workmanship and frothy canned beer. Fran saw desolate years opening up. As a result she became more brutally functional, more busy. Her lack of reproach was the greatest reproach of all. This was the heaviest weight upon Frank.

But look at him, she thought. Dousing the kids like that. He really is a little ginger bloke, with his paunch riding over his jeans like a water-filled balloon. His freckled body with wisps of red hair was wobbling as he hopped around the garden. He was red with the exertion, except for the dead-white parts of his face. They were hardened into premature old age, probably by his drinking. She hoped it was only by his drinking.

Last Christmas Eve he had terrified them all and killed the first batch of gerbils. She got a solicitor to write to Frank – she had a letter delivered to her own door – threatening him. Her brothers had offered to do him over. But Fran wanted to deal with him in her own way. She got the solicitor to say he would have to leave the house. He begged to be taken back.

In among the work, the ongoing work, the shouting down the street after kids, the hands-and-knees work at the factory, Fran had taken up drinking as well. She would match him can for can. She decided she'd share the bleary world view he imposed on the rest of them. He'd get only half as much beer and she would at least be sharing the madness. It seemed easier somehow.

"Honestly, Fran, you're a madwoman. How did your mother produce you?"

"Like a horse," she would say. "Squeezed me out, licked me and sent me out into the world. I'm an old grey mare."

He laughed. "Am I a stallion?"

"No, but you're My Little Pony."

And his face would fall. Unlike Fran, Frank had some difficulty accepting his lot in life. But he never had the energy to seek another, especially not by hawking around the tips.

A whiplash of water went over the creosoted fence. Their youngest, Jeff, was only eighteen months, but he had mastered the art of climbing that fence. He was a tiny duplicate of his father. The incoherent bullying was endearing in a child. He was growling as his father tried to worry him from his perch with the hose. Jeff wasn't having any of it. Without a backward glance he cocked one sausage-meat leg over the top. Frank soaked an old woman on the path at the other side. She was trundling along with her shopping trolley and hardly seemed to notice the wet in her heavy coat.

"Frank!" Fran yelled when she saw the old woman take the corner, very slowly, dripping miserably. The woman shook her head at Fran, not wanting to make trouble. She even gave her a slightly pitying smile.

Everyone knows my business, thought Fran. Everyone feels sorry for me with the four kids and Frank. But everyone feels sorrier for Jane, with one kid and no husband. Both facts riled her and she clenched her teeth, cradling her can.

To think, she wondered, I nearly had my own horse once.

Fran watched Jane step off the bus. It's funny, but I'm sure she's waving at the driver, she thought. To Peter she said, "Your mam's back."

Peter was studying the crazy reflections of his own face. They hopped like something bright on a computer. He looked up. "Does that mean I have to go home?"

Fran doubted it. When asked in for tea, Jane would reply, "Go on then."

"I bet that woman never bothers buying tea bags," Frank would tell Fran. Fran never replied. Frank had no right complaining about what other people drank. Jane had no manners, though. She was immune to hinting. Once Fran had told her she was going up for an afternoon nap and Jane had sat waiting downstairs.

Frank had noticed Jane walking from the main road to their gate. A smile of greeting played uncertainly on her face. He sloshed the water, aiming at her.

"Watch out!" Fran called, standing up. "He's waving his hose pipe at you!"

The younger woman passed through the gate and glanced at him.

"Must be my lucky day. But why's it turned green?"

Fran said loudly, "Lack of use!" They cackled, and Frank went back to fill the ever-emptying pool, gritting his teeth.

"Careful, it'll drop off," Jane said. Frank turned up the pressure. Peter ran to his mam. "Has he been any bother?" she asked.

Fran watched the boy grip his mother's wrist. She'll have him soft. She kept promising him a new dad. What was he going to grow up like?

Fran shook her head. "He's had a good play. Haven't you, pet?"

Dumbly Peter nodded. Back with his mam, he had switched his allegiance with that quick cunning of children. His eyes seemed to be asking Fran, Who are you anyway?

"We brought the pool out for them," Fran explained, "because that bitch over there – that Kelly-Anne – said they couldn't play on the grass by her window."

Jane turned. She knew all about that-bitch-over-there. Kelly-Anne and her husband lived right next door to Jane. He was Frank's apprentice and he went parading around in army pants thinking he was great because he was a part-time upholsterer. They were both under twenty-one and had been kicked out of their flat on the next estate for causing rows with the neighbours. They seemed to be doing their best to be getting kicked out of here, too.

"They look like weasels," Jane had said. "Both of them."

Fran didn't like saying anything nasty about people, she just nodded. She thought Jane was probably jealous of them really, a young couple who had stayed together.

Even Fran had had enough of the young couple, though. The young husband would come running out of his kitchen to yell at the kids, telling them to fuck off home if they got too close to his window. They would wake the baby up, he yelled at the street. But the baby screamed all the time anyway.

Fran thought Frank should deal with Gary, since he was his apprentice. One Saturday afternoon a befuddled Frank had been shoved outside to get on with it. Fran assumed they would have a rapport and would sort out the friction like gentlemen. But Gary started on Frank. He screamed at the man who was supposed to be training him. Frank kept an eye on the less-than-safe grip Gary had on his pit-bull terrier.

Jane said, "Remember how he yelled at Frank?"

"There's something creepy about that Gary," Fran said. "Frank reckons that he still won't talk to him at work. Not since that row on the street."

Jane went, "Oh," thinking that she wouldn't find much to say to Frank either, if they worked together, God forbid.

"He was like an animal." Jane sniffed and poured more tea. She enjoyed watching a good barney, though. That time she sent Peter indoors and stood by her gate, waiting for Frank and Gary to go for it.

"Don't threaten me," snarled the young husband. "I used to box for the army, y'naa."

Frank was bleary and shirtless. "Yeah? And I sleep with an axe under the bed."

Only recently another fight had begun when Fran was phoning her mam from the payphone outside Kelly-Anne and Gary's house. She was just describing a fellow cleaner at Fujitsu as a 'silly cow' and next thing she knew, Kelly-Ann – who'd been listening out of her kitchen window – came running out of her yard, squawking her head off. Fran was forced to hang up. The young wife had yards and yards of bright-red hair she couldn't do a thing with. ("*She* needs upholstering," Jane had remarked.) From where they were having a tea break outside the converted garage, Frank and Gary came running to see their wives at it hammer and tongs. Frank was hopeless but Gary leaped right into the fray.

Kelly-Anne's hair flamed silently as the young husband bellowed, 'Are you calling my fucking wife an ignorant cow?' His hands scratched privates in his army fatigues.

It was like most rows in Phoenix Court. Everyone shouting threats and abuse and then running off home to call the police on to everyone else.

"Oh, so she's at it again," said Jane mildly, staring at the pool.

"She's a silly girl." Fran sighed. "If she'd thought on, she could have had loads of help with the kiddie from some of the women round here. Hand-me-downs and that." Most of Fran's had been handed down to Jane's Peter, though, and Jane never gave anything away.

"She doesn't think, though."

"It's because he's not working full time. They get cooped up in that house. And he's got an army temperament." Fran gestured to the house next door to the young couple's. "Sheila and Simon are asking for a transfer. They can't stand it. And they've lived here almost as long as I have. They moved in the week crippled Mrs Wright in the bungalow got busted for vice. It isn't right they should have to move because of the likes of Gary and Kelly-Anne."

"Sheila and Simon will never get a transfer," Jane said. "Their house stinks inside. Cat piss and all-sorts. The council do an inspection, you know. You have to be clean. They look into everything."

"Oh, don't say it like that."

"But it does stink. Remember that party they had for Ian."

Fran's heart had gone out to Sheila at that party. Sheila and Simon had less than anyone on the Court and the buffet hadn't been up to much. She'd made up little sandwiches cut into diamond shapes, bread and marge sprinkled with pink and yellow hundreds and thousands. All the kids loved them and they vanished. Peter cried because Jane pulled him aside and said he wasn't to put anything off Sheila's table into his mouth.

Fran said, "Sheila reckons their little Ian is too scared to even play in the yard in case the army man sets his pit-pull on him."

"The army man!" Jane laughed. "He could only have been in for a year. What's that – basic training? But he wears those green pants like they were going out of fashion. I've got some news about the army man."

She bustled Fran into her own kitchen. Fran knew what sort of news Jane liked. She eased the kitchen door shut behind them so the kids wouldn't hear. Jane sat herself at the pine table and Fran asked, "Do you want some tea?"

"Go on then," she said complacently, as if she wasn't really brimming to tell her tale at all.

"Did you hear that racket last night?"

Fran blew on her tea. Jane had already gulped half a mugful down. "I heard something in the street," Fran cautiously replied. She had been craning her neck out of the bathroom window at half past one. "You know our house. Can't see a thing from here."

"Well, I was ideally placed," Jane said.

You would be, thought Fran. "Does that woman ever sleep?" Frank asked once. Coming back from the pub of a night he would look up and she would be staring out of her window at him. "Hasn't she got any furniture to sit on?"

"I think I heard that rough Helen over the road, yelling at someone at the top of her lungs."

"She was," Jane said eagerly. She had witnessed the whole thing. "She was out at the bottom of her yard holding a knife."

"I thought she'd seen a burglar."

"So did I, at first." Jane was withholding some delectable trump card. Fran could tell. She braced herself. "So I listened –"

"All I heard was Helen shouting that she had seen him, whoever he was, hiding in the bushes –"

"Bushes?" Jane frowned. "I thought she said 'bus shelter.'"

"Maybe she did. The sound was distorted round our way. But she said she had seen him every night for a week."

Jane scalded her throat, drinking too fast and laughing. "For a week!" she exploded and had to put her mug down.

Fran became impatient. "Was it a burglar, then?"

Jane composed herself. She struggled to meet the momentousness she felt the telling of the tale deserved. "Did you hear Helen shouting, 'I can see you hiding there, you effing wanker! And I'm not leaving the bottom of my yard till you piss off home – else I'm calling the coppers!'"

Fran nodded. "Yes, I heard all that."

"Well, I've got reason to believe that poor old Helen really meant what she said –"

"What?" Fran was lost.

"So he knew he'd been caught, because Helen shouted, 'Don't pretend it's not you, 'cause I can see you, with the dog,' and then he must have sloped off because Helen went back in. But then, from my window on the other side, guess who I see sneaking into his house at quarter to two in the morning?" She sipped her tea. "It was the army man himself, Gary!"

"He was the burglar?" Fran gasped.

Jane banged her palms on the imitation pine. "No – not a burglar! A wanker! Helen really meant a wanker! She caught him with his pants down in the bus shelter by my house, relieving himself...sexually, I mean. The dirty bugger."

Fran's forehead knitted up. The lower half of her face unravelled completely. "No!"

"I talked to rough Helen this morning. I went past there especially, going to the shop with Peter. I had to ask."

"And you're sure it was him with the dog?"

"It had to be, that time of night, didn't it?'"

"God!" Fran stirred her tea. "I'll use the other bus stop from now on."

"When I got off the bus just now I had a quick look at it." Jane shrugged. "I don't know what I was looking for."

"He can't be very...well...happy at home, can he?" said Fran thoughtfully. "And all the kids round here! He must be a right queer bugger. You hear about it, don't you? But when it's right on your own bus stop..."

"I want to know what he was doing with his dog."

They burst out laughing, although Fran didn't think it was a very nice thing to be laughing at. Frank came in to dry his hands on the tea towel. He took a can from the fridge and Fran groaned. Starting already at a quarter to three. She saw a bad night coming.

"Guess what," she said. "Jane's been telling me about that Gary, over there. Your workmate."

"Don't talk to me about him. He can't stuff a cushion to save his life." But these days Frank seemed edgy whenever Gary was mentioned.

Jane was mouthing at Jane: Don't tell him about it. She would be embarrassed having to explain the wanking stuff to Frank.

Fran smirked. "Someone saw him in the bus shelter last night, caught with his pants down and playing with himself."

"Oh?" He opened his can over the sink, catching his finger in the ring-pull. Beer gurgled over the draining board and he struggled to stop it. Cursing, Fran got up to help and he watched her try to save his drink. Frank rubbed the bruised knuckle on his sun-reddened belly. All the fuss diverted him from thinking about Gary.

Changing the subject, Jane said, "I got chatted up by that nice bus driver."

Mopping up, Fran turned. "The one with the jet-black hair?"

"Mm. He kept grinning and asking about my day."

"He's lovely."

"I know."

Minutes earlier Jane had been welling up with the excitement. Now it came to describing her experience she had run out of things to say. She put this down to Frank's presence, nursing his wounded can of beer.

Both he and Fran were looking at her expectantly. She listened to the shrill cries from the paddling pool. There wasn't much else to say. 'A really lovely bloke.' The juicy details suddenly eluded her, like the water running off Peter's bare limbs as he staggered into the darkened kitchen.

"Mam, I need a wee."

"At this rate," Fran said, "you'll soon get him a new dad. Getting chatted up on buses."

Jane picked up the clinging child. "I'd better stick to the bus stops. There's more action there."

"Ah, well," Frank gurgled and, with one of his flashes of coherence, said, "What you miss on the buses you pick up on the stops."

"No thanks," Jane said frostily. Just as she had when Frank had offered her a lend of his dirty videos, if she was feeling frustrated. Jane didn't mind a joke with Fran, but not him.

She said her goodbyes and went. Early today, thought Fran. It was only four.

Jane arrived home wondering where on earth she would find a Real Ghostbusters toilet with ectoplasm.

At least Christmas was still a way off. These were the dog days of summer. There was still time to look. But that very night the weather changed. Jane watched it from her window. Dawn drew up dreary and wet. It was autumn, right in time for the kids going back to school.

TWO

NOWADAYS PETER WAS WELL-BEHAVED. THERE WAS NEVER ANY TROUBLE when she took him to playschool. Jane had cured him of his tantrums and tears just in time for the start of the autumn term. As she said goodbye this morning, at the doorway of the wooden community shack, he just took a deep breath and turned away, hoping to find someone to play with.

She did worry about hitting him, sometimes. She spoke to her mam about it, to see what she thought. It was hard. Perhaps Peter's dad would have known how to control him. Perhaps a man's influence about the place would have lessened the load. She didn't know.

Her mam hadn't been very helpful. "Men can't discipline children. They get it all wrong. Your father was hopeless too. No, it's all left up to us, Jane."

As a rule Jane's mam, Rose, didn't hold with men. Yet in recent years a string of variously debilitated lovers had passed through her life on crutches, in slings, eye patches and wheelchairs. She called them her 'charity work.' "'hat I'm really looking for," Rose would say, "'s a dwarf. A really little man would be just smashing."

"You've had a dwarf,' Jane would snap. 'Mr Flowers was a dwarf."

"Not small enough. I mean a really little man. About six inches tall, that I can carry around in my handbag."

And Jane would look worriedly at her mother. Her mother would be doing the ironing, in thoughtful, heavy strokes. Rose took ironing in from people who were too busy to do it themselves. Jane wondered if her customers would be so keen, if they saw Rose spitting on her iron, smearing it steamily into cloth. That morning, though, Jane was perched at the breakfast bar, fretting about Peter.

"Sometimes he's lucky he's not dead."

Rose continued ironing. She managed to look glamorous doing even that. A photo of her stooped seductively over the board had appeared in the local paper. She had taken out an ad and business was booming. The kitchen and downstairs hall were tangled with clean bedding and shirts, bluey whiteness everywhere.

"I have to lock him in his room, just to stop me belting seven shades of shit out of him."

Rose clucked. "I thought you said he was going to playschool nicely now?"

"He is. It's when he's home. Just me and him."

"And you think you're taking things out on him?"

Jane began to say 'yes', then stopped. "Taking what out on him?"

"Your frustrations." Rose raised an eyebrow at her. Jane clinked cup to saucer.

"I don't have any frustrations." She fetched her coat from a pile of sheets. "And I don't need anything else in my life." She was meeting Fran in town and was going to be late. "And neither does Peter. Just sometimes, it gets a bit much. That's all."

"Hm." Her mother hefted a neat pile of shirts. "I've only done one arm on each of these. You've made me lose concentration." Ten crumpled arms hung down the side of the otherwise immaculate set. "By the way, Jane, have I told you about Ethan yet?"

Jane was shuffling through linen to the back door. "Yes, old Ethan with the wooden leg." Jane remembered the whole story. Rose never spared her the grisly details. Some old bloke keeping her mother waiting in bed, ready for him, while he screwed his wooden leg off. Sometimes Jane wished her mam was more of a proper mother.

Rose attacked the wayward shirt arms. "I'll say this much. A wooden leg means bugger all lying down. It's a bit strange getting used to the stump, mind. Anyhow, we're getting married."

"You're what?"

"I said I'd give it a whirl. I've nothing to lose."

Jane agreed numbly and the rest of her mam's news passed her by until she left.

This was where Jane had grown up. It was the old part of town, where the houses were turning grey. They had been built in the fifties, with pebble-dashing coming off in chunks. The gardens were bound in by iron railings, scabbed with rust. The wasteground hemming in their backs was being filled in with private houses, crammed in but nice. They were bright orange, four windows and a door, like a child's drawing, filling up the empty space. Jane thought about living in one. They called them 'starter homes'. Jane had a head start. She thought about ending up in one.

This whole part of town was nicer than Jane's. Nicer than the estates. She felt temporary in the estates. People never seemed to stay long. Her own house had been up fifteen years, she was the fifth family in it. But here, where the trees were named after famous poets of the past, people were growing old. Their heels were well dug in.

Jane mulled over Rose's predicament as she headed the short way to town. She thought of it as a predicament; a mess that Rose was getting herself into. A new engagement was fairly routine for her. Rarely did she follow them through. If she acted according to habit, soon she would be asking Jane's advice for shaking this peg leg off.

Something was disturbing Jane about this one, though. It was the nonchalant way Rose had announced it, just as Jane was leaving. Usually her engagements were a big joke, a bottle of plonk mid-morning. Yet Rose was almost coy about old Ethan. And, as she ironed that morning, in the rumpled whiteness of the kitchen, a large ruby had glinted and winked at Jane from the hand that drove the iron. Well, they would just have to see.

The café was in the arcade. The arcade smelled of many things. Piss on concrete, chlorine from the recreation centre's swishing doors, flower and animal scents from the pet shop.

It was dark in here and boys from the comp on their dinner hour were slouching around by the broken automatic doors. They gave her the usual perusal. And I can fettle the lot of you, she thought, elbowing through.

It was market day and the usual fleet of disabled person's dodgem cars and metal trolleys was moored outside Boots.

When she went in she could hear the pensioners still mourning the loss of their own wooden shack where coffee for OAPs was subsidised. Someone had burned it down. Jane couldn't help seeing the funny side of that heap of blackened chairs and tables outside the ruined shell. Make the old gits pay the same as everyone else. They get the same on a pension that I get for both Peter and me. Some of them have mattresses stuffed with fivers, too.

Fran was at a table near the back. A mock fireplace stuffed with dried flowers and a number of crowded tables separated them. Fran was with another woman Jane didn't recognise. She started to squeeze through, moving with a guarded smile towards them.

IT WASN'T OFTEN FRAN FOUND TIME TO WASTE IN CAFÉS. THIS MORNING she had left Frank in charge. He wasn't going to work. He disappeared beneath the duvet with his favourite upholsterer's joke: "Tell them to stuff it."

"They'll get you one of these days, you lazy thing."

She put the two toddlers on the bed with him, and took Tracey and Kerry to school. Then she was free for coffee and quiche with the girls.

Jane approached the table cautiously, prising a way past the hunched backs in anoraks, glad of the diversion. She decided on a casual air and to wait for Fran to introduce her new friend. It didn't work out that way. A twinge of nervousness took her and she burst out, "Hiya, Fran! Who's this?"

Fran blinked. She moved a strand of dark hair from her eyes. The woman next to her smiled expectantly.

Fran said, "This is Liz. She's just moved in where Mrs Griffiths who died used to live." At the back of Jane. Jane already knew. She had watched from her window all Sunday afternoon, judging the new arrivals by their furniture.

Liz looked as if she might be a bit stuck-up. She was difficult to put an age to. She obviously took care of herself: smart clothes and properly done highlights. Liz was wearing fuchsia and no one else in town wore those sort of clothes to go shopping in. A garish silk scarf was knotted at her throat. Lot of jewellery, too. Taking out cigarettes, offering them around, she gave off a metallic gleam, like artillery.

"Jane lives at the back of you."

"Oh," Liz mouthed. She and Jane were anxious for Fran to keep talking, or for the waitress to butt in.

Fran said, "Liz has got a little girl. She could be a nice little friend for Peter. I've been telling her."

Why do they do that? wondered Jane. Matchmaking for the under-fives. What's wrong with them?

"Sorry, I meant to say," Liz began. "Penny's actually seventeen. I tend to make her sound younger." They laughed.

"So where did you live before?" Jane asked, blunter than she had meant to be.

"In Durham," Liz said. "Quite near the centre of the city."

Several assumptions clicked into place for both Jane and Fran. She's come right down in the world, they thought. We wonder why.

"I do like these council houses," Liz said. "They're so much cosier."

Jane snorted. "Not when they're being fire-bombed."

Fran stared at her. "We've never been fire-bombed."

"I meant that it isn't always that cosy."

Liz asked, "So you get trouble on the estates still?"

The waitress was heading their way. Jane nodded solemnly.

"We've got a vicious gang across the road and they go setting fire to cars. One of them, the leader, is meant to be on a curfew. But he's been out one night recently and bitten someone's ear off. Down by the Burn. And just next to me there's an ex-soldier who keeps threatening to beat people up."

"So what can we get you?"

The waitress was stooped right over their table, nose pressed almost against her notebook, squinting with her pencil at the ready.

"Tea for three," Liz replied. "So it's still the same old place then?"

Fran and Jane exchanged a glance. "Same as what?"

Liz grinned. Her cigarette smoke was vanishing up the nose of the waitress as she scribbled. 'I mean, nothing's changed since the Seventies, when I last lived on a council estate.'

"Where was that?" Fran asked.

"Oh, in this town, still. In the Blackhouses. It's even rougher there."

"You've been right around the block then," Jane said.

"Aye," Liz snorted. "You're not kidding there."

They stayed at their table longer than they had planned to. Even some of the pensioners left before them. To string the time out they ordered cups of tea by turns, like teenagers skiving off school.

Fran told Liz about her kids' new gerbils killing the budgie. 'The poor thing must have been attracted to all the sand in the tank. It flew in and got the shock of its life. All these things popped out and jumped on it. It was pitiful to see. It sat on the perch three days with no feathers. Then it fell off, dead.'

"We had the drama of the budgie going on for days," Jane said. "Every time I went round I got a newsflash on its health. But they used to let it fly around where it liked. It was bound to happen."

"Only because Frank sawed off the bottom of its cage when he was pissed."

"I hate birds flying round the house. It's like that film. Sets me right on edge. If they're not crapping on you they're pecking your eyes out. But anyway, it's tea round Fran's kitchen every afternoon. I go round at about one. You'll have to come too, Liz."

Fran grimaced and looked round at Jane. She felt like saying to her, Thanks a bloody bundle. Why don't you tell her to stay till teatime like you do, too, Jane? But she didn't say anything.

"I probably won't get the chance," Liz said quickly, noting the look on Fran's face. There was an awkward pause.

Then Jane told them about her mother's engagement.

"Screwing what off?" Liz cackled. Her laughter was surprising, raising heads all round the café.

"His leg. He's got a wooden leg."

Fran at last took a cigarette. "Only one. I can't afford to get started again. Jane's mam goes out picking up men in nightclubs."

"She's not that bad. And it's usually the Navy Club. They've usually got something missing or wrong with them. She reckons that's what it's like when you're scraping the bottom of the barrel."

"She's off her head." Fran laughed. Her own head was swimming after a couple of drags. "Tell her what she gave you last Christmas."

"Last year it was a watering can. And the year before that, one pink glove."

Liz was stifling her cackles. "One? What for?"

"I don't know. She said she'd 'used' the other one. She drinks. Last year me and Peter went round for Christmas dinner and she never turned up till four in the afternoon, rolling in pissed with this bloke from the pub. She'd forgotten all about dinner and she gave me this watering-can thing."

Fran squinted across the room through plumes of smoke. She seized Jane's forearm as it went reaching for her purse.

"What is it?"

Fran kept very still. "Over there. Isn't that your bus driver?"

Jane looked over her shoulder, trying to look cool. There, at a corner table, out of place in his blue uniform, was her friendly driver.

"I never knew he came here for his break."

Fran told Liz, "Jane's got a thing about men in uniform."

"Not bloody soldiers."

The driver was looking their way just the same. Jane stared with the frankness she felt their connection allowed. He was as tempting in this private moment as he was in a public one.

"He's very nice," Liz said. "But I bet he's about five foot one when he stands up. They always are." She sighed.

"Who cares about height?" Jane remembered what her mother had said about stumps and lying down.

"Listen to her!" Fran laughed.

"Are you up to something you shouldn't be with him, then?"

"Chance would be a fine thing." Jane smiled. "But he's always nice to me."

Liz called for the bill. "Go over and talk to him."

"I can't."

"Go on!" Fran urged. "The only other time you'll see him is on a bus. Take your chances."

"I'll ask him for some change," Jane decided. "He's bound to have plenty on him. He always does on the bus."

She stood up and began to weave her hesitant way towards him. Fran and Liz automatically glanced down, so they could listen and not be seen observing. The waitress came over and insisted on standing in the way and talking.

"Hiya again."

Jane felt foolish, hands resting on the chair opposite him. The bus driver looked surprised to be interrupted here. His face came out of the *Daily Mirror*, still burned red, with eyes deep as black coffee. He smiled, apparently recognising her at once.

"I was going to ask you for some change. For a tip."

Any strategy she had had in mind flew straight out the window. Jane's courage had failed. She wanted to get away as soon as possible.

He fiddled for change. Then he spoke. "I saw you earlier on."

Her heart slipped a bit and she said, "Oh."

"I didn't like to come over because you had company."

"That's all right. They wouldn't have minded. We weren't doing anything special."

A nag of conscience for this. Because they were doing something special. Quiche in here was her one treat of the week. He couldn't have spoiled it if he tried, though.

"I recognise those two. They live just by you, don't they?"

She was shocked. He's been checking up on me! It didn't seem half as sinister as it might have.

"Yes, Fran and Liz. Liz moved in last Saturday."

"Liz, is it?"

"I don't know her very well yet. She seems all right. A bit flashy, if you ask me."

He was peering past the bent heads, catching a glimpse of Liz and Fran looking back at him with now unconcealed curiosity.

"I don't suppose you could..." He laughed and shook his head. "Could you introduce me to her?"

Jane's hands gripped the chair back very hard indeed.

"God, I don't even know your name?"

"Jane," she said.

"Jane. Would you mind introducing me to your new friend?"

His eyes never left the gap he had found through the crowd. He never even glanced at Jane. Not even when he asked her name.

"Right," she said.

THREE

THE WIND RUFFLED PENNY'S HAIR AS SHE STOOD IN THE GREY MUD UNDER a goalpost. She lit a cigarette.

It's been an epidemic this summer, her mam had said. Burning things down. First the Portakabin in town where the pensioners went to drink tea and then Penny's new school. Penny gazed at the ruined section of her new school. In the early-morning drizzle it glistened and its smell was acrid in the air.

"Newton Aycliffe's rough," her mam warned, with the air of someone who knew the place of old. Apparently they had both lived there in the late Seventies, early Eighties, but Penny couldn't remember that at all. No, that wasn't true. She could picture the Royal Wedding and some kind of street party in a cul-de-sac.

Since then, though, mother and daughter had lived in Durham. Penny had always loved their house there. Her window looked out over woodland and you could just see the cathedral if you stood on her bed. Theirs was a house on the end of a terrace of converted miners' houses.

All you could see from upstairs in the new house in Aycliffe was

Woodham Comprehensive and its slushy, trudged-over playing fields. When they lost their house in Durham it was her mam's idea to come back to Aycliffe. She got them down on the council waiting list and it took almost a year for their number to come up. They were given a place in Phoenix Court, on the Yellowhouses estate, between the blocks of flats and Burn Lane. "Better the devil you know," Liz told Penny.

Do I know this place, though, Penny wondered when they moved in the thick of autumn. The first day she wandered around, trying to make it seem familiar. The pink asphalt of the play park rasped under her feet. The corner shop smelled inside of cheese and crisps and lager; not at all of Indian spices like the one she was used to. Everyone had their front room windows open so you could hear the tellies blaring at night.

She wondered whether her mother felt she was taking a backward step, moving back to a council house and a town and a way of life she'd left nearly fifteen years ago. Liz turned red.

"Of course it's a backward step," she said. She was unpacking her chinaware from crumpled *Northern Echos*. "Do you think I want to do this?"

Later, painting the bathroom and laughing uproariously because they'd spattered the bath, the mirrors and the floorboards with hot-pink sploshes, Liz said, "It's exciting to have somewhere new to do up, don't you think. Sometimes I felt stifled in that old place. You could *smell* the oldness there."

Penny smiled but she was keeping her mouth shut on the subject of the move and just helping out as best she could. The move was unavoidable. They had money troubles and they had lost their house. That was all there was to it. It was just them, mother and daughter by themselves. Both of them had to muck in.

They managed the move well by themselves, bringing all their belongings in shifts down the A1 in Transit vans. They crammed everything into a house almost half the size of the one they were used to. 'We'll have to chuck loads of this old junk out,' Liz fretted, throwing open yet one more cupboard in the old house, dismayed to see boxes of books and clothes and records that had gone undisturbed for years.

"We can't get rid of anything," Penny said. At seventeen she was in a phase of sentimentally rediscovering things. She had a craze on fishing out all Liz's scratchy LPs from the Sixties and Seventies. To the mother the cupboards they had to clear were nothing but a headache. To the daughter they provided a nostalgic musical jamboree. Penny found herself yearning for times she couldn't remember, and for times before she was born.

That summer was the one following Penny's botched O levels and spent it in a minor alcoholic daze to a soundtrack of Janis Joplin, Bob Dylan and Rod Stewart. She wore an old suede coat of her mother's. When she passed only three of her nine exams, Liz put it down to the threat of upheaval. They had been trying to sell the house in Durham since January, and revising in her room, Penny was continually disturbed by prospective buyers. But Liz wasn't one to blame herself. The thing for Penny to do, she said, was resits.

Resits in Newton Aycliffe. Liz was sitting her own test there, too. She was trying to fit back in. Only she knew how much she had changed in the interim years. That's exactly what the Eighties were, she thought: interim years. And then she looked at Penny and thought, That poor bairn grew up in my interim years.

They took the little money they could make from the old house and, with all their possessions in tow, set up in Phoenix Court. They were fired with determination: Liz to get to know the neighbours, to feel a part of it, and Penny to get her exams and two A levels on top, English and Art. She wanted a decent job afterwards. For the first time she could see the sense in having money.

The comp across the Burn from them was a school not unlike the one in Durham city she was used to. At least that is what she told Liz. 'It's fine. It's a nice place. And the sixth form is quite separate anyway, and they treat you properly, like grown-ups.'

Liz pursed her lips. She knew exactly what reputation the comp had in the town. And she knew that it was best not to be in the precinct at lunchtime when the kids from the comp were on their dinner hour. She could see that Penny was protecting her. It made her sick that her daughter felt she had to.

Having smoked her cigarette right down to the filter, Penny squelched it in the mud and plunged her hands deep in her cardigan pockets. Her back to the wind, she had to toss her head to keep the hair from her eyes as she surveyed the fire damage to the home-economics department. That was a subject she had always despised, back at the old school. When she started the comp at eleven she'd had terrible rows with the hag of a teacher who told her that her hands were dirty. Penny had been in tears by the end, denying it, and the teacher marched her to the sink to scrub them herself. The water was scalding. The school soap was globby, yellow, antiseptic. All the girls were laughing. "See! Your fingernails are black!" the home-economics mistress shouted. "They're always black!" Penny was sobbing. "They're already clean!" And eventually the teacher had given up in disgust.

Here there was a black oblong of scorched earth. Not for the first time Penny said a silent thank you to whoever did this and prevented her having to resit HE. Oddly, four or five burned cookers stood among the wreckage. They looked like rotting stumps of teeth.

The town clock bonged out nine o'clock from the far side of the field and Penny stirred herself to go in. Actually, she was keen this morning. Young Mr Northspoon was starting them on EM Forster.

Her first morning there had been grim. The lino in the sixth-form common room was dirty yellow and fleshy and it put her off. She never told Liz but that first afternoon she skived off down the park. The skiving could easily become a regular thing for her again. In Durham she had routinely sloped off, but with more shops to go round there had been less chance of walking into her mam. Penny loved the indoor market there, freezing cold, backing on to the river, reeking of damp, dead pheasants and old books.

In Aycliffe there was the park or the new covered-over bit of the precinct. That was where Noble Amusements was and, although she hated fruit machines, she found herself going on them again and again. The air was smoky and everyone else was over sixty. The music was the cheesiest she had ever heard and by the end of September she was thinking she must find somewhere nicer to skive to. Next door there was a café run by Christians where they sold arts and crafts: wreaths and baskets of dried fruit and flowers. She couldn't bear it in there, she found. Everyone smiling.

She was at a bit of a loss really. The lessons she skived didn't worry her much and, somehow, she managed to get work in and no one bothered her. She slipped through, she thought. The bits about the sixth form she liked so far were: having a locker she could fill up, having full run of the art rooms when she liked, and being able to slip in and out of the school whenever she fancied.

The only lessons she was always there for were English. They were a group of six and had two teachers. They began with Mrs Bell who, in their first few weeks, rattled them through selected highlights from Lawrence, Eliot and Hardy. But a few weeks into the term there was a new member of staff. In their very first lesson together, in a tangerine-coloured room at the top of the school, he declared he was losing his teaching virginity with them. Joanne, sitting next to Penny, gasped. She said afterwards that the new teacher thought he was being risqué. But Joanne was just snotty, Penny thought, because she lived in Heighington, a bijou village out of town. Penny didn't think Mr Northspoon was trying to be risqué. She thought he was marvellous.

That first lesson seemed to evolve quite naturally and easily into a class discussion in which they all pulled their chairs round in a circle and talked about their first-ever snog.

Mr Northspoon was in a sharp black suit with a beautiful shirt. He had his legs crossed and listened patiently to all their stories and had them all laughing, tapping one hand continuously on the air as if he was dying for a cigarette.

Alison Bradley fled and Mr Northspoon said it was probably because she was sweet sixteen and never been kissed. Penny thought he was out of order, especially since she knew Alison was pregnant, but there was still something enthralling about Mr Northspoon. He was young and auburn-haired, he had this great floppy fringe…and he set his head in his hands to listen and gestured eloquently and sometimes wildly and he laughed, he laughed loud and infectiously.

What she remembered most was that he even told them a little about his own first snog. For the first time he looked sheepish and talked vaguely about rolling around under hedges down the Burn. It turned out that he had grown up here in this town, too. He talked about how, on this day of his first snog down the Burn, right near here, some boy was torturing sticklebacks he'd caught with a net in the stream. He was nailing them to a tree trunk and watching them squirm themselves dead. Mr Northspoon said he stood by this boy and watched him do that, on the day of his first-ever snog.

And Penny suddenly found herself telling the most embarrassing story ever. With her friend Deborah Watts in her bedroom back in the old house. She was ten. Debs had said, "You don't even know how to snog.'"And Penny went, "Yeah, I do. Course I do." Deborah's speculative eye roved Penny's room and lighted on her *Girl's World*. A ghastly life-sized plastic bust of a Barbie doll with all this hair you were meant to do up in styles of your choice and a face for scrawling make-up on. Deborah went, "Go on. Snog your *Girl's World*." Penny had done so, and this is what she told the class. The others sniggered appreciatively and a little uneasily, but Mr Northspoon had been delighted. That was the note he had ended their first lesson on. But before they went he gave them each a soft-back copy of *A Room with a View*, which he said was the most wonderful book ever about somebody's first snog.

Somehow Penny had found out that his name was Vincent and that he was generally called Vince. It was the kind of fact that slipped into one ear and simply stayed there. She thought it was an old-fashioned name, like something out of the Fifties.

On her way to his class that morning she dropped her tutor group's register off at the secretary's office as asked. She bumped into him down there, slipping blithely through the dark corridors, through the press of small bodies. He was in a purple jacket today, rubbing shoulders with everyone, giving genial shoves when necessary, heading in her direction. He's more like one of us, Penny thought as they walked straight up to the secretary's door together. He grinned and gave a little 'after you' nod, clutching his *Room with a View* to his chest.

Penny knocked briskly and led the way into the typing pool. Before she knew it, she was asking him, "How did you get to be called Vince?"

The secretary was scowling at them. She was wearing ski pants and always looked as if she was trying really hard not to pee.

"It's my dad," Vince said. "He's a teddy boy. He thought it was a teddy-boy name. He still is one."

"This town's still in the Fifties," Penny said.

Then her teacher was talking to the secretary, asking after redirected post. The secretary was still scowling, but less when she talked to him. Penny left the register on the desk and left.

Throughout that lesson, as they talked through the Florence chapters of the novel and Vince tried to explain what Mr Emerson was getting at when he took Lucy aside by the Giotto frescoes and gave her a good talking-to, Penny was still mulling things over. She was surprised Vince had gone telling her about his father. Another barrier had gone down: he was just another bloke in a typical Aycliffe house. Penny knew he lived just by the school. One night last week she had left school by the wrong exit, following him. She went to the shop for fags and saw Vince duck through the crowds of kids, looking not much different to the other sixth-formers, and hurry across the grass, through the garages, and up a back gully into the yard of a terraced house. He lived in the old part of town, Penny saw.

FOR HIM BREAK TIMES WERE MURDER. THE OTHERS SAT ROUND TABLES and grumbled and smoked and drank foul coffee. The staff room was across from the sixth-form room and their music shook through the walls: the Smiths. He felt reincarnated, somehow having got it wrong, snapping his Kit-Kat with a twinge of spite. Shreds of chocolate fell on his immaculate white trousers. Looking up, he saw Mrs Bell at the coffee machine, stressed, jabbing all the buttons. Snatching up her cup, she actually muttered "Thank you" to the machine. She came over and plonked herself down by him.

The others were caught up in a discussion about admin.

He was off in a doze, thinking about Mr Emerson by the Giotto frescoes. It was Denholm Elliot he saw, as in the film. Gently the old man set his voice booming in the cavernous spaces and told Lucy plainly that the things of the universe just don't fit together. That their awkwardness causes world-sorrow, and that all you can do is unpack your sorrows from your old kit bag and...what was it he suggested? Lay them out in the sunshine. Oddly, the sun was coming through the clouds at that point, tepid and yellow. The music through the thin walls was 'This Charming Man': Morrissey on about how he'd go out tonight if he had a stitch to wear.

The geography teacher handed round pictures of his new baby. He was the thinnest person Vince had ever seen. He wondered vaguely how he could have the strength to squeeze anything life-producing from himself. Beside him and looking burlier than ever in a red tracksuit, the PE teacher was scowling. When Vince had been working his way up through the years here, ten or more years ago, that bastard had made his life a misery. Since the beginning of this term they hadn't exchanged a word. It would come. Vince realised the PE teacher was actually scowling at Mrs Bell. She was lighting her second cigarette of the mid-morning break.

In solidarity he lit his own, reaching into his bag and pulling out the black Sobranies, just for effect.

That Penny was a bit forward, asking him things all the time. Still, it showed that he wasn't coming across as stand-offish. The business about Aycliffe being stuck in the Fifties was sharp of her, too. He could remember his own moment of realising that an abnormal number of houses in this town had Elvis memorabilia on the walls. Elvis clocks and mirrors all mixed up with crucifixes and Cliff Richard calendars. When he eventually got away, it turned out that the rest of his life, the small part of the world he'd seen, wasn't all like that. What he wanted to tell Penny now was how circumscribed her world was. How this town would do her no good. How it had two faiths, Elvis Presley and God Almighty. While she was here it would always be under a dead king and an absent father.

HER FATHER HAD BEEN AN INSOMNIAC. ALL NIGHT HE WOULD SIT UP IN the kitchen and use the endless hours to catch up on the washing. He liked to pretend he was in a launderette. For the company, he said. You could pretend that the most fascinating people were there, or were just about to walk in. Those are places filled with dead time and so it wasn't time you could think of as wasted. When she thought back, Penny remembered Dad often talking about wasting your time, wasting your life. He said that was the only real crime.

When she was small and couldn't sleep, Penny would slip downstairs and wordlessly come to sit beside him. She would bring a book and read, or they would both watch the washer. Before she grew sleepy and mesmerised, they might strike up a conversation out of the blue, as strangers might. In this way Penny's father was, he explained, teaching her how to deal with all the ordinary strangers in the wider world.

Once when she was nine she came down and found him in his coat and shoes, watching the washer. She spoke to him straight away.

"I feel strange, Dad."

"Hello," he said. "I thought it was too quiet in here tonight." He rubbed thoughtfully at his beard. "Maybe you could use the machine at the far end. I think I noticed somebody emptying it a minute ago."

Penny wasn't up to pretending that night. "I feel really strange." She sat down and spread her fingers, fat, squashy fingers that could break her dad's heart to look at them. Her black fingernails made his insides twinge whenever he saw her hands. Penny was staring at her damaged fingernails now as if they were to blame for how she felt. Her dad took off his anorak and put it around her shoulders.

"How strange?" he asked.

"Sort of tingly. Tingling."

"Oh."

At this moment the machine's cycle stopped and there was silence. He felt for the stacked ten-penny pieces they kept on the bench and pretended to feed more into the washer. These coins they saved, usually, to spend on boxes of After Eight mints. They had a craze for these and ate them all through the night, talking and dipping their hands into the snug emerald boxes, pulling the mints out of the envelopes, writing messages to each other and leaving them about the house in the black slips of paper. They loved getting these tokens from each other, stowed like litter all about the place, on scraps of paper, sticky with smears of peppermint cream.

"Tingling?" he said.

She took a deep breath and used a word she had learned only recently in a Susan Cooper novel. "I think I've had a premonition."

"Oh?" He made it sound like the most natural thing in the world, popping an After Eight into his mouth.

Penny nodded grimly. "I can see that I'm going to be something big."

He said, "What you've got is growing pains."

"It was a premonition. It's more than being tall."

"What then?"

"A guru or something."

He was impressed. He gave her a big hug.

When Penny was twelve she once had to go outside to their Ford Capri to find him. In the dark street he was pretending to be stuck in a traffic jam. That was more dead time he could cheerfully waste. She climbed into the passenger seat and watched him mime bored exasperation. Then he turned to her with a worried look.

"You haven't locked us out, have you, Pen?"

She jangled the keys.

"Is it the tingling again?"

She nodded. "I'm having another premonition. It's bigger than just being a guru, I think." She looked out the window, down the street. Through the black trees you could only just see the cathedral, lit up gold and green on its hill. She always thought of it as the colour of frankincense and myrrh. "Dad," she went on. "When you were a kid, did you ever think that you might be the Messiah?"

He gripped the steering wheel with a faraway look in his eyes. Eventually he said, "I was never sure that what I was going to be would ever really be me." He shrugged and laughed. "Does that make sense?"

"It sounds straightforward enough. Straightforwarder than what I've got."

"Go to bed." He smiled gently. "Second Coming or not, you still have to get to school tomorrow."

AT THE END OF THE MORNING PENNY WAS THERE WITH HER HEAD IN HER locker once more, putting books and files away and wondering where to go for lunch. Today was a good day because she had a fiver and she was thinking about going into town. Maybe she would even ask around and see if anyone in the common room was up for a walk and a laugh.

They were a pretty uninspiring bunch in there. Boy scientists and girls in dark skirts who did history. She didn't have many friends yet. Somebody was playing Ice-T on the crappy old tape deck. Some of the more interesting lads were ranged around the end of the room, and she saw them look up sharply when the door beside them flew open and Mr Northspoon came swishing in with a stack of photocopying. He pulled a face at the music and then sought out each member of his English group, thrusting handouts at them. They were pages Xeroxed from other Forster novels, from articles on him. "I forgot to give them out before," he repeated as he went round. When he got to Penny he said, "How can you bear to stay in here with Ice fucking T?"

She thrilled at the word as she hadn't since she was eight.

"Ooops," went Vince. "Can't you get them to change the music?" He whirled round. "Here, boys," he called and went up to them. They were taller than him, all in dark cardigans. "Can I put something on?" Bemused, they stood back and let him flip through the records and tapes. Here there were things left by generations of sixth-formers. It was a tradition scrupulously kept up, this donation of successive eras' favourite music. Vince found a faded copy of David Bowie's *Hunky Dory* album and turned it on with a triumphant grin.

One of the boys in cardigans nodded. "That's meant to be smart, that is."

Vince looked at him. "It's just wonderful."

Penny watched him walk back towards her. "I was thinking of going into town for lunch," he said. "Do you want to come? I can't sit watching them boring bastards in the staff room eating coleslaw sandwiches again."

Penny was nodding, aglow and – she suddenly realised – tingling madly. "We can go to the Copper Kettle. It's all there is."

They escaped as the dinner bell rang, ahead of the rush, through the technical department where the machines in the workshops clanged and buzzed laboriously and the smell of oil hung about like an abattoir smell.

Over the fields it was drizzling. Penny waded uncertainly while Vince plodged ahead. They kept up a companionable silence for a while.

Behind them the school was warmly lit, each classroom giving off its separate yellow glow. From here it seemed peaceful, but they knew that inside it would be full of noise and the tang of sweat and paper and smoke. Penny was lagging behind, looking at it. She heard the squelch of mud as Vince came back to stand by her. She stared at the orange brick building in the middle of school, the circular deaf unit they all called the Magic Roundabout, because it seemed the whole school revolved around the deaf kids in there. Sometimes the kids who could hear chased the deaf kids just for the fun of it. They got jealous because the Magic Roundabout had better carpets and double glazing and two videos. There was one belligerent kid who had no ears at all, only two frail wires coming out the holes in his head.

"You haven't got long to stay here," Vince said.

"I've only just got here."

"I know. But, really, this is just the time in between. Enjoy it, but you'll like it more when you get away. Wherever you go."

"I haven't thought about afterwards yet," she said, with a shiver.

"Afterwards it will all be better."

The precinct was a five-minute walk across the field, through the old houses and across the car parks. Vince started telling Penny about the Queen visiting, about the time of her Silver Jubilee. She'd come down in a helicopter on to the car park where Kwiksave was now. His infant school had trooped all the kids out to stand at the railings and wave crayoned Union Jacks. "My teacher, the immortal and terrible Miss Kinsey, had us terrified in case we acted out of turn. Death to anyone who made a show of her in front of the Queen. I wouldn't care, but the Queen was only coming to open up the borstal. It wasn't to see *us*."

No one had quite reckoned on the gale-force winds brought down by the Queen's helicopter in such restricted space. Kids were blown over, the home-made flags shot off somewhere, and Miss Kinsey herself dashed backwards, screaming helplessly, into the cordoned-off road. Vince had felt sorry for her, wanting so much to greet the Queen and looking, once the wind had stopped and the mayor and the royal party came past nodding, like an insane woman.

Since then and since he had last lived here, the town centre precinct had had all-sorts added to it. Whole new shops with rent so dear they stayed empty. The indoor bit for the Christians and gamblers. A gym, up the ramp, above Kwiksave. The precinct had arrived at this state through a gradual accretion. In the Fifties it had been a high street, paved over in the Seventies, built up in the Eighties, and taken over by the cheap shops in the Nineties. The cheap shops like Boyes and Winners and Bill's Bargain Basement had become Vince's favourites, with all their tat and tawdry cheeriness.

They were walking past Winners now as Penny pointed out that she hated seeing all these women in ski pants and anoraks. "They may as well come out in what they sleep in. And they don't look like they wash their hair."

"Don't be so snobby and picky."

"It depresses me, all this, though."

"Aye, but think of them looking at you," he said, "thinking, look at young Lady Shite over there, in her trendy black jacket and her PVC rucksack. Thinking she's smart because she's about to piss off to college."

This chastened her for a moment. "I never said I was going anywhere. I could just end up on this town like any of the other lasses. With a double pushchair and toddlers piled four deep. I'm not setting myself above no one. I know where I'm from."

"Good," he said. They were held up then by a couple in their twenties, sailing complacently out of Woollies and cutting across their path.

"I bloody hate that," Penny said, "when the bloke has hold of the woman by her waist or shoulders. Like she can't keep herself upright."

Vince rolled his eyes and said in a singsong voice, "I thought it looked quite gallant."

They were walking in the wake of the happy couple.

"He's got his hand cupped right on her arse," Penny said. "Like he's scared she's going to shit."

"Touching cloth." Vince grinned. "My mam used to say that, I remember. Horrible thing to say."

"Have you got a nice mam?" Penny asked. She felt they were roving all over the place in this conversation and it exhilarated her.

"She's gone now," he told her. "It's just Dad at home."

"The teddy boy."

"That's him. Look, is this the place? I'm actually dying for the bog now."

This is the one, Penny thought, gazing at the great steamy window of the Copper Kettle and its dried flowers on the windowsill.

"Could you order me some quiche?" Vince asked her as they shoved inside. He shot off through the crowded tables and Penny was met by a young waiter in a frayed black waistcoat. He was small, girlishly featured and his hair was greased back, but not quite properly: there was a dry calf-lick sticking out of his crown. He looked at her and she saw he had a twitch.

"Is there room for two?" she asked, amazed he could hear her over all the noise. It was intense. They seemed to have walked in on the most animated points in all the conversations in the room. But that was what it was like in the Copper Kettle. They even got people here who came in by themselves and shouted loudly to no one in particular. That was mostly Saturday afternoons, when they let the people in the hospital up the road out for a wander.

The waiter was in a bad mood. He glanced round, led the way and flicked his tea towel at an empty table. It was pressed between the backs of women clustered around their own tables. From one came piercing laughter in waves as someone held court and everyone indulged them. Penny was intent on the dirtiness of the table the waiter had brought her to. There was a layering of tablecloths, crusted with stains and crumbs. She jumped when, as she was sitting down, somebody grabbed her elbow from behind.

"Mam!" she gasped, looking round.

Liz gave her a shrewd look, her face red with laughing. There were three others sitting with her. Penny recognised two women from Phoenix Court and someone who was surely one of the bus drivers. Her instant reaction was pleasure, that her mam had found a place here so soon. She could have a cackle with someone.

"Have you had the same idea?" asked Liz loudly. At this point Vince had found his way to their table and was settling into a place of his own. Liz raked her beautifully painted eyes over him. "I mean, about having lunch here?"

"Oh, yes." She hesitated, caught between Vince and Liz. She hated formal introductions. "This is my English teacher, one of my English teachers."

"Vincent Northspoon," he said, raising himself and offering his hand. When Liz took it she jangled her bracelets and announced to the others, "Penny is doing A-level English. And this nice young man is going to teach her. She's going far, this one."

Vince fell back into his seat.

"Do you often go to lunch with your students, Vincent?" Liz fixed him with a stare.

"Not often, no," he said, faltering slightly. "But I don't believe in keeping different people and things separate. I can't compartmentalise my life. We're having a laugh."

Obviously, for Liz, this reply had seen him through some kind of test. "And so are we," she said graciously.

The others were greeting Penny. From under her dark bob Fran gave a friendly smile. Jane went "hiya" somewhat grudgingly, Penny thought, and the bus driver seemed genuinely pleased to meet her. Liz winked.

"I'll leave you to order your lunch in peace," she said. "We're discussing serious things here. We're planning a big night out."

As her mother turned away, Penny sighed.

"Your mam looks young," said Vince, flicking the menu. "Ugh, God! Look at this. Mince on toast."

"They've got quiche on, anyway."

"And is there a dad at home?"

She shook her head.

"Maybe we should introduce my dad to your mam," Vince said. "We could be like the bloody Brady Bunch."

"Great," she said distractedly. Vince's novelty value had already worn off. "What are we having?"

The small waiter was back beside them. He looked on the verge of a stinking migraine. With their order taken, he slipped crossly away.

"He's sweet," Penny said. "Makes me feel all protective."

"I bet he'd be furious to hear you say that."

"I don't care."

"He wants to wash his hair." Vince peered over heads to see him.

"I'd take him home and run him a bath and strip him." Penny was looking wistful.

"Well," Vince said smiling, "maybe I wouldn't kick him out of bed for eating crisps."

Penny's eyes went wide.

There was a great peal of laughter from her mother. Liz swung round in her chair and broke in as the giggles at her own table were subsiding.

"Oh, I've just told the most awful joke. I'd forgotten I knew it. It just came out and I'm so ashamed of myself."

"Go on," Penny told her with lips pursed.

"Have you heard about the new Tupperware girdle?" She raised an eyebrow and tittered at Vince. She's still testing me, he thought. "It does nothing for your figure, but it keeps your fanny fresh."

That said, she returned to her original audience, snorting. Penny was horrified to see Vince helpless with that infectious laugh of his. It reminded her of that nice first lesson, when he made them all laugh. This seemed to diminish that lesson. Worse, his giggles threatened to set her off.

"Don't encourage her," she hissed. "She's getting worse."

Vince made a very teacherly effort at composure. But his eyes, Penny thought; the unspoken stuff just lurking there...

"I wish that little waiter would hurry up." He said it with eyes cast down, and they waited for their quiche now in quiet.

THEY SAID GOODBYE TO LIZ'S PARTY OUTSIDE BOOTS. THE OTHERS WERE heading off to catch the Road Ranger back to Phoenix Court, the bus driver was going back to the depot, and Penny supposed she ought to return to school.

Vince had turned thoughtful. As farewells were said he was staring at the market stalls, their tarpaulins heaving in the wind.

"Is something the matter?" she asked him.

"I'm off for the afternoon," he said. "And I've got some business I've been putting off ever since I came back home."

"Oh," she said. "Is it nice business?"

"I'm not sure anymore." He looked at his watch. "It's in Darlington. Someone I have to see. Look." He glanced around almost furtively. "Why don't you come on the bus to Darlo with me this afternoon?"

She had maths. A resit lesson. She couldn't bear it. "All right. Where are we going?"

"I want to have a nice afternoon round the shops and I want a couple of pints first. And then I want to see...the person I've got business with."

Her interest was roused by now. "And I'll be your moral support?"

He smirked. "Aye. What time do the buses go?"

"Twenty-five to and twenty past." She knew exactly: those were buses were one of the few routes out of Aycliffe for her. "Round the back of Kwiksave."

They sat on a bench to wait. Penny stared thoughtfully at the rest of the bus queue. She recognised a couple of faces from her new street. There you go, she thought, fitting in already. That bloke with the tattoos from the flats. He was there with a bairn in a pushchair. An ugly-looking baby with an old look about it. He stood with an old woman in a fur-collared coat. Her eyebrows were drawn on too heavily. They were arguing about who was going to spend the coming Christmas with whom. Without even looking at the blue-tattooed man, the older woman muttered, "I just want a nice quiet do, after all the fuss last year. You've all got to come to me and Iris. All of you."

The man with the tattoos looked doubtful. And then the bus came. As Penny and Vince took their place in the queue, Vince said, "I adore eavesdropping. It makes you feel so glad to be alive."

Penny thought he was staring at the blue man. "Do you know him?"

"Kind of."

"Is it him you've got business with?"

"God, no."

Penny was offered half fare by the driver. "But I'm seventeen!"

"Sorry," said the bus driver. She frowned and pushed a button, doubling the fare.

"Honestly," Penny sighed as Vince led them up the grey spiral staircase. "First I couldn't get served in a pub, then they wouldn't give me fags, and now this!"

Vince sat heavily on the front seat at the top. His favourite place. "Hark at Peter Pan," he said.

Behind them the old woman was breaking some news to the man with tattoos and they listened in on this as the bus lurched into the grey wind. The rain started up again.

"Mark, I've got to tell you. She asked me to tell you. Sam's pregnant again."

A pause. "Oh. By him? By that copper?"

"Who else? She's been worrying how to tell you..."

There was a longer pause as the bus wound its way through Aycliffe Industrial Estate, where all the buildings were squat and grey and had gleaming silver logos on their fronts. Penny was watching the slag heaps and miles of metal piping glide by and Vince found he was staring at her fingernails as they fiddled with her bus ticket.

"Do you always paint your nails black?" he asked.

Immediately she curled her fingers round to hide them. "They aren't painted," she said quietly. "They're natural."

He felt a roll of sympathy in the pit of his stomach. "Did they get crushed?"

Penny gave a sigh, preparing to give something away. "When I was tiny, when I was first born, my dad took me out of the incubator and out of the hospital, into the car park. He held me out to the moon and shouted and cried...and we were struck by lightning."

"Oh..." Vince fell quiet.

Now they were on the outskirts of the industrial estate, coming down Fujitsu Lane.

Behind them the man with the tattoos said to the old woman, "Tell Sam I'm pleased for her, Peggy. If another bairn is what she wants."

Vince rolled his eyes. "It's babies everywhere you turn, some days."

Then their bus met the motorway, bringing them to the flat stretches of yellow, drizzly fields that stretched out the distance to Darlington.

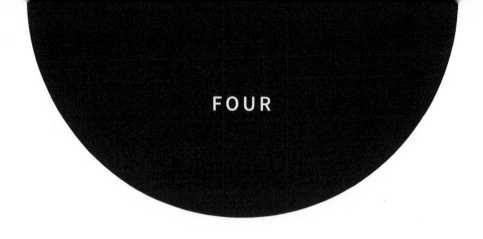

FOUR

SHE STARED FIERCELY AT HERSELF. THE LIGHTS ON BOARD THE BUS AT night were blue like a butcher's freezer. They made her reflection turquoise, hollowed out. It slid through the glossy dark all the way home and kept her company. At one point Penny thought miserably, I am my own best company. Then she put a stop to that. Look, she told herself, I've had a nice day, a nice time with lovely and interesting people. Now it's time to go home. This is the last bus home. It's midnight almost. There's nothing more to be had out of this night. So why was it she felt so let down? She wasn't even sure what was making her glare at her own reflection. She felt that someone had got her all stirred up, only to let her drop.

Buses at night made her nervous. Penny bided her time until home and consoled herself that at least the 213 went right to the stop outside her house. At least she wouldn't need to go traipsing round the streets, still unsure of her own estate's geography. But if that was the best she could salvage from this evening, then to hell with it. Was that the most she could expect from life – to get home safely?

Don't knock it, she thought. I'll settle for safety just now. Voices came from upstairs and further back down the lower deck. Voices raucously enjoying themselves on the last bus home. Whoever they were, whatever they were up to, Penny found them unnerving. She wished she was in a gang. Purposefully she had sat right behind the driver. He had a thick red neck and his bald head was white as a knuckle under the lights. Whenever she looked at him for reassurance – measuring his dependability whenever she got a twinge of nervousness – he seemed to sense it, and turned to give her a sly wink. He was in the same uniform as the nice bus driver, the sexy one her mam and the other Phoenix Court women had befriended. But he wasn't the same at all. Hyde to the nice driver's Jekyll, he drove double-deckers through the dark and ferried the town's dregs round the estates.

Darlington hadn't been as much fun as Vince had promised. It was grey and wet, full of charity shops, age-blackened buildings and cemeteries. From the moment they arrived Vince had looked troubled, set upon his mysterious business. As they passed the afternoon in bookshops and wandering the back streets Penny was aware of his nervousness and dread. It was as if he was reorienting himself, unwilling to explain anything to her. She wondered if it was something criminal he was into. Then she thought, surely not. If he was into something dodgy, then he'd never be teaching. It might, of course, be drugs. He was in Darlo to get some stuff off someone. That made sense. She started to feel sick with fretting as they sat in a vegetarian café by the marketplace, by which time Vince was starting to perk up, going on about, of all things, the nature of desire and love. As he talked and the sense of what he was saying slid over her head, Penny gazed at him and wondered if he was stoned or tripping now.

"What do you think, Penny?"

She shook herself out of it. "Hm?"

"I asked if you thought loving, desiring, wanting someone could last out years of not seeing them." His hands were tracing patterns on the oilcloth. "What do you think?"

At first she felt toyed with. Then she thought, he really wants to know what I think. "It..." she began. Oh, I don't want to sound trite, she thought. But what do I think? And she realised, what she believed in did sound trite. "It takes a lot to shake feelings like that off," she said. "And I think love continues. It moves into different forms, or becomes something else. But it's still there. And what happens to it then depends on the people involved." She swallowed.

"Wow," Vince breathed. "You should be on *This Morning* during the phone-ins with Richard and Judy."

She flushed. "Cheers," she snapped.

"No, honest. That was good." He sipped his tea. "You sound like you've thought about this stuff."

Penny shrugged.

In Dressers' book department Vince whisked her from shelf to shelf, telling her who was rubbish and whom she ought to be reading. He would pluck books out seemingly at random, flick through them and announce his verdict. Dressers was old-fashioned, its floor wooden and groaning as he dashed about.

"You've read everything," Penny said.

"Nah," he said, thrusting something else at her. "But enough to know. It won't make things *right*, reading good books. It won't make them easier. In fact, it usually makes things harder." He passed her a paticular novel he thought she should read.

"Great." She went to buy the book, just to placate him. In the queue she asked, "Are you always a teacher?"

"What? But I'm being a friend now. Honestly, if you read this stuff – the best bits – it's all here. Honest. Friends always recommend books. If they can do that and be unconditional with their respect and love and support and tell you that you look nice when you might not...then that's all right."

"Uh-huh." Penny nodded as she handed her money over, wishing Vince would keep his voice down just a bit. The lady behind the counter didn't look impressed.

Then he announced they should go to the Arts Centre in Vane Terrace to see a particular show, a dance piece. She had never been to see a dance piece before and, to start with, had a vision of some sort of ceilidh thing, where she'd be obliged to whirl and skip about in a barn with people watching. Vince appeared to pick up on that as they walked down the narrow and seething Posthouse Wynd and he told her, "It's like a play. About an hour long. People with superbly proportioned bodies running about on white lino, probably. And there will most likely be a huge fridge or something in the middle of the stage."

Now the 213 was circling the deserted town precinct. They had reached Aycliffe with Penny hardly noticing. She'd have to watch out or she'd be missing her stop. Wake up in that terrible bus station in Sunderland. Upstairs the noise was louder, as if they were all unduly excited by the sight of Aycliffe town centre. Penny groaned at her own prissiness. I'm only jealous because I'm not drunk and I've not had a nice enough time.

Vince had bought her a couple of pints. She was surprised, really. It seemed as if he had no recollection of their teacher-pupil dynamic. Now he sat them at a low, round table in the foyer of the Arts Centre and made them both drink pints of fizzy lager. He was looking to Penny to get him through something. When conversation lulled at one point, round about half past five, he hissed somewhat desperately, 'Talk to me! Distract me!' Penny had asked him about college, where he had gone, what he would recommend. Vince warmed to this, telling her a whole load of silly stories about the things he had got up to. Just when he'd got into his conversational stride, he jumped up and hurried off to the box office. Penny watched him chatting to a young woman who stood between the till and an oversized vase of arum lilies. Vince was asking about someone, asking if they weren't working tonight. When he returned with two tickets for the show – it was called *Fridge* – he seemed disappointed.

He waved her money away. "My treat," he said, and fell quiet until it was time to go in and see the show.

Penny wanted a body like that. She wanted to dance like that. She wanted to come out under lights in front of all these people and she wanted to be lithe and bendy and braced full of tension and supple brilliance. She wanted to wrap herself around the beautiful body of the male lead. Until the final moments, when he crept off into the huge fridge in the centre of the stage and closed the door, her eyes were on him, licking in every detail.

Outside again, where the bar was now fuller and louder, busy with the night-time crowd, the cinema-goers, the drama youth group, the poetry workshop, she told Vince she had loved the show. She was glad he had brought her. He said bitterly, 'I was right, though. Another fucking fridge piece.' They were at the bar, where a woman on a high stool held court and talked about flamenco. "Sorry, Penny," Vince said sheepishly. "I'm horribly cynical and queeny sometimes, aren't I? It's only put on. No, I'm glad you liked it, pet." He ordered two more pints.

They sat by a large window and Penny looked out at the park in Vane Terrace. It was sinisterly Victorian, box trees and holly beyond the Arts Centre's driveway. And then she saw someone was standing beside their table. He was collecting the empties, but he was staring down at Vince.

All in one go Vince looked scared and relieved. He was on his feet in a flash and then he didn't know what to do. The man collecting the empties seemed pleased to be clutching his tower of empty pint glasses and his plastic basket. "The woman at the box office said you might be in tonight," said Vince. He tried to laugh. "We both look like we've seen Banquo's ghost, don't we?"

Both Penny and the man collecting empties said, "Who?"

He was about Vince's age, Penny decided, but he dressed younger. He was in a white Adidas top, the ones with stripes and flashes and irony. He wore his jeans slouched down, his hair clipped short and he had a nose ring. Vince commented on this.

"Had it years," was the reply. He was a boy, Penny thought, in a way Vince wasn't. They might be the same age, but this was aspiring to boyishness and Vince was not. There was a surliness about him, too, that seemed as much a part of his outfit as the trainers with their tongues sticking out.

"This is Andy," Vince said to Penny. And all at once he seemed genuinely relieved. As if something he had worried about had turned out all right. But what had happened?

"I'll finish with this lot...I'll be back in a second," Andy said. And he was gone in the crowd. Vince sat down with a sigh, brushing the hair out his eyes with both hands.

As the 213 weaved and plunged down Burn Lane and entered her own estate, Agnew Two, Penny devoted a moment to inventing excuses for her lateness. She should have phoned. But Liz trusted her. In the summer she had been out all hours, coming back the next day sometimes. These were the dark nights, though. By their nature they became more hazardous. She thought, Oh, here I am, backwards and forwards on the bus to and from Darlington. It all seemed a horribly futile exercise, going somewhere and coming back. What happened in the middle ought to transform or replenish you or do you some good. Had it really? Here she felt a stab of spite towards Vince. He was doing something else. He wasn't just slinking home unchanged. He had stayed and was, presumably, being transported into some other state. Oh, I'm tired, Penny thought. And I don't want anyone to be happy.

The bus seemed to be groping its way blindly to the top of Phoenix Court. She got up ready to ting the bell.

Andy had sat at their table until closing time. When Penny started drinking soda water, the two of them switched to gin and tonics. They were talking more freely, enjoying themselves, enjoying each other. Penny watched. They were laughing and, when the other wasn't paying attention, giving sly, appraising looks. Gauging each other. Penny was drawn in, aware of something private going on but not shutting her out. She felt suspended, sitting there. Vince and Andy ordered tequila slammers for them all to end and together drilled Penny on the procedure. The salt on her fist, the exact force of the slam on the yellow table top, and the etiquette of sucking a lemon wedge. "Got it?" Vince asked. "Lick, slam, suck...on a count of three. It has to be all together."

"It's our favourite thing." Andy grinned. "You get licked, slammed and sucked. One, two...three!"

And, still smeared with wet salt and lemon juice, tequila burning their throats, they hurried out into the night, which had turned freezing. Almost without a word they escorted Penny to her bus stop. She asked if Vince was coming back to Aycliffe.

With an eye on Andy, Vince explained that he wasn't. He was heading off up to North Road, where Andy had a room above a taxidermist's shop.

Penny nodded. "You might as well get off now," she told them. "It's a long walk up North Road. You won't make my wait any shorter, staying here till the bus comes."

"Are you sure, pet?" Vince asked. He raised his eyebrows in concern. A smear of lemon on his cheek was bright under the streetlight. Penny had an urge to wipe it off. Andy stood a couple of paces back, bouncing on his Adidas heels, eager.

"The 213's due any minute," she said and smiled. "Go on. Have fun."

Vince smiled almost shyly then, and suddenly both he and Andy were gone.

The bus groaned and hauled itself shuddering to a halt at the stop outside Penny's garden gate. She jumped out and thanked the driver, smiling with relief, and he winked at her again.

As she turned she saw that there was something dark bundled up in the corner of the bus stop. Was it someone sleeping there, or rubbish piled up, or...? She thought it might be a big animal. It growled at her.

Penny stepped back, and, as a van went by on the main road, there was a sudden burst of light and she could make out the shape of a bloke sitting on the ground at the back of the bus shelter, clutching his little dog to himself. The man's face was turned to her, twisted up as the headlights swept over it, and she realised that she knew who it was. One of the neighbours from round the back, the one who went marching about the place in his combat trousers.

"Hello," she said uncertainly. And then she thought, bugger this, and dashed off across the grass and round the corner. The grass would be clogged with dog shit and things you couldn't see in this light, but she was past caring. At last she burst through her own garden gate and fiddled for her backdoor key. Then she saw that all the downstairs lights were on. Liz was still up. Waiting up and worried. From inside came the muffled sound of a record, an old one. Rod Stewart, Penny thought. The odd thought struck her that maybe, when her daughter wasn't around, Liz allowed herself the luxury of being nostalgic.

"It's nice, this," Jane was saying. "I get so bored at nights with no one round."

Liz went to turn the record over. "But you say you do a lot of reading?"

Jane drummed her fingers on the six-high stack of novels she was borrowing. "Oh, I do. I read these one a night. But you finish one book, and you start another, and you read that, and you finish it...nothing seems to happen in between." Jane looked down at the novels. Glimpsing their titles, the promise of their cover illustrations, she felt with a flush the inadequacy of what she'd said. When she had a book on the go it was all right. She was in that world. It was somewhere to go back to. A place where everything fitted together.

"Well, it's nice to have friends to visit as well." Liz sneaked a look at her watch. Jane had been round for seven hours. She had followed Liz into the house on their return from town. At first Liz had assumed she just wanted to see the house, to see what things Liz had. Nosy, but natural enough. And of course the house was in chaos, with boxes and crates still blocking the hallway, the settee under plastic wraps. Jane had plonked herself down on it, drinking tea and eating biscuits, rustling the plastic all the way through the evening. She seemed impressed by Liz's belongings. She sighed with pleasure at her ornaments from around the world, Liz explaining that each knick-knack had its separate story, and she smiled at the records Liz set about unpacking for the first time from her cardboard boxes.

"All a bit before my time," Jane said.

"Are they?" asked Liz tersely. She was tired and worrying about Penny. Jane was trying to give her a crash course in what went on in Phoenix Court. She'd already talked her through Fran and Frank's marital problems, all the scandal that went on round the flats when someone's bairn vanished last Christmas, and the tale of Jane's mam Rose and her one-legged lover. "I don't think she should encourage him," Jane was saying as Penny let herself into the kitchen. "I mean, she throws away so much of herself on these men. She never gets anything back."

Penny was surprised to hear anyone else there. "Who's that?" she shouted through.

Jane, misunderstanding, explained as she followed Liz into the kitchen. "My mam. She's marrying a bloke with a wooden leg."

Liz put the kettle on. She gave her daughter a searching look and said in one breath, "You've met, haven't you? Jane, Penny, Penny, Jane. Penny, I've been worried sick."

Jane laughed. "It's rubbish, Penny. I've been here all night and she's never mentioned you once. We've had the sherry out."

"Actually, you're wrong."

There was an awkward silence. Penny slung her coat off and hugged it to her.

"So, where have you been, Penny?" Saying this, Liz felt terrible. She never talked this way to Penny. She was worried, but she was also aware that she was performing for Jane's sake. Jane was nodding. They were mothers together, wanting explanations.

"I went to Darlington with Vince...the man you saw me with." Penny felt pinned to the Formica bench.

Jane took the last drop of sherry and prepared to go at last. She said, "You've both been lucky today. Your mam was asked out by that lovely bus driver."

She hadn't kept the resentment out of her voice. They all noticed.

"Are you going to see him, Liz?" Penny asked.

"You call your mam by her name?"

"Um...sometimes."

"My mam would kill me if I did that. Different generations, I suppose."

"Something like that. Are you going to see him, then?"

Liz handed Penny a cup of tea. "I doubt it. But the lasses round here are organising a night out. Jane's been egging us on. Tomorrow. I'm going out then."

"You're mad not to see the bus driver," said Jane, pulling her coat on. "I suppose it means he's not married, anyway..." She did her zip up thoughtfully.

"Doesn't prove anything," Liz said, opening the door. "What people claim to be has nowt to do with anything. People lie."

"She's a philosopher," Jane told Penny.

"No, I'm not. Good night, Jane."

Jane blinked, aware she had said something wrong and not sure what. "Thanks for the books. I'll probably pop in tomorrow, then."

"You do that." Liz forced a smile and hustled her out. She slammed the door behind Jane and rounded on her daughter. "Well?"

Penny was looking shamefaced. "I haven't done anything silly."

"Are you sure?"

"Not the silly you think."

"And Vincent?"

"I got the last bus home by myself. Vince stayed in Darlington with his boyfriend."

"Oh."

"Yes, oh."

"A disappointing day, then."

"Mm."

DAYLIGHT CAME BLEAKLY OVER THE ESTATES. THE GAPS BETWEEN THE sandy-bricked buildings were sludged with leaves turning to paste. There was a searing brightness in the air as the milk boys pulled up, sitting on the back of their van, clambering off and dashing about at first light.

Fran was earliest out, doing the five-till-seven stint at Fujitsu. It was as if all Phoenix Court was hers. She felt that way about all the streets, walking through town to the factory. By the time she returned each morning to get the kids out of bed, the estates would be coming to life, cars starting up and steaming, crowds coughing and stamping at bus stops. At seven each morning it was as if Fran relinquished her world to everyone else. And at seven her shoulders ached already from wielding round her super-Hoover, her superb industrial cleaner, her futuristic hobbyhorse. The one thing she loved about her morning job was her newfound skill wheeling about the floors and gangways at Fujitsu with this powerful machine. She rode it on the polished floors and she rode it like the wind.

This morning while Fran was gone, her neighbour paid a call. Frank was woken too early by a hammering at the back door. He was used to being prised from his bed after seven, the same time as the bairns. Then the house would be warmed through and Fran would have breakfast on the go. Today he jolted awake, alarmed by the noise downstairs. He shambled down to find Nesta from next door framed in the glass.

"Can I have milk?" she asked when he opened the door.

Frank couldn't bear the sight of her. Her complexion was like tinned rice pudding, its broken veins and acne strawberry jam stirred into it. She wore a navy anorak and her fawn ski pants were gathered at the knees.

"We've got no milk for the baby and the milkmen didn't bring ours."

Frank looked past her, to see if theirs had been delivered. Two bottles stood on the sludge of old leaves. She nodded her rapid thanks and hurried away, remembering her own dislike of him.

Free milk, Nesta thought excitedly, hurrying across the grass. Free milk like in school when that's what they gave you at breaktime. And there was bird crap on the tinsel tops. You poked your straw in and it tasted too warm and creamy because it had stood outside too long. She stopped at the house where the new woman had moved in. Fran had told her she was called Liz and she looked as if she had a bit of money put by. She was the glamorous type. Nesta couldn't stand that type. They didn't want that type here. Clutching her new bottle of milk, Nest crept closer to the front window of Liz's house, the window that looked out on the grass and the kid's play park. She narrowed her eyes to slits and stared inside.

In the living room Liz was kneeling in front of the biggest mirror she had, watching TV out of the corner of one eye, concentrating on her hair with the other. Her wig sat on its pedestal before her and she teased skilfully, slowly at it. Nesta's eyes boggled at this, and at the sight of this woman without hair, without make-up, kneeling in her kimono. Absently Nesta stroked her own hair. Then there were footsteps in the play park behind her. She turned to see Jane crossing.

"Nesta? What are you doing?"

Nesta broke away from the window and hurried back to the path. 'Milk for the baby!' she called out, as if that explained everything.

Jane shrugged and left it at that. She couldn't get on with Nesta. You couldn't get a sensible word out of her. Jane had more things to worry about. She had to cross town to pick up Peter from his nanna's, where he had spent the night, and she reckoned that old feller with the one leg had spent the night there again. She wasn't sure how she felt about Peter coming under his influence. By the time she got to Rose's, to find Peter having his Weetabix at the breakfast bar and staring in awe at the old man's leg by the coat rack, Fran had already returned from work.

By eight the school buses had started to come and go, bright blue and rowdy. Fran's eldest were dispatched while she waved from the roadside with her youngest two round her ankles. The toddlers were interested in a dead dog lying on the grass verge. Fran went to see what they were dancing round and then recoiled in shock. The poor thing was past helping. She thought it looked like the pit-bull that belonged to Gary. She didn't fancy telling him his dog was dead in case he accused her of killing it. She hurried her kids away and phoned the police from the box.

Little Lyndsey said, 'Tell them blood. The blood coming out its mouth.'

When she finished talking to the police, declining out of habit to give her own name, Fran turned to see Gary marching out of his garden. He seemed ready to say something, but changed his mind and walked away. Let him find out about the dog himself, Fran thought.

"Time to get inside," she told the kids. "There's something I want to ask your dad before he goes out to work."

To their surprise, Frank was dressed and in the kitchen when they got back, checking the beer cans in the fridge. As soon as she was indoors, hearing the kids going on and on about the dead dog, she wished she could have done more about it. She hated seeing animals hurt. And what if Gary walked that way and saw his own dog dead like that? She should have broken it to him gently. Maybe she'd pop over after. That's you, Fran, doing turns for everyone, she thought.

She ushered Lyndsey and Jeff into place for breakfast. She poured their extra-milky tea. "How come we've only got one pint?" she asked Frank and only then realised they were her first words to him.

"That bloody Nesta from next door came round while you were out. She says she can't afford milk. So I gave her it." He completed his first emptied can.

"She's been round here every day for a week! I told her no more."

"I didn't know that. What do you want me to do, go round and take it back?"

Busy with cornflakes, Fran waved him away. Lyndsey and Jeff were chatting between themselves. "That would be something at least. You'd give her the stair carpet if she asked, you're that daft. You're addled."

Frank gritted his teeth and rubbed his belly. "She's got that baby. If she can't afford milk –"

"If she can't afford milk, she should lay off the Woodpecker. So should that dopey husband of hers, that Tony. Some people will do anything to get their booze."

"I'm getting ready for work."

Fran shouted after him, "You can look after the bairns tonight. Me and some of the lasses have decided we're having a night out tonight. You're staying in and you're not getting drunk."

He turned around. "You've organised this quick."

She snorted. "It's about time."

"I see."

Fran went to the sink and turned the taps on, making lots of noise. The noise drummed away the tension in the air.

At last he said, "I want you in by eleven."

Then he was gone, leaving the kids kicking each other under the bench, and Fran silently watching over the sink as it filled. All you've got to do, she told herself, all you've ever done, is ride out the worst of it. It was what she was best at. She could cling on for dear life. Anyone else would have got shot of Frank years ago...yet here she was. When things got tough, that was when a grim resolve came over her and she dug her heels in even harder. Her mother said she'd learned her stubbornness from the horses she'd broken in with her brothers. She had subdued them all to her implacable will in a way those strapping boys had never managed. Fran simply held out for people. Until the age of nine she had, with the grimmest intensity, thought that she was herself a horse. Something of that hadn't quite left her. When she and Frank made love he always felt gripped to her, that his heart would burst before she would let him go. And she in turn felt that she was carrying him and she made herself strong and content to be ridden like this, by him.

She lifted the plates one by one from warm soapy water and watched the scum of grease slide into the froth.

HE WOKE TEN MILES AWAY FROM HOME IN A STIFLING ROOM. WHEN HE opened his eyes, the air was dark orange because of the curtains, which hung in musty velvet folds. On an armchair misshapen by their thrown-off clothing, a marmalade cat was sitting. It stared unblinking at Vince. It nodded at him once and then was gone, out of the door they had, in their haste, left open.

He had a peculiarly guilty thought about abandoning Penny on the streets of Darlington. But she could look after herself, surely? Odd that his first thought – after last night of all nights – should be of her. Maybe he had dreamed about her. He groaned, feeling yesterday's events wash over him. He could taste lemon and tequila and something less definable.

His tongue, his eyes and his cock all felt tender and bruised and he moved carefully, aware that the slightest twitch might break the delicate train of his thoughts. It might unhook him from yesterday's surprises and render them untrue. His memories always took some reeling in. But when they came it was with a clarity he could relish, and one he was convinced nobody else ever knew.

The light in the room was a treacly amber and it was dulling him somewhat. He could work out what time it was. The day before seemed caught in flight, etched in the air before him. He couldn't see where the arc of his memory ended. Which meant that the story was going on still. He was still embroiled in something. So it didn't matter what time it was, whether he was late for work or not. There could be no question of going in. He was busy.

There was a line of warm sticky heaviness down his left side and leg. A trickle of sweat on the flat of his stomach. Andy was still deeply asleep, by the look of it, glued to him. He was on his back, impassive, as if determined that sleep should have no effect. For all that his expression seemed peaceful and content.

He could feel their bodies sticking in other points of contact. Their feet were tangled warmly together like shoes. His palms itched to be back around his lover, for the feel of him. Vince could feel his cock shrugging and thickening itself, leaning out towards the sleeping Andy. Gently Vince pulled himself free of the semi-embrace and moved across the bed. He was determined to make that call.

In the hallway there was a payphone. He remembered that. He looked around for something to wrap around himself and decided not to bother. Andy lived alone. He had nothing to be ashamed of here.

This was something he had promised himself long ago he would never do again. And yet it was bliss.

The hallway was dowdy and grey. He nicked ten pence from the money box and rang the school. He got the secretary and made himself sound terribly afflicted with cold. Her voice in his ear was tinny and nonplussed. Shamefacedly Vince clutched at the plastic coil of the phone's lead and looked down at the carpet. He stared at his cock, bulging absurdly over the phone table, as he muttered excuses. Almost without interest he was saying, "Yes, do give my apologies to Mrs Bell, and say we've reached the trip into the countryside in *Room with a View*. She won't mind doing that bit with my class." He put the phone down and hurried back to Andy's room.

He snuggled down separately, burying himself in the bulky oppression of blankets. Why did Andy need so many? It was sweltering in here. He'd always been like that. Like a hibernating beast, Vince thought, sleeping all day. Which was why he was happy with a night-time job.

Oddly the memory of the things that irked him about Andy brought home to him the ease of slipping back into his life. Walking down North Road and feeling like a couple was the beginning of it. Falling wordlessly into this lumpy nest upon arrival was the obvious continuation. But the relief of an old lover...Vince knew all about that. In college he had fallen back in with old lovers once or twice. A few extra nights in fallow spots, to resume relations, remind themselves, to pass the time. Ex-lovers seemed always to be around and available. Eventually, in a town as small and incestuous as Lancaster, he had worn the whole scene dry. Yet he hadn't made love to Andy since they were both eighteen.

Suddenly he wanted to wake him up. He felt a burst of optimism, like a physical sensation in his chest. He looked at Andy and hesitated. This is a holiday, he thought. A proper holiday. Already at school he felt both too old and too young. Somewhere between the pupils and teachers, doing his own thing. At least here he was with a peer. The only one he ever needed.

Andy's head and shoulders stuck out of the duvet like a statue upon a tomb, cast in orange and blue shadow. It always amazed Vince how people looked different in bed. He couldn't believe that the perfection they had then never lasted. It never seemed to carry to outdoors. Why didn't people remark upon Andy's beauty all the time? Because here it was plain as day in the half-light. He was seized by a rush of affection and stretched out under the covers to grasp Andy's chest in a hug.

Andy's head whipped round as he started awake. Never had Vince felt that Andy was his until this moment. Andy always woke like this, as if at gunpoint. As if he never trusted anyone. Now he smiled, his mouth stretching his whole face into a triangle, with those green, glinting eyes alive in the corners. "It's you," he said to Vince, feigning surprise.

Vince squeezed his chest. You're mine, he thought. And realised that was part of the charm; the unlasting spell of the beauty of the other in bed with you. In that moment they have chosen to be yours. They are vulnerable and there for you. He decided this was exactly the point. The beauty is fleeting because the next thing that happens is that they go. You end up alone. But...there must be more to this, because here was Andy again. His again. Looking vulnerable. Andy always looked unsure what to say around Vince. No matter how much they had done together or how much they ever loved each other, he always felt inarticulate. It amused Vince, seeing Andy struggle to pitch their conversation. He would follow Andy's lead.

'I thought you'd come to tell me last night that you were seeing that girl,' Andy said at last. So Penny was the first thing on his mind this morning, too. "I thought she'd turned you."

Vince reached for Andy's hand and clasped it. Their fingers were dry and flaky with each other's come. Last night they had made love too eagerly, perhaps, as if it was something to just to get over with, like the lick-slam-suck of the tequila, before settling down to the real business of clinging hard to each other and whispering away each other's pounding headaches in the middle of the night. Vince had a sudden vivid recollection of the night's final embrace, his face in the taut whiteness of Andy's neck, the length of their bodies pressed hard, too hard together, as if in contest. Their stomachs were wet and Vince could feel one of their pricks softening between them, he wasn't certain whose, and Andy was crying, heaving out dry sobs. Now he couldn't remember what had begun that storm.

"I'm here, aren't I?"

"People never come here," Andy said, letting Vince take his hand back, letting him begin to touch the rest of him. He watched as Vince started to tug back the voluptuous warmth of all the bedclothes, exposing them. He stared at Vince as he knelt by him, his urgent cock. "People never want to come back to a taxidermist's."

Vince gave a little laugh and bent to put his mouth to Andy's prick, drawing it out of itself. Andy took hold of him under his arms and hoisted him up in a morning kiss.

"Morning dog breath," Vince said.

"I don't mind," Andy said.

For a few moments they rolled about like this, pushing the covers right back to allow themselves room to play in. They let the conversation drop and there was a sense of their using these embraces to stretch life into their limbs. To wrestle the sleepiness out of themselves. These were warming-up exercises. Soon, however, this cool, almost rehearsed rigour was replaced by a determination and a pressure that brought up its own fresh sweat. They began to tear at each other, breathing hard. Vince embarrassed himself by groaning out loud and long when Andy got right underneath him, probing with a strong, practised tongue under his balls and then right into his arse. Automatically Vince arched his back right up to spread himself further apart and let Andy inveigle himself inside in a way they once, some years ago, rowed about. Vince had been dead set against it. Andy had desired it in the way his own noises now showed. He came up again to lay Vince's legs along his haunches and, taking his reddened, angry cock in his hand, made him come in one, two, three savage jerks. Vince sat up, cross and smarting, immediately. They held each other then, both a bit surprised at how frantic it had all been.

When they got their breath back, Vince said, "You never came."

Andy shrugged. "Doesn't matter."

"That used to make you all bothered."

"I was reading something that said it did you good not to."

"Yeah?" Vince was sceptical. "Here." And he started to kiss Andy again, trying to replicate the moment before. He reached for his own cock and found it still as hard, and started to pull at it, wanking just as Andy had shown him, the way he did himself. And then Vince felt a bit ridiculous, found himself faking his own excitement now that his own moment had passed. Andy beneath him was delirious, however, soaked with sweat and falling back on to the sheet, tossing his head as if in fever. Vince was losing his grip, getting cramp, found himself muttering encouragement. Next thing he knew Andy had slipped his own hand down, taken his own cock from Vince, and was doing himself. He left Vince braced between his knees, watching with a smile as suddenly Andy seemed to break something inside; his eyes went wide, and then he shot spunk all over his chest in copious amounts. Its first lucid stream laced down the side of his face.

Sudden as it had begun, his fever subsided and he wanted another hug.

"I think," he said groggily, some moments later, "this place puts people off."

"Yeah?" Vince tried to get up, wanting to be up and about now. But Andy was holding him down, tender but strong.

"A few months ago I was seeing an older man. House of his own. Good job. He would never come here. Mad me feel I had no life of my own."

"I can see that," Vince murmured.

Andy turned to look right at him. "Are you staying tonight?"

Vince clasped him, the once familiar, everyday weight of him. "I don't see why not."

Andy grinned. Tasting his own saltiness down the side of his face, he wiped at it. "We'll have a night out then. We'll go out on the town. We'll dress you up nice."

PENNY WALKED INTO THE LIVING ROOM JUST AS LIZ FINISHED PREPARING herself to face the day. She was doing her eyeliner and 'Sympathy for the Devil' was playing, not quite loud enough to drown out the telly. She took great care with her make-up every day, even those days when she wouldn't be seeing anyone. As if to keep her vigilant, mirrors were everywhere in the house, except in her bedroom. Liz felt that if she slackened the effort at keeping herself perfect it might make her ill again, and she didn't want that. Now everything had to be in its right place, her eyes drawn in exactly, and then it would be all right.

She turned to smile at Penny. "Good morning!" she said loudly.

Penny was shrugging herself into her cardigan. She scowled. "You look gorgeous as usual, for this time in the morning."

"I'm a morning person."

"You never used to be." Penny made for the kitchen. "Can you turn the music down?"

Liz followed her. "As of this week, I am a morning person. I'm changing all the old things I don't like. And wasting time being grumpy and looking a fright until eleven is the first thing to go."

Penny tutted. "Thanks a lot."

"I wasn't talking about you. You look lovely in the morning no matter how you feel because you're so young. You couldn't look horrible if you tried."

Penny thought her mother was pushing the Julie Andrews routine a bit. She had already seen herself this morning and she looked a hag, no matter how young she was.

Liz banged the grill pan into the oven, cheerfully making toast. "I have to make more of an effort to be forever young these days."

Sometimes Penny thought Liz had what bordered on a mania to do with age and ageing. They had already talked at length about what ages Penny thought Fran, Jane, Frank, everyone round here was. It was as if Liz was always competing to look better for her age than everyone else.

"Is that why you do your make-up with the Stones playing?" Penny teased. "So that you'll look as fresh as they do?"

"Tell you what," Liz said. "I admire them for still going. They could look like skeletons and they'd still sound marvellous. It does me good to see people hanging in there."

Penny was making coffee, sluicing the cafetiere under the tap. "I admire John Lennon for being dead. Before he could get too old. He got out the right way."

"So I should just lie down and die now, then? Is that what you mean?'" Two red spots had appeared high on Liz's dusted cheekbones.

"Oh, get away, Mam! I'm talking about pop stars, how they should give up the ghost. Like Rod Stewart. Or Cliff Richard. Take off their long hair and underneath they'd just be like any other scraggy bloke of fifty. Like some old bloke off the bins."

Still Liz was looking stung, taking the toast out from under the grill. The sides weren't equally done and she had to scrape all the slices over the sink.

Penny tried to make it better. "I think you're lovely for your age. You know that."

"Hm."

"And you've said the same thing about Cliff Richard's turkey neck."

"Hm."

"It's just like the whole world is full of people wanting to be teenagers. And most of the time I feel about sixty."

Liz looked at her. She decided to abandon the toast. 'Someone isn't happy this morning.'

"I'm all right." Flustered, Penny went to make the coffee.

Her mother decided to have a dig back. "I know what it is. You're in a narky mood because you found out that your pretty boy was queer."

Penny was lighting a cigarette and managed to singe the ends of her fringe. "Why do you always bring everything back to sex?"

Liz raised both eyebrows and took her coffee. "I do not. I don't care about it any more."

"Yeah. Right."

"You know best, Pen. Obviously you know it all."

"It's like that joke yesterday. About keeping your fanny fresh. You enjoy that, don't you?"

Her mother smirked. "What? What do I enjoy?"

"Being embarrassing."

This hit its mark. Liz lowered her eyes. Penny just wished she'd kept her trap shut.

At last Liz said, "So I'm an embarrassment to Lady Shite, am I?"

"Vince called me that yesterday! Is that what I'm like?" She was appalled.

"We're on about me here. Listen. Am I really an embarrassment to you?" Liz's fuchsia lips were set, grim.

"You know you're not. I didn't mean it like that."

Liz swung her legs round and jumped off her stool, shoving her almost untouched breakfast things into the sink. "No, you've got a lot to be embarrassed about. I'm not surprised. I've put you through too much."

Penny knew then that she had to put a stop to this. It was a destructive mood, this one, and Penny knew it of old. It was a downward spiral. If Penny left her like this, Liz would stay at home today and think herself embarrassing and foolish until she found herself unable to go out. And nothing would talk her round.

"Mam," Penny said, very decisively, making sure she had Liz's attention. "You've never put me through too much. You really haven't."

Liz wouldn't be easily talked round. "But the kids must say things at school."

"Not a word. They never realised. They don't know. People accept things anyway. And you know I can cope with anything. You've taught me that, Mam."

Liz took two steps across the lino and hugged her. Penny sighed. Disaster averted. "You're calling me Mam! You haven't done that in...ages."

Penny looked sheepish, gathered up in her mother's broad embrace. "You've never claimed to be anything different."

Her mother let her go. "You're a smashing lass, Pen."

She shrugged. "I know."

"There's one thing I've got to tell you though, Pen."

"What?"

"You've burned a bloody hole in my mohair with that fag of yours."

FIVE

SHE TUGGED AT HER SLEEVES AS SHE CAME DOWNSTAIRS. WHEN SHE wasn't bending her arms they didn't look too short. Perhaps the jacket would be all right. It was smart enough for a club, anyway. It would do. It wasn't as though they were all going to dress up to the nines. They were going for a quiet drink in a club, that's what Jane had promised. That's all Fran wanted to do. They weren't going raving or anything. Her jacket was fine. The doorbell went on ringing.

Behind the misty glass of the front door she caught an impression of the squat form of Nesta from next door. Even through the frosted glass you could see the black roots in her self-bleached hair. Fran knew for a fact that Nesta had done her own bleaching with Domestos and a paintbrush. Nesta had told her so, proudly. She wasn't going to pay a fortune to sit in a hairdresser's window and look stupid. She'd do her own for next to nowt. When Fran opened the door Nesta gave her a loose grin and said, "I've brought you a pint back. Tony's been given some money." She pressed the bottle on Fran, shouldering her way into the hall.

"Thanks," mumbled Fran and followed her neighbour into the kitchen.

Nesta turned to eye the black velvet jacket. "Are you going out?"

This was what got on Fran's nerves about Nesta. She came on like the doziest cow you'd ever meet. Everyone said she was intellectually subnormal. Jane had been in school with her. But when you got her on her own there often seemed something shrewder than that about Nesta. Conniving was the word, Fran thought. She'd perk up and stop being slow if she was going to get something out of it.

"I've been trying my glad rags on. I haven't dressed up in ages." Fran found herself being cagey. No one had invited Nesta to come out with them. No one had even considered it. They would have to buy her drinks all night and then she'd only be sick at the end of it. Like the time she'd thrown up on the nightie she was trying on at Jane's Anne Summers do.

The black jacket made Nesta stop to think. At last she said, "Yes, they used to be quite fashionable, didn't they?" Fran looked blankly at her. She felt herself shrink inside the jacket. Oblivious, Nesta continued, "When they were in, I used to have one of every colour. Wine red, evergreen, tan, navy blue. You get them turning up in car-boot sales a lot. People chucking out their old clothes." Nesta was an expert on the car-booties.

I can't let her get me down, Fran thought. I'm wearing this and that's all there is to it. I've got nothing else and she's not exactly Selina Scott, is she? "Well, I think it still looks nice."

Nesta made her way to the kettle. "But it makes you look fat."

Fran marched neatly over and slapped Nesta's hands away from the flex. "Right, that's it! If you're going to be rude like that you can bugger off home, Nesta. I'm not having you come in here to slag me off. I've given you milk every day this past week because you won't do your own shopping. You needn't come round here again."

Nesta was shocked. Fran was never like this. She stood quite still, not used to this treatment. Fran controlled her breathing and carefully put down the half-empty kettle. Nesta's brow crumpled. "I'll go, then. I might see you tomorrow." Then she hurried out the back door.

Fran sat down at the pine table. She stroked the velvety material thoughtfully, running a fingertip around a cigarette burn on the forearm, one she hadn't noticed before. She laughed softly.

Her eldest daughter Kerry had, only recently, told her off. "You're a mess, Mam. The other kids' mams are fashionable. Why don't you get smartened up? Get your hair done?"

"There's more important things," Fran said. She had been too upset to say anything else. Kerry tutted and walked away. Now, Fran caught her reflection in the kitchen mirror and grimaced to herself.

"WHO OWNS THE TAXIDERMIST'S?" VINCE ASKED THIS FOLLOWING ANDY down the stairs wrapped in a towel. His skin was cooling now, but still lobster pink from the hottest, hardest shower he had ever had. Andy had joined him and they'd fooled around some more in there. He hadn't had so much sex in ages. Not in months. Feast or famine, that's how it always was with him. With the odd little picnic on the way. Andy was the same, he said. They were making their way down to the kitchen at the back of the shop in search of tea, and the thought had just struck Vince that never had asked who owned the place where Andy lived.

"Oh... Some bloke. He's not here much. The shop is hardly ever open."

Andy's voice came wafting up the hallway, part of the musty air. It was cold here, and dark, quite different to the cosy nest of Andy's room. Strange truncated animals jutted out of the stair walls. Each of them grinned, tongues lolling, as if their heads had been rammed though the plasterboard and they were pleasantly stunned. Vince felt funny, stranded on the stairway, glancing sideways at a drooling fox as he said, "Is there any tea?"

Andy reappeared. "Got it. Get back upstairs and get warm." He was in his red silk dressing gown.

"Look at you, Noël Coward!"

"Just get back and shut up." Andy gripped the creaking banister on his way up. It always amazed Vince, the number of outfits Andy had to dress up in. All his money went on clothes.

"It feels good to be here again." Vince had an urge to have a poke around the taxidermist's shop. "I don't know why I stopped coming here."

Andy reached him. "I don't know either. You never said why."

"One of those things."

"I was starting to bore you?"

"God, no! I thought...I should be looking for something else."

"Thanks a lot."

"You stopped scaring me. You weren't strange any more. I let you drop for your own good. Because you weren't making the same impression." Vince thought again, wanting to make it sound better. All he could add was, "Um."

"I think I see. You thought you had used me up."

Vince was shivering badly now. His skin was rough and white. He looked down earnestly into Andy's foreshortened face, its eyes tilted upwards, full of cinematic menace. How could he have thought him no longer scary. "Yeah. And I was moving away. I was over on the other coast. Bloody miserably damp nasty Lancaster."

"You loved it there. Don't pretend you didn't."

"And how do you know that?"

"You stayed there over four years. You never came here."

"It didn't mean I was having a lovely time," Vince said. "It was just where I was. Where my life was."

Andy hesitated. "Why didn't you let me come over? To visit? I mean, I know trying to keep something going long-distance is difficult, but we could have just seen each other...gone out, or..."

They kissed greedily under the single beady eye of the fox. Tea bags dropped, one by one, onto the stair carpet.

LIZ WAS HAVING A MARVELLOUS TIME, TRYING ON NEW FROCKS. IN THE only decent clothes shop in town she was kicking up a fuss.

"No, I don't want any assistance. Just give me the garments and let me decide for myself, thank you."

"But the limit is five, madam. You have eleven."

"And what if I buy the lot?"

"Are you sure you don't need another opinion?"

"I'm wearing the things. I only need my opinion, thanks." With that she yanked the curtain shut. "You can count them when I come out. I'm not nicking anything."

The sales assistant sighed and walked away. She stood idly at her counter with no one left to please. Occasionally, over the music, Liz could be heard laughing at herself as she tried various new combinations.

The assistant concentrated on straightening the racks and picking bits of fluff off the carpet. Then Fran appeared with all her kids in tow. She asked the assistant to watch Lyndsey and Jeff and, like Liz, waved her assistance away, disappearing into a cubicle of her own with the maximum five garments.

She held them to herself, watching her reflection in solitary confinement. Sighing deeply, she examined them against her, one after another. As yet she didn't dare look at he prices. Someone on the bus had said this place was meant to be good value. It was the first time Fran had been. It was a seconds shop, but she couldn't see much wrong with the stuff. Maybe she could afford something...just something not too...

Fran was caught by the chuckling in the next cubicle. Then a familiar voice went, "Oh, dear! You couldn't get away with that." At first Fran thought the voice was talking to her. She thought it was the voice of her conscience. And then she recognised it, and realised it was a voice speaking to itself.

"Liz?" she asked.

"Yes? Hello?"

"It's Fran. Are you getting something for tonight, as well?"

"Hello, Fran. Yes, I am. And I look a slut at the moment, so forgive me if I don't pop through to see you."

"I'm getting something for myself." Fran ruffled through the items, rejecting the slutty skirts, the gold and black dress. "Something new."

"Good on you. What sort of thing?" Liz's voice became muffled as she struggled out of one skirt into the next.

"I don't know what sort of place we're going to."

"Me neither. It's all Jane's doing. We should have asked her."

"It'll be some kind of pick-up joint."

"But I've already discarded the slutty stuff."

"Is that how we should be then? Slutty?" Fran was enjoying herself now. She shrugged off her anorak and unbuttoned her blouse. "Are you going out on the pull, Liz?"

"If I've nothing better to do. But Darlington is full of creeps."

Fran started to concentrate. Her mam always said she had lovely taste in clothes, when she put her mind to it. Suddenly it seemed important that she prove she hadn't let it go. 'We need something plain and classy.'

"Not sluttish."

"No, classic, alluring..."

"Hm. Alluring like...an old movie star sort of thing..."

"Aye, no frills...sort of plain..."

"Tarty."

"Slutty."

"Tarty it is."

"WHAT DOES IT MEAN WHEN YOU SAY YOU'VE GOT A TALENT FOR SOME-thing, anyway?" Penny was asking earnestly. "I mean, really, I could be talented in millions of things."

She was sitting in a poky office with her careers consultant, a small man who seemed to be made entirely from plastic. A fleshy, rubbery plastic partly melted. They were sitting by the radiator and discussing Penny's vocation.

Shrugging good-naturedly, he set about stuffing his pipe with tobacco. His other subject, besides careers, was photography, for which he coaxed girls of all ages into modelling the various hats he collected. The school couldn't afford photography equipment, so his small department was scrupulously self-financed. A blind eye was turned. As Penny spoke he examined a new hat someone had brought him from a Blue Peter bring-and-buy sale.

"So we can't find one thing that I excel in, or that I really want to do. So what? Does that mean I have to compromise and do the same old thing as everyone else? Does it really?" What she wanted to tell him was that she was cleverer than that. She knew she was. But she had no way of measuring that. She had no way of showing it. These were frustrating times. Penny felt got at on two sides: by the implacable rationality of the careers master, and by the secret and sure burgeoning of her own talents. She knew they were there, but not what they were useful for.

Her careers consultant took a long drag at his pipe and slowly set the lime-green hat on his own head at a jaunty angle.

"You see, Penny," he began at last in a quavering tone, "everyone must be good at doing something. Why, I once knew a boy who, like you, seemed stuck for a vocation in life –"

Penny was thinking about typewriters. "I'm like a shift key!"

"Pardon?"

"The shift key on a typewriter that makes the upper-case letters available – that's what I'm like. It's exactly how I think about things: on a different level!"

The careers consultant regarded her serenely, half his faced shrouded beneath the lampshade hat. She wasn't pretty enough to model, he thought, and went on. "I gave this talentless boy a block of wood. Out of desperation, you see? A perfectly ordinary block of wood and a chisel. And when I came back to him, he had made me the most wonderful antelope you have ever seen. Vocation, you see. He had found his at last. A beautiful creature... I think I still have it in my filing cabinet. It is one of the great successes of my teaching career. That and my portfolio, of course. These days, I believe that same boy is very high up in the town council."

He rose to his feet. "So, Miss Robinson, you have some serious thinking to do. Some serious thinking on practical matters. We shall talk again soon and, if you are still keen on typewriters, we can have a look into some secretarial courses together."

"Thanks for all your help," said Penny and left.

Upstairs she stuffed her head in her locker. It was mid-morning break. Someone in the common room was playing the Cure. She strolled over and asked the boy in dark-framed glasses standing by the speakers if she could put something on. She dug out Vince's tape of *Hunky Dory*.

"That's really classic, that," said the boy who had been forced to remove his Cure album. He was talking to another boy in dark-framed glasses and a cardigan. 'Changes' stuttered into life over the speakers. "He influenced everyone; the Cure...yeah, everyone."

Penny liked to think she was bringing some style into their lives. "Bowie is God," she said.

And they nodded respectfully, as they would for a recently deceased aunt whom they never really knew or understood. "My dad reckons this LP is a classic," he said.

Penny already knew. She had lived already. Her shift key, the perennial tingling, whatever she liked to call it, had elevated her way above the trees and houses. This was, after all, the term following her great summer of experience.

That summer in Durham she had had her romance with a boy called Rob. Rob was on probation for something that sounded like 'feathery'.

"Fucking chickens!" Penny would crow.

"I was robbing houses," Rob would mutter, abashed. "Keep your voice down."

"Chicken fucker," she'd snicker. "You smell of stuffing."

With him Penny had entered the late-night high life of the ill-lit medieval town centre and discovered that the very hippest of her peers spent their summer evenings on benches with bags of glue and bottles of Woodpecker.

"Losers," she told Rob after their first night out. "How can glue sniffing solve anything. Ha ha ha!" Rob didn't get the joke. He clung grimly on to her, unsmiling all the way home. She was tottering about, having sniffed too hard that night, and eventually she threw up in a shrubbery.

"There's a technique to sniffing," he said, patting her back. "You have to respect the glue."

"It's all over my jacket," she groaned. "Like spunk. Never again."

Rob's advice about 'respecting the glue' confirmed for her his status as an arsehole it would be safe to chuck by September. "Respect the glue," she would mutter to herself. "Typical!" Rob looked affronted. "That's typical of your sort," she would accuse him. "I suppose you respect the government and magistrates, too." Rob scowled at her. He thought she didn't know what it was like to be on probation.

To all and sundry, that summer, Penny would announce, "Rob's really sweeping me off my feet."

It was a whirlwind. Experience everything, she was instructed by her innermost drives. At the peak of summer she found herself sucking, sniffing, chewing, drinking, laughing, frotting, coaxing, snorting, smoking, bleeding, gorging, sighing, retching, fucking, and starting at last to sort the sheep from the boys. And tingling always, shift key firmly depressed; shift lock, in fact.

At the beginning of September, Penny kicked leaves down the road, all the way from the whirlwind, into autumn, and back to school.

remembered spending a lot of time indoors, and then standing at the bottom of his garden, waiting for the taunting fly-overs Fran's brothers made on horseback.

"I think Fran's going to start spending money. Going out more."

"Get her a new armchair."

"I did last time."

"Get her another one."

"There's only me and her who sit on chairs."

"Get them recovered."

"Nah."

"I was just suggesting..." Gary let it go. He remembered that they weren't supposed to be speaking, having threatened to do each other in.

"That bloody family of hers." Frank spat too, but it was thick with beer and clung to the can. "Them and their horses. Giving her ideas."

"You've given her all she needs."

"I thought so."

"Yurp," Gary asserted, consolingly. He bent to start work again. He held up some material. "This is a new print, this. She'd like her three-piece recovered in this. I won't say owt if you whip some."

"I don't pinch stuff."

"I just said –"

"And you don't either. You're unemployed, remember." Frank swapped cans and glared at his apprentice.

"Yurp."

"Bloody horses! Giving ideas. Bloody cushions!" Frank slid sideways n the Styrofoam. "I'd take her out, for fuck's sake."

"YOU'VE GOT EVERYTHING YOU NEED?"

"I think so."

"I'm looking forward to this now."

"It'll be a laugh."

"You look lovely in that. We'll get you cracked off with someone. No other."

Fran laughed. "Thanks anyway." She peered into a dark shop window. Terry had been right. "I'm walking round in an anorak I've had ten years

IT WAS TWO GARAGES KNOCKED INTO ONE. THE WALLS INSIDE WERI
with artificial light and clouds of sprayed colour. Cushions and I
dismembered settees were strewn about, with acrylics, fabrics, a
wound in waiting piles. Everywhere there was foam rubber. Jau
squares of sponge, fleshy slabs rounded at the corners. The room
soft, comforting room. Here sofas were put back together. It was a s
for the badly upholstered.

Frank was slumped on a mass of Styrofoam, knocking the
of a can against his teeth. His cigarette smoke rose in a blue pl
the naked light bulb above him. He wasn't meant to smoke in he
materials were dodgy.

Gary was wrestling with unwieldy cushions through his dinn
He was in mourning for his dog. He hadn't told Frank anything a
about finding his dog dead and surrounded by policemen at the
the road first thing this morning. He had no idea how the dog
out overnight. He worked continuously, stretching covers over
them back, zipping them carefully up with pursed lips. His hand
absorbedly over cheap fabric.

They hadn't spoken at all this morning. Frank had been lyin
stewed to the gills. Gary's only comment had been to zip up zips v
than his usual vehemence.

They hadn't spoken properly since Fran's argument and t
about the axe. Frank would instruct Gary in his work – he was
supposed to be teaching him – in as few words as possible. Ga
reply, "Yurp" or "Got it", and take his duties over.

It was Frank who broke the fractious silence. "Does your w
a lot?"

The question startled Gary. He dropped his latest cushion
pile and wiped his mouth on the arm of his camouflaged jacket

"She never goes out. We've got the kid. I don't go out." He s
concrete and rubbed it away with a corner of his next cushio
walk the dog...of a night and that's about it." For a moment ther
forgotten, and mentioning his dog almost made him break do
was no way he'd let Frank see him upset. Ammo to the enemy.

Frank remembered how difficult it was being newl

and my hair's all –"

Liz was dashing off to the bus stop, swinging her carrier bags. "Get a wig then!" she cried.

Fran ran after her. "Look! Look who's driving the bus!"

The bus stopped and, pulling up for them outside the fish shop and the video shop round the back of the precinct, the bus driver grinned at them.

"All aboard!" he shouted.

SIX

VINCE HAD A SUIT THAT HIS FATHER HAD BOUGHT HIM WHEN HE WAS seventeen. They went shopping together in the Metro Centre in Gateshead when the sales were on. Thinking back, it was the last real thing they had done together. In the spring of that year his father realised that soon Vince would be leaving, that by the end of the year he would be gone. The father would be on his own in the little house by the playing fields. He held no illusions about Vince's attachment to him. He knew that, given one sniff of freedom and the life beyond, Vince would be gone. Father and son had only ever been held together by a kind of tacit, improvised trustfulness.

His father wanted to buy his son a suit for the interviews he would be having at universities. He couldn't be there himself, he couldn't drive his son to all the different towns, but he wanted to do something. He didn't think a boy that age should want his father there with him, anyway. One breakfast-time he tried to bring this up: how much support would Vince be needing to do this, this breaking away? And Vince looked up from his cornflakes mystified, as if he'd always assumed he'd be on his own. Worse, for his father, as if he'd assumed he was already on his own.

There was a vigorous practicality in his father. He'd been through the army. Grown up in the Fifties. He'd worked with men in garages. He'd known times of austerity and rebellion. He'd done it all on Teesside, where such things struck harder. So he could submerge his deeper upsets and resentments and concentrate on the proper things he could do for his son at this time. Arranging for a van, for example, to transport his few things to college in the autumn. Making sure he got his head down and revised hard enough to pass his exams in the first place. His father could see this process as some kind of endurance test and, that way, he could understand it. Vince had to run the distance. And that included smartening himself up for interviews.

At seventeen Vince would have been happy to turn up looking a state but his father wanted to see him right. At seventeen he barely even thought about what he was wearing, slouching around the place in faded jeans and those bloody green trainers of his. He'd had them for years and he wore them in all weathers. His father was a dandy, sprucing himself up teddy-boy style for the big club every Friday night in his drainpipes, midnight-blue jacket and shoestring tie. He manicured his quiff in the mirror in the living room. Vince's father knew what you had to do to pull the lasses and get on in the world. He stood and stared and sighed at Vince's wilful negligence of his own appearance.

The day he drove him up to the Metro Centre, his father took a long appraising look at him while they had cappuccinos in a Grecian-style café. How much like his mother he was! Almost a man...well, he was a man, really. And there was that pale skin, the orange hair, the same mouth. Vince's dad remembered the very day Vince had told him he didn't want his father kissing him any more. It wasn't long after his mam had walked out. Looking at Vince's mouth now, across the table from him, his father could forget that the voice coming from it was broken. He could find himself wanting to kiss it. As your kids got bigger, your thoughts got funnier and more complicated. Sometimes you didn't know where you were. And there was the kid, completely headstrong, set on what he wanted. It was always the parents that got left mixed up, wasn't it?

"Drink up," his father said. "We'd better go and see what we can get you."

Vince would have liked to look in the bookshops that afternoon, but Dad didn't read. He barely watched television. Anything that entailed sitting down longer than ten minutes without eating or drinking was suspect in his world. Whenever Vince was reading he could be sure Dad was doing sit-ups on the top landing or tinkering with his car.

"We've got to decide what sort of suit you'll need and how much I can afford to spend."

They headed for the escalators, and Vince realised he was scowling. He really didn't want his father going to any expense. He didn't want to be any more indebted to him than necessary. He hated the thought of his father standing there when he was being measured and trying on suits. Dad attempting to impose his own vision of his son on him... Vince liked to play himself down in his green trainers and his 'Meat Is Murder' T-shirt.

As they headed down the brightly lit hallways of the Metro Centre, Vince's mind was made up. He was having cheap and he was having tacky. Something he couldn't respect or feel grateful for. Sometimes he got into these moods. I'm a spoiled cunt, I am, he thought savagely as they went through Next, Top Man, Principles, Burtons. I'm purposely turning up my nose at everything he suggests. It's all I ever do. Why do I treat him as if he's always got to be making up for something? He was the one here for me. He did me right. But no matter how hard done by he thought his father was, left behind with an ungrateful son, Vince was far more angry on his on account. He felt that no one had ever talked to him. Someone had taken a look at him and simply assumed what he wanted: this is the kind of life you want, a boy like you. All he wanted to say was that he wasn't a boy like him. He clung doggedly to a private self, an inner self they didn't see.

His earliest book was one of fairy stories, an anthology whose spine wore away with overuse, far outlasting the building sets, the electronic devices and mechanical things his father bought in ensuing years for them to share. And in the book was a retelling of *Pinocchio*. For Vince it had always gone without saying that he and his father were Gepetto and Pinocchio. The tale underlay their everyday lives as surely and obviously as genetics. It was something he never questioned, even as late as seventeen.

When Vince looked back to his first suit, the one he wore at seventeen, it made him cringe. It was a lightweight, satiny material of blue and white checks. He wore it everywhere, even to school, with the sleeves rolled up to his elbows like someone out of *Miami Vice*. And his hair was streaked with gold, cut spiky, blown back on top, grown long, almost halfway down his back.

Vince got his place at Lancaster without even having to go for an interview, but his father still wished Vince had chosen a nicer suit.

In Darlington on the afternoon of their reunion Andy pulled out scores of old photos and laughed at Vince, such a child of the Eighties. Vince had his head in his hands, cursing.

He was wearing the suit the first time Andy met him. They met in Sunderland, at Roker Park. It was 1987, the year of David Bowie's Glass Spider tour, and they were on the same bus party from Darlington. Their relationship was cemented that warm, drizzly afternoon, standing in the pressing crowd, right at the front, right under the shadow of the sixty-foot-tall perspex spider that Bowie was going to perform on. Doggedly they kept their pole position in the stadium crowd and talked and talked for the hours until the evening concert was due to begin. Vince shared between them the cheese-and-pickle sandwiches his father had packed for him.

When Bowie came on, just yards ahead of them, it was with irony and aplomb, in his own lightweight, satiny suit, his own teased-up, bleached Eighties hair, but he was also a terrible disappointment. It seemed that he had lost his edge. All his weirdness just seemed put on. But, jostled and pulled around by the mass of swaying bodies, Andy and Vince kept looking at each other.

Andy had come dressed in what Vince would soon recognise as only one of his many outfits. He had a separate guise for everything and, for that first meeting, he was done up as Bowie in 1976: the black suit, white shirt, powdered face and slicked-back hair. Bowie when he had integrity and a bone structure you could chop sticks with. Vince was looking increasingly less at the stage, more at the boy right by his side.

At the end of the concert there was no encore, because it had started to rain. Vince was thoroughly pissed off. Bowie's one last chance to reprieve himself was the promised encore: singing 'Time' and being crucified on angel's wings at the very top of the perspex spider. He'd done it at Wembley. Oh, but not in Sunderland. Course he wouldn't do it in Sunderland. Vince stomped out of the stadium, through pissy-smelling underpasses, making for the car parks. All the while Andy kept pace with him. Their ears were ringing, they realised when Andy stopped to buy a T-shirt from a bloke by the exit.

They stood on the sparkling tarmac of the car park outside. Andy said, "I don't really want this. I don't know why I bought it."

Vince was craning his neck, concerned that they'd never find their coach, or that it had already gone. "It's a souvenir, I suppose."

Impulsively Andy said, "You have it. I want you to have it." He held the T-shirt up. Bowie with that teased-up golden hair.

Vince smiled. "Cheers. Do you know where our coach will be? I forgot where they told us."

"Let's go and look on the main road."

The main road was right on the coast. The sea was high on Wearside that night, crashing in thin waves on to the path and the road itself. There were coaches and stragglers tunelessly singing 'Let's Dance' everywhere up the road.

"What if we don't get our coach?" Vince said, starting to worry.

Andy had pulled his leather jacket back on. The wind was unsticking his slicked-back hair. He was strolling nonchalantly, gazing out at the black sea. It was as if the rush and panic of the other seventy thousand people flooding out of the stadium at midnight hardly touched him at all. He was walking, leading Vince further down the coastal road, away from the noise. "It would be all right," he said. "It would be all right even if we did get stuck here. My nanna lives down in Shields. Two miles down the road. She'd put us up."

"Oh." Vince marvelled at how easily he could come up with contingency plans.

"Do you really fancy sitting on a coach with fifty Darlo Bowie fans singing 'China Girl' and throwing up in the gangway?"

On the way the tour guide had made the whole coach watch a *Freddie Starr Live* video. Vince didn't relish the thought of more of the same.

They carried on walking in silence. He looked behind to see the lights of the coaches swaying and bobbing, moving back towards the motorway. That reminded him of something. As the coaches roared past on the coastal road, their lights rearing up and receding, excitable faces pressed to the window, something came back into his mind irresistibly.

"It's like Pinocchio," he said, putting the T-shirt over his head as the drizzle worsened and the great lit-up coaches went thundering by.

"You what?" asked Andy, who was starting to think they really had missed their coach. And it was his fault. They would have to get a taxi to his nanna's. She would have to put them up in her back parlour. Even wet and tired Andy found the idea strangely exciting. He huddled into his jacket and turned to Vince. "What did you say about Pinocchio?"

In the downpour Vince was blushing. This was part of his private mythology. He said, "In *Pinocchio* there's that island where they tempt all the bad boys to go. The bad lads' land. It's where they think they're gonna have this smashing time with gambling and booze and messing around, and then they all turn into donkeys. Pinocchio goes there, tempted by his friend Lichinoro, who says they can go and have the time of their lives."

Andy was smiling, watching the traffic. "I remember."

"Anyway," Vince went on, "in the book I had, it described this bit with all the wagons going off to the shore, with the boys bound for the island, for the bad lads' land. And it said there was a fat jolly coachman hanging off the front, taunting Pinocchio for being scared. And all the boys clinging on, laughing. It said that the wagons' lanterns were swinging and lurching in the darkness and horns were hooting. And Pinocchio was jumping up and down going, 'Wait for me! I'm coming too!'"

He fell quiet. Andy was nodding. "Like he was feeling he'd missed the boat."

"Summat like that." Vince was starting to feel daft, as if he'd given too much away. His ears were still ringing and he noticed that they had both slipped further into a broad Geordie accent. As if they were being bluff and easy-going with each other, but in those exaggerated accents there was also a guardedness, a put-on roughness that hadn't been there an hour earlier when they'd both shrieked themselves raw down at the front as Bowie sang 'Heroes'.

"Here's all the coaches bound for bad lads' land," Andy said. "And they've left us behind! Bloody typical, that!" He was soaked to the skin. "Listen. Next phone box we come to, I'm ringing Nanna Jean and she'll book us a taxi for nowt. She'll pull in a favour and get us in warm and dry before we know it."

"Smart," Vince said. Actually, he wasn't sure if he felt he'd missed the boat at all. In terms of the Pinocchio story, he felt that, since the Blue Fairy was nowhere to be found, since she'd gone and never put him right, he'd gone straight from wooden boy into being a donkey. And in the meantime he had never been a real boy. He was cursed into being a doltish, lascivious donkey... Getting vaguely stirred up by the idea of maybe sharing a room with Andy in this nanna's house. But he'd be happy just to talk to Andy a bit longer. Andy listened to what he was on about.

"I'll have to phone dad, too," Vince said, as a box came into view. By now all the coaches had gone by and they were none the wiser as to where theirs had been.

The phone box stood opposite Marsden Rock. This was a rock the size of the Albert Hall, two hundred yards out to sea. In daylight you would see it swarming with a myriad irate seabirds. In the dark all you got was an impression of bulk and seething life. As Andy used the phone first and told Nanna Jean he was coming and bringing a friend with him, Vince shivered and stared at the massive rock, thinking that could be the bad lads' island there. The place the lights went lurching and bobbing towards.

VINCE WAS BEING SMOTHERED IN A REEK OF PERFUMES. IT WAS LIKE BEING a kid again, slobbered over by one of his aunties. All his dad's sisters made a fuss of him once his mam left home. But in 1984 they all upped and left for Australia, all five of them. They married five Australian brothers. His dad had never approved, although it was still his dream to go out there some day to visit them. If he had the money he would be hard pressed to say which trip he would spend it on, Australia and his sisters, or the Graceland pilgrimage. When Vince was younger it had always been promised that his dad would take the pair of them on holiday when the time came. It never had. Vince added that lost holiday to the stock of things they had never done together.

He was standing in the doorway of Boots, under the hot gush of the fans, waiting for Andy. I'm really wallowing in the past today, he thought. He watched as Andy laughed with the girl who was serving on the make-up counter. Sometimes Andy could make anyone laugh. He was there buying make-up for himself, so he could do himself up like a Goth. He had explained to Vince that tonight they were going to the nightclub round the back of MFI. Flicks, it was called, although the fake scrawling of the neon logo made it look like Fucks. Tonight it was retro Eighties night and, in Darlington, that meant a night out for all the town's Goths, most of whom didn't realise that they were being retro. They just liked the music and the dry ice and the Snakebite at a pound a pint.

Andy came back to the doorway and they left the shop. Vince was glad to gulp in the bus fumes of the main street. "So you're dressing up as one of the Sisters of Mercy then?"

Andy nodded. "It'll be excellent." At the moment he was in a Take That outfit, one of those cropped T-shirts to show off his stomach, despite the time of year. His anorak was cropped too and it had a fake orange fur trim.

Vince asked, "Can you get away with wearing make-up in Darlo at night these days?"

"Course. And I'll look dead hard anyway. You'll see."

Andy was leading them towards Skinnergate, towards the charity shops. Vince understood that the days Andy was up early enough, he cruised the second-hand clothes shops. Inside his wardrobe there were the faint smells of face powder and strong detergent. An old people's smell, Vince thought, that smell of second-hand shops.

THAT WAS WHAT NANNA JEAN'S HOUSE SMELLED LIKE, LATE THAT NIGHT in 1987 when she let them into the hallway. It was from his Nanna Jean that Andy got all his second-hand habits. It was all waste not, want not with them. While both Vince and Andy saw their lives in terms of feast or famine, it made Andy scrimp and save, but Vince pissed everything he got into the wind.

"Ha'way in, pets," Nanna Jean had shouted, lumbering up the hallway, showing them into the parlour, where the old stove was on. The place was full of heat and steam from fresh baking. "I've put some pies in for the pair of you." Vince stood uncertainly by the doorway. Andy smiled at him. "Mind," Nanna Jean said, "if I knew you were coming, I'd have baked a cake." She laughed at herself and went off into the scullery to see to things.

She was a huge woman. The tiny dimensions of the house by the docks helped that impression, but to Vince's eyes, she was a monster. She was in a tentlike black frock, with a well-scrubbed grey pinafore over the top. Her hair was in a bun and her feet were dainty and pointy as if they had been bound that way. She called out harshly from the back, "You pick your moments, you do, Andrew! At the moment I'm all worked up because of old Iris. Remember Iris, who I used to go down the Spiritualist church with? Aye, well, she's not well." Nanna Jean reappeared in the doorway with a tray of fine china, cakes, and the biggest black teapot Vince had seen.

"What's the matter with her?" Andy sat on the hard-backed settee.

"She's going to die, bonny lad. Now move up so your nice-looking friend can get on there with you. The pies will just be a minute or two."

Every detail of that night came back to Vince whenever he thought of it. It was a lovely night. Nanna Jean sat there and regaled them with stories right into the early hours, feeding them and encouraging them both to talk. Yet all the while Jean was thinking about Iris, her best friend from before the war years, and that she wouldn't last out the winter. And it turned out that Jean knew Vince's dad's family too, which Vince thought was a weird coincidence.

"Nah, pet!" Nanna Jean patted his knee. "It's a small world, this one. You watch, when you get a bit older. You're always crossing each other's paths in this world. You can't stop it. And that's nice. And anyway, if your family came from up here, round this town, then there's none more likely to know someone that connects them than me."

"She's right," Andy said. He was finishing home-made steak pie with a sickening amount of tomato sauce. "Nanna Jean knows the whole world."

"And who I don't know I ring up on me phone." She patted the heavy, old-fashioned phone beside her armchair. "Any family with five sisters and one son is bound to stand out. Aye, I know your people, hinny. And Northspoon is a name that stands out an' all. You're from a decent lot, you are."

She looked at Andy and nodded. Vince started. Something had passed between them.

Minutes later she was up on her tiny feet again, casting an immense shadow on them in the dusky light. It was past four in the morning. She gave Andy quick instructions for making up a bed in the back parlour and then retired to her own. And then she said to them both, "Don't worry about getting up in the morning. Lie in. Don't worry about anything. It's been a long night. It's been a special night. Now you two are new friends. It's good. I'll be seeing you tomorrow, lads."

That night they lay on settee cushions and clean sheets in the back room. Vince stared up at the window, at the vase of plastic violets on the sill. And, under the candlewick bedspread, he and Andy held hands all night, their hands red and slippery with sweat and confusion. When the sun came over the terrace backs, into the yard and through the net curtains, Andy was pressing his first kiss on to Vince's shoulder. Vince turned to meet it.

SEVEN

WHEN SHE WALKED INTO FRAN'S KITCHEN AT NINE O'CLOCK THAT EVENING, Jane's eyes shone with an eagerness brought on by Babycham. Fran wasn't used to seeing her in make-up. She looked oddly overemphasised.

"I haven't had this thing on since the honeymoon," she announced, twirling quickly on the doormat. It was a lime-green dress that made the best of what she had. Fran applauded. Taking her cue, Fran praised Fran's new outfit.

It was something she ought to have done straight away. She should have been shocked by this young and expensive look of Fran's. But Jane was a coward. To her, Fran didn't look quite right got up like that, and the lie nearly stuck in her throat.

Fran's black frock was all the things it was meant to be, classy and alluring and ever so slightly tarty. Nervously submitting to inspection, Fran had the air of a plain but respected actress receiving an award at a glitzy ceremony.

"You look gorgeous," Jane told her.

Fran's make-up – pale fuchsia lipstick, eyes ringed black like an

Egyptian's – was pure 1965."

"You're like one of those sex kittens."

Fran snorted. "It makes a change from being an old dog."

Jane's deprecations were stifled by Liz's entrance. She burst into the kitchen, rattling the blinds, and gleaming from head to toe in skin-tight gold lamé.

"Not a word!" she cried.

"No," said Fran. "It's...stunning."

"It's very gold," Jane said. "You're like something off the telly."

Liz went to stand under the lampshade. "In the shop they called it Golden Sunrise."

Jane muttered, "More like the Crack of Dawn."

Frank put his head round the door. "Are you going then?"

"Just about." Fran shot him a look. "You'll be all right with the bairns?"

"I've set them off stuffing cushions. And I won't start drinking until all of them are asleep."

"Make sure you switch the central heating off, too."

Liz paid their bus fares with a flourish, instructing them to grab the back seats. It was only when Fran and Jane were sitting down, the engine throbbing right underneath them, that they saw that Liz was talking to the driver – their driver – and telling him where they were off to.

To distract Jane, Fran said, "I seem to spend most of my life on the bus."

Jane watched Liz finishing her little chat. "I hate the back seat. It always smells of pee."

Moving down the aisle towards them, Liz cut a tight swathe of gold through the debris and used tickets. Jane turned to the window. It was dripping with frosty condensation.

"He's a sweetie." Liz checked the seat for stains and flung herself decorously down.

Jane said, "There's Nesta, talking to someone."

They all peered out to see Nesta nodding slowly at someone in a camouflage jacket.

"She's talking to that Gary," Fran burst out. "The traitor! I'm glad we never invited her now."

"At least he hasn't got his dick out this time. Nesta would die. How's your bus driver, Liz?" Jane tried to ask this lightly.

"He's not my bus driver. He's all our bus driver. I mean, he belongs to all of us. And he says he wishes he was coming out with us tonight. We all look terrific, he says."

Then the bus pulled away and Fran cried out, "Bless his heart!"

THEY STARTED THE EVENING OFF WITH A BOTTLE OF BULGARIAN RED IN the graveyard just off North Road. Vince and Andy passed it between them on a park bench, wincing and taking the wine like medicine.

"It's cold and it's rough," said Andy, "but it'll get you pissed." He looked proudly at Vince and the way he had dressed him up. Late-Eighties grunge, Andy called it, a faded tartan shirt left undone on top of a green fisherman's jumper. Green faded, ragged jeans. It was as if Andy had set inverted commas around Vince's one-time scruffiness and made it wonderful. They looked smart together, Andy thought; Vince all scuffed and slouchy, Andy sharp and made up like someone out of Depeche Mode.

"I won't make myself too ill." Vince glanced thoughtfully over the smog beyond the gravestones. "I'm going back home tomorrow. I've got all next week's lessons to prepare."

"Oh."

"I can't miss any more days."

"You're sounding like a grown-up."

"Mm."

"Do you realise how much you've talked about coursework and marking and schedules today? You can't help it. It's already sucked you in."

This, for Andy, was an outburst. Vince said, "It's inevitable, I suppose."

"The old Vince wouldn't have bothered. He'd have just told his class to write something nice about themselves or paint something. You've turned into a real teacher."

"Maybe I have."

"Just...oh, it doesn't matter."

Vince could sense that Andy was reining himself in. He was keeping hold of the bottle and picking at its white label, very bright in the gloom. Vince could feel the first of the wine fumes knocking about in his head.

Andy said, "But doesn't it make you feel weird? Going back to the same school? Living with your dad again?"

"Of course it's weird. I'm treading water. Magnificently well, but I'm treading water all the same." He lit a cigarette so fiercely that it broke, gaping hot smoke in the open air. He threw it away. "I'm stagnating."

Andy ripped the label off the bottle in one piece. That one point of brightness was gone, crumpled in his fist. "Do you think it's a realistic thing to do? Coming back to Aycliffe?"

"Probably not." Vince felt vulnerable in front of Andy, and uncomfortable, as if this was the final, impossible intimacy. "The truth is, I was scared. Scared of doing anything else."

"Thought so," said Andy simply. He said it as if being scared of the world and everything in it was an ordinary way to be. This annoyed Vince. It always had.

"Anyway," Vince tried to change the subject, "I've never felt very realistic. But I did once think I'd end up doing something better than staying in Aycliffe. I used to imagine that I was being filmed during every moment of my life. I was acting out the part of someone else, called Vince, in a long, long film with no edits." Andy smiled at him, as if he was it all up for his amusement. But when Vince thought about it, what he said was absolutely true. He spent years thinking that he was in a film. Every now and then the film would end and the credits would roll over him in some significant pose, the camera slowly pulling backwards into the clouds. He remembered once lying on his back on a hillside in Durham. From there he could see all the swamps behind the cathedral. He was eight and had run away from his dad, who was there for a bikers' weekend. The helicopter shooting him backed away steadily into the sky as the cast list rolled upwards, leaving him just a speck in the distance. And he never got to see the name of whoever was playing 'Vince'.

Andy said, "It's no wonder."

"What?"

"You are like you are. You've got the biggest and most damaged ego of anyone I've met."

Something in Vince flared up. How dare Andy, who spent his days hiding under a duvet, tell him anything about ego?

To Vince it seemed the only natural way to grow up, that very deliberate alienation he had practised. Andy was chuckling as though it was something sweet. Vince wanted to say it was just a way of making the world seem funny, even when it was hurting you. The world can be abrasive, but not profoundly disturbing. If you can regard it as a mildly off-putting illusion, then you can spend your time undermining and subverting that illusion.

"Here." Andy thrust the bottle at him. "Drink the rest and start being less coherent."

They wandered through the gravestones towards the jagged railings. As they did so Vince was thinking (although he never mentioned it, so as not to upset Andy) about planes in space. They were walking upright, vertically. It was too obvious to mention. Yet they were cutting diagonally across a dark field crammed with bodies lying on their backs, staring upwards.

He wondered what they thought about him and Andy, all those bodies. They would be as impassive as Andy that morning in bed. He as dead as they, they as alive as him. He made himself mordant, zombielike, Gothic, on purpose.

Here they were prowling an acre of recumbent forms, deliberately picking over those who, in a lifetime, would have been acutely aware of their own singularity, would have had worries of their own. Here they could no longer afford to be so choosy. They had thrown in their lot. Looking up in regret, maybe envy, surely with mixed feelings, these bodies couldn't condemn love? Not when they could sense it so nearby. Vince decided that by now, unable to condemn, they understood.

Before clambering over the railings into the street, Vince muttered into the dark, "I bet they're having a whale of a time down there. One long, unremitting orgy. I bet heaven is just like teatime at the Marquis de Sade's."

Andy hauled him over. "I can't take you anywhere, can I?"

FRAN, JANE AND LIZ STAKED OUT A CORNER IN A BAR THAT HAD BEEN MADE to look like a ship's deck. "A pirate ship, eh, Jane?" Liz winked. "Remember *Frenchman's Creek*?"

But Jane didn't. Their reading didn't overlap entirely. Sipping a double vodka, she advised, "Stick together, girls. It's going to be a rough night. The packs are out."

The place was full to capacity. People were standing eight deep at the bar, swaying in time to the music. The crowd was reflected back in the misted-up mirror behind the optics. Lots of suits, the smart-jumper brigade with their tight perms and moustaches, and then a few ravers in hooded tops and greasy hair. All the men stood in tight clusters, sticking together for now, fists around their glasses. Now and then their eyes would flick along the length of the bar at the women and at other men, as they talked about something else. This was the serious part of the night, the part in which they would discuss, decide, and realise just how pissed they were going to get.

The women kept to smaller, yet louder, groups, all dressed young although the age range was wider. There were schoolgirls who had overdone their make-up because the club they were going to had funny lights and they wouldn't show up otherwise. Older women with highlights in their hair blown rigid under driers. There was more laugher from the women than from the men. They weren't at ease, but they were confident, half enjoying, half ridiculing the attention in those nervous, shifty glances.

"God, it's like the jungle!" Fran had decided not to drink. "I forgot about all this."

"Show me Tarzan." Liz was not joking. "All the men are horrible. Greasy little things. Why do they think we want them with all those muscles?"

"I like muscly men," Jane said.

"That's because of the books you read. They've made you think you want something big and strapping when, really, you don't at all."

"But I do! And you read those books, too!"

"Honestly," Liz went on. "They go pumping metal, or whatever they call it, they waste all that time and energy, and then they haven't got the life left in them to pump anything else. They come out of it looking hideous. Fat necks and red faces with bulging eyes."

"Nice bodies, though," said Fran. "I tried to get Frank to go weightlifting. He looks like a Care Bear with his kit off."

"And," Liz ranted, "weightlifters have got tiny whatsits. It's the one part of themselves they can't expand. It's sad, but the more they build themselves up, the worse it gets. That's why they all get bulging eyes, trying too hard. What time is it?"

"Late." Jane was well on her way by now. She had dropped the frostiness from earlier. "We'd better collect our tickets and get across to Flicks before it packs out. I want to dance."

"Let's get on the cocktails. That'll get us going." Liz moved to go, sliding across the plush. "Hang on a sec. Everything I've just said, I take back. Him by the bar. He's built up. And just look at the packet on that!"

Fran hurried them out while the body builder with the overdeveloped packet passed crisps among his circle of mates.

THE ENTRANCE WAS ROUND THE BACK OF MFI. ANDY RAPPED SMARTLY on the door, which opened to reveal a bright-red room, heavy with smoke.

The bouncer shouldered backwards to let them in. He glanced from beneath a broad brow, his pan-shovel hands making irritable pincer movements while he waited to block the doorway again. Goth Night made him uneasy.

In the red foyer there was a window at which the cloak attendant lounged, dangling her jewellery over the edge. As Vince and Andy approached, she pulled a wad of chewing gum from her mouth, reaching tonsil-deep with well-manicured nails, and stuck it deftly into the top left-hand corner of her window frame.

"Well, boys, it's weirdy night up there. Weirdy night tonight. We've got every freak, drug addict and queer in town milling about upstairs."

"Oh, we know." Andy passed his coat across. "That's why we've come. It's our favourite."

"Right." She seemed to be taking note of them for the first time. "I thought you might have been expecting to be bopping to Jason and Kylie and what have you." Her eyes narrowed to slits and she tested the water with, "Because it's not that night tonight and the girls here aren't the sort of girls you might be after."

Andy gave a conspiratorial grin. "As a matter of fact, we're both quite queer ourselves."

"Are you now?"

"Yes. Very queer indeed, actually."

Vince ushered him to the stairway, where there were posters of the Hollywood greats tacked every few yards up the furry wallpaper, leading them towards the source of the low, hypnotic music.

"BLOODY SMART, THIS!" JANE WAS ENTHUSIASTIC AS SHE AND LIZ WAITED in the doorway. The wine bar was full to overflowing and Fran had gone in by herself to ask about tickets. "Freebies and everything!" Jane shuffled out of the way of some people waiting to leave, toppling into Liz, who manoeuvred them both towards the potted plants.

"I'm not so sure it's right."

Jane said, "My mother says it's Ladies' Free Night every night –"

"No, I mean the whole idea of a ladies night. It seems sordid somehow. Lure in a bit of skirt with free tickets –"

"Bugger that! I'm on a tight budget."

Forced to wait by the rubber plants, Liz was sobering fast. "So am I, pet. But I wonder whether we ought to be capitalising on our femininity like this?"

"What, you mean, like selling it?"

Jane was breathing thick liqueur-and-vodka fumes into her face. Liz took a step back. "Yes. No. I mean...oh, you're right. And it is a tart's night out, anyway."

"Too bloody right!" Jane yodelled, startling some smart suits just easing their way inside. She leered at them.

Liz was rescued from her moment of lucidity and doubt by Fran, who cut sharply through the crowd carrying three golden tickets.

"We're in!" Liz grinned, snatching hers. She called over to Jane, who had her face squashed against the glass doorway, "Jane, we're in!"

"Yes, but it's –" Fran began but Liz took command, grasped both her companions firmly by the crooks of their arms and marched them outside. As they headed for the main road, Fran tried again. "But it isn't their usual. They gave me the usual tickets, but they said it isn't their usual."

"What's their usual?"

"I never asked. But they said that tonight it was Goth Night."

"It was what? It's a what?" Jane was struggling to make them slow down.

"When they all dress up in black. You know, Goths. I got the tickets, but I didn't know whether you'd still want to go."

Jane looked confused. Liz beamed. "You're wearing black anyway, Fran, so you're OK. And if the rest of them are, it'll just make me and Fran stand out more, won't it?"

THERE'S A PARTICULAR DANCE THEY DO, VINCE THOUGHT, ALL THE GOTHS.

He was sitting at a wickerwork table, resting a bottle of Pils on the glass top and watching the dance floor. It was swathed in purple mist to about knee height and peopled by a series of thin silhouettes, all of them waving their arms in the air, moving very slowly.

They seem to be beseeching. They keep looking at the ceiling with pained expressions, raising their arms and clawing above their heads, then sinking back in resignation. Like Christopher Lee at the end of a Hammer horror. It's not as if there's anything up there worth beseeching. A few lights. But they're all at it.

He watched Andy, standing in his own private space, doing much the same thing. Perhaps a little better than the others, Vince reflected. They were rocking gently and thoughtfully to Dinosaur Junior. Again it struck Vince as odd to see someone you'd been sleeping with at a distance on a dance floor. Their mystery is regained; suddenly they look independent and divorced, yet available. Sometimes he thought it might be nice to keep every lover at arm's length, all the time.

He started to look around, beyond the dance floor. It was dark but every now and then he would catch sight of the occasional bleached blonde head on a body slumped on steps by the bar. Next to the bar there were lots of white faces, painted white with cheekbones carefully accentuated. People with drinks were bumping into each other because they didn't like to take their shades off. They apologised shyly to each other with shrugs and smirks.

Now the DJ was playing the Cure. More bodies on the floor, eager to reach up and worship the light fittings. Vince sighed. He had been here before. Nothing much had changed. Something about Andy and Andy's attitude over the past two days had almost convinced him that this time would be different somehow. Classic, even. Vince was beginning to distrust his own perception of what 'classic' meant.

He wanted something to look back upon in his old age. Something about which he could declare, "I was there. I was doing that then." He wanted something to write his memoirs about. At times he felt that the whole of life was geared around doing enough things to fill up all your memory-time in old age. He wasn't going to have children. Classic memories, classic thoughts, and the power to vocalise them. That was what he wanted for his old age.

At other times he couldn't imagine living beyond the age of twenty-four. It seemed obscene somehow.

Fran, Jane and Liz were shuffling their way into the darkness. They squinted into the smog, assessing the state of play.

"I don't really like it." Jane had to shout over the music ('Boys Don't Cry', which she remembered from the Youthy years ago).

"They tried to warn us," Fran said.

Liz seemed delighted with the place. She pushed through the knot of figures standing by the door and made for the bar. The others followed.

At first Vince was mildly surprised, as others were, by the sight of the three women coming in and ordering exotic cocktails on the wrong night. Then he recognised them as Penny's mother and her friends from the café yesterday. This is it, he thought, standing up. This was something different. Bauhaus were crashing into 'Ziggy Stardust'. His heart skipped a beat as he went to tap Liz on her golden shoulder.

She was caught in verbal mid-stride, carefully enunciating a list of cocktails across the sloppy bar. She turned open-mouthed to Vince. 'Penny's little friend!' she gasped. Fran and Jane shoved in closer, glad to have something on which to concentrate in a place that felt threatening.

"Vince!"

"That's it. Are you here with friends?"

"Is Penny here?"

"No; this is the old mothers' night out. I've never been in here before. Is it any good?"

Her dress really did stand out against all that black. She was a shining gold from the highlights down. Even her face looked burnished and colourful.

"Do you want to dance?"

Liz beamed. "To 'Ziggy Stardust'? I'd be delighted."

She left Fran and Jane to order the drinks.

Fran found them a table in a dark corner. There was only one other person, a drunk girl with very short hair. She was glaring into her handbag. "Men are all bastards," she told Fran and Jane as they sat down and she stood up to go.

"We know," said Fran with a smile.

"I've shrunk one of them to fit inside this bag. As revenge." She held out her velveteen handbag and gave it a vigorous shake. "It's an antique bag. He'll probably ruin it. Bastard!" She lurched off towards the exit sign.

"Drugs," Fran said. "Make them say the strangest things."

"Why do they cover all their nice black clothes in flour?" Jane asked.

"God knows. So they'll look old and dusty."

"Ha!"

"I know what you mean. But we can't be that old. Look at Liz."

They looked at Liz, slow-dancing with one of her daughter's friends, forming the only couple on a floor of solitary shamblers.

"But she's...she's a floozy."

"I suppose so. But I don't feel very old at all. I hope they play the Stones tonight."

"I would never want to be as young as this lot ever again." Jane blearily took them all in.

"They're probably older than you are now, some of them. What are you; twenty-six?"

Jane thought. "But what I've done has put me in a different age – a different generation. I've been married and I've had a kid. That makes me like all of this lot's mother. At least in the eyes of the world. I'm responsible now, aren't I?"

"Right now you're arseholed, pet. Worry about all that in the morning."

VINCE CAUGHT ANDY'S EYE FROM ACROSS THE DRY ICE. HIS CHIN WAS propped on Liz's shiny shoulder and Andy was glaring at them both from beneath his blue spotlight. Vince ignored him and went back to talking to Liz as 'Aladdin Sane' began. Another slow dance.

"Why didn't Penny come out?"

"She doesn't go out much. I worry about that. She's not like her mam at all."

"No."

"Vincent, pet..."

"Yes?"

"Penny told me about you being bent. I'm pleased you told her. It wouldn't have been nice for her to get a crush on you. You did well to nip it in the bud."

Vince frowned. "It just sort of came up in the conversation. There was no particular reason –"

"You what?" The louder part of the song had begun, breaking into their conversation.

"I said, I just told her. Because I wanted to. Not because I thought she fancied me."

"Oh, but she does. I think we have very similar tastes, me and our Pen. You're very nice."

Out of the corner of his eyes Vince noticed Andy stalking through the milling crowd, across the floor's glowing squares, towards them.

Vince stepped away from Liz. "Well, thank you for that, and thank you for the dance."

"The pleasure was mine." Liz bowed just as Andy reached them.

"Who's this?" he asked with a mocking leer.

"This –" Vince began, but Liz caught his arm and interrupted.

"I'm sorry, but I've got to leave you. Somebody's just walked in."

"That was Penny's mother," Vince explained as she shot across the floor to the bar.

"I REMEMBER ONE SCHOOL PARTY. IT WAS THE FIRST TIME I EVER GOT pissed. We smuggled booze in under our coats." Jane was, by now, turning sentimental. "One lad had to get his stomach pumped. We took all the tinsel off the tree and wore it round our necks like them Hawaiian things, or Wonder Woman. Someone yanked the tree right over and there was hell on the next day."

Jane's voice dwindled away. Someone was striding towards their table. He was in blue jeans and a bright white shirt, open-necked. His skin was ruddy, healthy as a Red Indian's.

And he was being intercepted by Liz, who appeared before him in a shower of gold. Together they seemed to abandon the idea of visiting the ladies' table and went off to the dance floor instead.

Jane watched her bus driver disappear. Her mouth fell open. She had forgotten all about nostalgia. "She's done it again!"

VINCE AND ANDY RETREATED TO THE SIDELINES. VINCE WAS SUDDENLY intent on getting drunk. When he placed his elbows on the table he could feel spilled beer soaking through the material, spreading up his arms.

"Surely you can't be jealous," he said. "That's ridiculous."

"Why did you leave me out there by myself?"

"You *like* to dance and mope about by yourself."

"Occasionally it would be nice to have my boyfriend with me. So people can see."

"Oh. Right."

"For Christ's sake, Vince. She could be your mother."

"No, she couldn't."

Andy started fiddling with money for more drinks. "Can I get you anything?"

Vince looked for his own money. "Yes." He paused mid-rummage, looked up and smiled. Andy bent down for the expected kiss.

"Andy...we were only dancing."

THE MUSIC WAS GHASTLY. BUT THEY WERE OBLIVIOUS. A SPACE HAD cleared for them in the smoke, as if they needed more room for their colour. They were very still, holding each other, barely dancing at all.

"I came down after my shift finished. I finished early tonight."

"Did you?"

"I wanted to find you."

Liz nodded. "What's your name? We only know you as our bus driver."

"Cliff."

She nodded again, as if she knew already.

"Yours is Liz, isn't it? Elizabeth?"

"Just Liz."

They carried on dancing, dancing very slowly and wondering why they were dancing like this. And what it meant.

At the end of that song, on a low, rumbling, drawn-out note, Liz seemed to collect herself in and, Cinderella-like, tried to pull herself free. He smiled and drew her back, into the next song.

Incredibly, Liz was trembling.

I've made her tremble, thought the bus driver. What does this mean? And at their table Fran and Jane saw that they were dancing still and they wondered, What does that mean? Vince and Andy were drinking and keeping to themselves, casting only occasional glances at Penny's mother and the spectacle she was making of herself. This was one of the few times that Vince wasn't thinking, What does it mean?

Cliff the bus driver was, at that moment, thinking to himself, This woman has an erection.

Liz at last seemed to relax again. She steadied her weight against him and looked him the eye. "There's something you ought to know."

The bus driver nodded tersely. "I know."

"That I'm a man?"

"I've known for a while." He smiled at the confusion in Liz's face, at the thought of the erection under that gold lamé frock. "I've known that all along. But it is nice to be convinced, I must admit."

Liz gripped him more tightly than she meant to. "Does it show? Does it really show?"

"Nobody ever has to show anything they don't want to. It's up to the rest of us to guess."

"I knew that. I know that. You guessed well."

The song went on.

EIGHT

PENNY ALWAYS LOVED HER DREAMS AND SHE WAS SURE THEY WERE better than anyone else's. A bad sleeper, she had trained herself to go off into a kind of trance, sitting motionless with her dreams superimposed luridly over everything else. There was no way she was missing out on dreams, no matter how little she slept. And as she dreamed, her blackened fingernails tingled.

Tonight she was sitting very calmly at the dining-room table, staring into her own reflection in the framed picture opposite. Around her head, almost out of range of her vision, floated three objects. They were an egg timer, a little man made of china and a brass coffee pot.

In her dream she allowed herself a quick smirk.

Once you had the knack it was very easy to keep all these things together in your mind. You simply had to stop up the holes in your head.

She closed her eyes and made herself sink.

Out on the coast road in the night, she was walking along and looking out to sea. The North Sea was still and black. Beside her the road was quiet and, as it dipped and rose with the lie of the land, these few bleak miles between Shields and Sunderland, she watched the tireless seabirds commute between the vast rock out at sea and the Roman remains beyond the road. The Roman remains were weathered and copper-coloured, looking like an abandoned wedding cake, its icing picked away. Penny decided to cross the road and examine them. And on the road, she realised then, there were a number of dead dogs. They lay at awkward angles and blood was pooling around their open mouths. A woman was whimpering, her anorak bundled up around her, visiting dog after dog, nudging them, shaking them, coaxing them with clumsy words. It was Nesta, her hair silver and dry in the moonlight. She was setting a bowl beside each dog and taking a milk bottle out from an inside pocket, pouring them each a small drink. Penny crossed the road, ignored by Nesta and the dogs, wanting to say, What if a car came by? But she crossed and said nothing, making for the grass, for the tussocky hills and the Roman remains.

Looking back, the pale bowls of milk on the road looked like satellite dishes. In the long grass there were shouts and squeals of fright and merriment. She squinted and, just by the sheer drop of the cliff, Fran, Frank and their four kids were shouting and running about, each with a butterfly net, recapturing their gerbils.When one was found, they'd pop it in an empty lager can.

Penny climbed up to the crumbling, muddy remains of the Roman fort, and by one of the entrances she discovered a miner's lamp and a diving suit. It was like the Famous Five. Next thing she knew, she's slipped into the suit, which seemed to have a vital, rubbery life of its own. Her helmet lamp flashed on and she plunged into the Roman doorway which, as she walked in, became the entrance to a steeply declining tunnel.

God, Penny thought. Not this one again. She was revisiting the scene of her most shamelessly Freudian dream. Worse than the one about riding down the street on her mother's sewing box. These were the underground caverns where, in one recurring dream, the Big Fat Wailing Worm lived. It lived in Lambton, brought back from the Crusades by a local knight, chucked down a well, grown to monstrous proportions simply to terrify Penny. It pursued her across moors and into houses, where she would slam doors on it, making it pull backwards and forwards through thresholds, eventually burning down the house with its friction and its wailing. But this wasn't one of those dreams.

Beside her, Andy's Nanna Jean was standing in a clean pinny and her usual immense black frock. Penny had no idea who she was, but she seemed friendly enough. Jean was explaining that this wasn't an awful white wailing worm dream. "But you have to go right under the water, through the caves to the rock, hinny," said the old woman.

A question popped into Penny's head. "How is your friend?"

"She's dead, bonny lass," said Jean. "She walked out under the ice. Best way to go. Now you go on, catch up with the others under there."

Penny gulped and struggled onwards. She left the old woman far behind as the tunnel grew thinner, the walls slicker and colder. She was potholing now, she thought, with a grimace. She remembered hearing something about fish with no eyes. Down here, they didn't need eyes. Down one hundred and twenty feet: she counted every one and soon she was where she presumed sea level began. Then down again, wading purposefully, training her lamp on the walls, throwing crazy shadows. On the bloody orange walls were stencilled bits of bodies, as if someone had been drawn around, like a template. There were pictures of madly galloping horses, antelopes, dog creatures and things that were half seal, half penguin. Penny stared at them as she went along, hunting for drier land.

And then, suddenly, she was hauling herself on to a dry, sandy shore. She must be far beneath Marsden Rock. She couldn't quite believe she'd climbed so far down, across and up again, even in a dream. Then, Vince was helping her to her feet. He was in his sharp purple jacket and suddenly she felt clumsy in wetsuit and flippers.

"Hiya, pet," he said. "I thought you were stopping in tonight."

Penny asked, "What was it you were saying about not believing in world-sorrow, and not believing that things fitted together?"

"Did I say that?" He sounded puzzled.

"Yes, in a lesson."

He shrugged. "That was a lesson. That was E. M. Forster. This is real life."

"You don't believe that!" she said accusingly. "You think you should live out what you say in lessons. You aren't cynical!"

"No," he said. "I'm not."

Vince glanced over his shoulder, into the darkness beyond the beam cast by her headlamp. He nodded at the black pools of water. Penny turned sharply, picking out Andy, crouched on the water-worn shore. He was holding out his hands, laughing softly at something in his palms. He was still dressed up Goth for his night out, his leather jacket creaking in the near silence. He motioned Penny to come and see what was in his hands.

Unsteady on her feet, Penny shuffled away from the wall and focused her light on Andy. Vince followed behind. As Andy's face turned brighter, Penny could see the little creatures dancing on his palms, hopping lightly from hand to hand. Tiny black horses, dog-things, antelopes, seals and penguins. Some were clinging on for dear life, hooking fragile legs on his huge, clumsy fingers. They kicked and stamped in the air and against his flesh, colliding with each other, haring about, glowing. More of them were pattering over slimy rock, coming to him.

"He has a way with animals," Vince said, and the sound of his voice made Penny jump. She looked up at him and jumped again. He had donkey ears and a donkey tail and his eyes had a sexy and lugubrious cast to them. "Andy's in touch with his animal self," he said. Vince reached into his purple jacket pocket and produced three green apples. An expert juggler suddenly, he tossed them into the dark for Penny to catch.

Then came the braying of a horn, the wild lurching and flashing of gas lamps and, with a terrible clatter of hooves, a carriage appeared on the road leading into the rock. A stage coach painted gold, with flashing leaded panes, pulled by a troop of white, steaming donkeys. The vehicle was filled with boys, pushing and shouting and laughing. The coachman brought them to a halt and waved his riding crop at Vince and Andy. Above his tightly knotted scarf, Penny saw, the coachman's face was brightly tattooed. "It's our lift home," Vince told Andy. Andy scooped as many little creatures as would fit in his pockets and then he was off, running after Vince, to the carriage.

Penny watched them go.

As they rode off, vanishing up into the island at last amid howls and jeers, she set about balancing the three apples round her head. They were all the vividest green, an invisible thread connecting them through the cores, keeping this perfect triangular formation. Penny levitated them, one single perfect crease in her forehead. Gravely they revolved about her as she exerted her own gravity.

As the fruit encircled her head she sat back and grinned, relaxing now. She clapped her hands and the triangle held in place, its shadow smudging blue on the dark wood of the polished table.

"Father, mother and the holy ghost," she said in a singsong voice. "Me."

Then there was a knock at the door and the fruit dropped, thumping one two three against the wood as if plucked and flung.

Penny brushed away her shock, settled her heart rate, and went to turn the kitchen light on.

"Who is it?" she asked through the kitchen blinds, fingers resting on the key in its lock.

"Jane." Her voice sounded thick, as if she had bitten her tongue.

Penny paused. Before opening the door, she offered a brief prayer. If I'm going to be bludgeoned, let it be quick, if this isn't really Jane but a psychopath...

"Your mam's not with us."

Jane was slumped against the doorframe, coloured a brilliant emerald with the dark foliage of the garden behind her. Fran hugged herself nearby, looking embarrassed.

"She's making her own way home, pet," Fran said. "She'll be home soon."

"We got a taxi," Jane gold her. "Guess what it cost!"

"What do you mean, making her own...?"

"It was twelve quid." Jane pulled a face. "I spend less on food for a week."

"Why didn't she come home with you two?"

Fran said, "Jane here had a head –"

"She got off with someone, that's why. Guess who?"

"She what?"

"Yes, she did. With the bus driver. With my bloody bus driver!"

Fran took Jane by the shoulders. "Come on. Time for home."

"And he's called Cliff!"

Fran marched her out of the garden, calling back to Penny, "Sorry about this. She just stayed back for a lift. She'll be in soon, pet. Night."

The gate slammed and Penny watched them disappear around the corner.

IT WAS THAT TIME OF NIGHT WHEN THE WHITE LIGHTS IN TOWN, FROM the cinemas and take-aways, were all switched off. Only the streetlamps burned. Everything was flat and dull and yellow as Vince and Andy linked arms down North Road, following the cracks in the pavement.

They kept in step. "We're walking at exactly the same pace!" Andy shouted. "And we didn't even realise it! Fucking brilliant."

"Smart." Vince concentrated on the gaps in the paving stones. Paving-stone width didn't quite correspond to the length of their strides. On a first step their toes would nudge a crack, then the other foot would land dead centre in a crack, then the first foot land half across a crack, then...

"We're not even walking with equidistant paces, either. Frightening, isn't it?"

In his enthusiasm for the sound of their own joint footsteps, Andy couldn't hear the others behind them. Vince could. To him they sounded too stealthy. He tried to urge Andy on, to get them home. He always found himself in this position, trying to see things through to the end.

They paused by the church, where a turn-off led up and down a dip in the landscape that concealed the industrial estate. Here you could see the sky pulled in tight over a low horizon that was made of a single row of Georgian houses. They were square like cartoon teeth, some of them punched in. A gas tower rose out of the dip, a huge metal drum gazing over the town from within its metal cage.

"I used to think you could go up to one of those and puncture it with a knitting needle. And the skeleton would still stand," said Andy.

There was a terrible cracking noise as someone smacked him round the head from behind. Those following on had caught up. Andy slumped into the church railings.

Vince watched him buckle, head forced between his knees. He gave a grunt of surprise. Then he saw three men in heavy hooded tops and loose tracksuit bottoms. Closest to him, one with lank hair, green in this light, had his car keys bunched across his knuckles.

Andy groaned, shaking his head from side to side. It's all right for you,

Vince thought. You've already been hit. You're exempt from responsibility. You don't have to do anything now. He bunched his fists by his sides.

"What was that for?"

The two behind Car Keys had been shuffling away. They had seen the dark trickle of blood running from behind Andy's ear, shocking as a split in his white collar bone. They snorted at Vince and moved in close again. "Fucking queers!" Car Keys grinned.

"How can you tell?" Vince asked.

Car Keys smacked him across the mouth with his empty hand and Vince fell, taking the kick to the stomach surprisingly well. He hooked his fingers into a pavement crack, as if trying to see down it.

"Cocky little bastard, inne, lads?"

Vince let his forehead rest on the concrete. God, this is so banal, he thought. What's the matter with them? It's not as if we're getting beaten up by interesting people. Why doesn't Andy bloody well do something?

Car Keys kicked him again, in the groin, and Vince sent his stomach splashing into the road. He was hoisted up by the armpits against the railing and slumped there, his body below gut-level making no sense at all.

"We don't want him choking on his own spew, do we?"

Andy was trying to speak.

"What's that one saying?"

He was holding out his palms.

"Fucking cocksucker!" They laughed. "He's begging for it."

Car Keys went over to Andy, gripped his head and pulled it into his own crotch. Andy twisted his head aside. There was a crack, then an acrid smell, the sharp ozone scent of pain and pissy tracksuit. "Suck it. Go on." They laughed again, then Car Keys pushed him away. He fell into Vince.

"Come on, lads!" Having exhausted their range of possibilities, the little gang went away.

"Vince?"

Vince had been pretending to be dead. He was thoroughly ashamed of himself. "Yeah?"

"For a while there, I couldn't see."

"Shit!"

"It's OK now." He shifted his weight on to Vince's legs. He had to whisper. The whole road was rocking from side to side for both of them. Vince whispered back, breathing with difficulty.

"We'd better move. If the police find us lying like this, *they'll* fucking beat us up."

"Right." But Andy put his bleeding neck down on Vince's stomach. He too was suddenly fascinated by the weedy cracks in the ground. "When I could see again, there were things crawling out of the pavement."

"Yeah?" Vince sounded as if he was trying to sleep.

"Glowing things. With arms and legs and heads."

"He hit you round the head." Vince's hand reached up, touching his shoulder. "Sorry."

Andy reached the worried hand with his own. "Little animals. When I could see again, I saw little animals. They were climbing into my hands."

"I'm sorry, Andy. I'm sorry."

Vince curled over and was sick again.

HAVING LEFT JANE SPRAWLED ON HER BED IN HER BEST GREEN DRESS, FRAN at last went home. Before passing out, the younger woman had looked around the almost bare room and said, "It feels strange without Peter here. Even though he's asleep through the night and I usually get lonely. I can hear him breathe through the walls. The house seems alive." Then her head hit the pillows. Peter was with her mother Rose and, presumably, the man with the wooden leg.

Fran left her breathing coarsely through alcohol fumes. One arm hung limply off the bed. It had dislodged a stack of paperbacks. Their golden titles and authors gleamed under the streetlight poking under the blind. Fran left quietly.

The street was nearly silent. No trouble tonight. But there was that odd tension in the air. It had been around since midsummer, the time of the riots in North Shields. Here there was an air of expectancy. Fran felt the whole town was asking for trouble. She shivered as she passed the bus shelter, but there was no one in there.

She unlocked her kitchen door in a rush of panic and stepped into the dark warmth, wondering how Penny felt. Her kitchen's slatted light was still glowing. She was up and worrying about Liz. Fran recalled that image of Liz and the bus driver, kissing, pressed close, on the dance floor. Liz had been leading the dance. Was that because she was taller?

With her door securely locked behind her, Fran went about turning lights on. An expensive night. She'd had a good time, though. Not too bad. She was a bit tipsy and not very disappointed and she still looked great to boot. Great-ish.

In the living roomed, basked by the light from the hall, there was Frank flat out on the settee. The two youngest, Lyndsey and Jeff, were crooked under his arms. All three slumbered peacefully, wrapped up in each other. The carpet was littered with empty beer cans and storybooks.

She frowned at him. She wasn't drunk. Keeping pace with him had increased her tolerance. His tolerance was beginning to disappear altogether, whereas she was going from strength to strength. She picked up Lyndsey to carry her upstairs.

Frank woke and smiled. She said to him, "Thanks for looking after the bairns. You look like an Athena poster, all lying there. Help me with these two."

He struggled to sit up without disturbing them. He remembered something. "Oh, yeah. We set the gerbils free by mistake."

VIA PHOENIX COURT, SERPENTINE WALK, GUTHRUM PLACE AND FINALLY Sid Chaplin Close, Penny was striding purposefully out of the estate, where the houses looked ghostly and squat and dark, with eyes made of satellite dishes squinting at the sky. She got to the main road, which was by now devoid of life, past the new petrol station, and made for the countryside. Beyond the woods stretched farmland for miles around, curiously silver and unthreatening in the night. The fields were passive, crops inhaling and exhaling with the breeze. She followed the winding roadway, kicking the stubborn grass of the verge, up and down the dips in the countryside. Very sensual curves, she thought, and imagined strolling the length of a giant's spine.

Oh, Gulliver, Gulliver, please roll over!

Shit, I left the lights on in the house. Never mind. It'll put the burglars off.

She was walking to clear her mind. The mind she had worked so hard at cluttering. All I want is stability, she thought. I did think we had it. But no, he wants more.

Why all of a sudden? What's going on in his – sorry, her – tiny mind? She never tells me anything now.

"It's just us, Pen," Liz had once said. "You and me forever now."

And now Penny was thinking, Am I just being jealous?

"We'll be here for each other," Liz once promised. "Mother and daughter."

"Whatever," Penny had replied. "But yes, we will."

When she was twelve her father told her about the facts of life.

They were sitting in front of the washing machine at four o'clock in the morning. He had a mirror placed on top of it and he was shaving off his beard. Penny listened and watched with great interest. She had never seen her father with a bare face. Even in the ancient hippie photos, the ones with her mam, back in the sixties, he had his beard. It had grown and grown and now he was sick of it. As he talked about sex and love and trust, they had the Beach Boys' *Pet Sounds* playing. When Penny imagined the kind of relationship she was meant for, the kind of love she deserved, it was always to a faint strain of Beach Boy harmonies. Sexy boy sopranos in concerted voice, promising her the world.

"You see, Pen, there's this thing that they tell you is out there in the world, and they call it sex. Apparently it's something that men do to women and it's how babies are born. And it's the thing young men are encouraged to go out into the world to find, like a good job, and when they find it, they're supposed to marry whoever it is that gives it to them.

"Then they can start having sex with other women, if they like, and go out to look for that. Most of them feel obliged to. A lot of men believe it is the women who give them sex and many vice versa. They don't think about it much, but it just kind of happens. It's a process involving the penetration of the female by the erect male member and the discharge of various fluids.

"Love, too, is something they are told is out there, and sometimes they go looking for that as well."

"I see," Penny said thoughtfully. She had been told all this already, at school.

"What I want to say is this, Pen. Sex is not something 'out there' at all. It's not something you hunt or that you are forced into finding, hiding or secreting. Neither is love. Sex is a thing that makes you fall in love with another person, another body, for an uncertain span of time – however long, however short – and you have that time to accommodate that person into your physical space in whichever way you both prefer. Sex is open and free. Admission free to the public, open to all comers. It is not something forced on you from the outside. Ever."

"Right."

"The same thing with love. Love is a thing that can make you have sex with another person, another body, for an uncertain span of time. That time is for accommodating that person into a particular place in your heart. Usually they stay there."

He finished shaving and turned to face her, looking very strange with a complete face. "I'm telling you this now because it is something I will never have again. I've done everything I want to. I've shared that private space. Now I'm just making myself comfortable with the space I have left. And I'm going to be looking after other people."

Penny stood looking out over the new golf course. Flags were bent in the rinsing wind. The moon was out and thick with suds.

He changed so quickly. As if he had died and come back as someone else. I thought I had a chance to catch up. I did have a chance. I fell in love with him all over again. He was my hero...my heroine. I was so proud. He became so much lighter as a woman, younger and funnier. It's nice to have a mam like that. I've had both parents...and only had to get to know one real person. He's a bargain. He was all for me, she was all mine. He promised.

Penny wept a little at the foot of the golf course and glared at the moon. "You're going there, Penny. You're going to the moon." When had he said that? She knew that he had, but couldn't remember when. Typical him. Typical her.

"Fat fucking chance!" she yelled at the moon. "I'm not going where he wants to go. If he wants to start fucking around and being tarty, that's fine. I'm no longer part of his space. I know where I'm going. And I'm not going to the fucking moon!"

And then she remembered exactly when her father had told her about the moon. Penny could feel the night breezes on her baby face, and she could picture herself there. Later father said they were struck by lightning. For hubris, he said. Daedalus and Icarus, and they hadn't even left the ground. And lightning from the moon was transformative, he said. Hence the change in their fortunes. The savage blast from the moon, which only the nurses who came running observed, that explained her dark powers too. And the moon had wrought an extreme change in her father. It had made him Liz. These were the unacknowledged, uninterrogated truths of Penny's life. These were the stories.

And what a load of bollocks, she thought. Fancy believing that! She felt embarrassed now, blithely explaining to Vince on the bus that, as a baby, she'd been struck by lightning. I've made myself look silly, taking other people's stories for granted.

There was the sound of an engine. At first she thought the moon was powering up to blast her again. But she looked down the bumpy country lane and saw a small white bus heading towards her, towards town. Strange time for that, she thought, as it came closer, moving fast. She saw it was almost empty. One figure was standing beside the driver. Like Boadicea in her chariot, racing into town.

The bus hurtled past and Penny flung herself back off the tarmac, into the ditch. For a moment she had been transfixed like a rabbit.

Within seconds the sight and sound of the bus was gone. She was left with muddy shins, a slightly sprained ankle, a bitter aftertaste.

Reinvention, Penny thought. Things are moving.

NINE

VINCE WAS WINCING AS HE CAME DOWNSTAIRS, LOOKING FOR ANDY. IT was just past seven in the morning and neither had been able to sleep. A milky weak sunshine came through the wire-netting windows into the taxidermist's shop.

Everything downstairs looked flat in the dawn, filmed with dust. Birds of prey stared at the floor with their wings pegged out, half-ashamed by exposure. Voles and hedgehogs clung to their mildewed logs. The single leopard stood arrested in pride of place in the window. He was crammed with fake, lumpy bones and patched here and there with scraps of old fox fur. Affronted by the light's intrusion, his eyes raked the street.

Andy in his Noël Coward dressing gown had the collar pulled up like a boxer before he goes into the ring. Perched on the butterfly case in the middle of the grey and yellow room, he was rotating his neck slowly, breathing raggedly. He'd switched the gas heater on and the air was warming. Salty and vinegary at the same time, it had a comforting smell, with a mustiness Vince supposed came from the animals.

"Hiya." Vince took him a cigarette. They couldn't find matches and

Vince knelt painfully to the heater to light both from its orange grille.

Last night they had elected not to go to Casualty. Vince thought that, when they eventually arrived there, right across town, they would only get embarrassed, sitting in a roomful of real and terrible cases. People with bits missing, heart attacks, accidents. He thought they'd feel shamed into doing something dreadful to themselves, to justify the visit. So they struggled back here and mopped themselves up.

Andy had no qualms about tapping ash on to the shop floor. Vince mentioned it. "It doesn't matter," Andy said. "Everything in the shop is dead. The room is full of ash and dust." It was true, the heat was stirring the air up and it was full of particles which could have come from anywhere.

Vince found an ashtray anyway, under the counter, by the till. There, too, was a whole row of glass bottles. They had home-made labels and he found their colours enchanting. In the new light they shone and he found himself, without even thinking, stuffing one, no larger than a Body Shop tester, into his pocket.

His head felt twice the usual size. Someone had put a football inside his skull and inflated it through his nose. His flesh was pulpy and about to peel away. He had checked in the mirror already and his cheekbones were nowhere to be seen.

When he sat beside Andy, Andy was saying, "Just when you feel great, when you feel calm and nothing could get at you, there's always some cack-handed fucker to come along and shove you back on your arse. To remind you that you're just a piece of shit on the pavement. Just like they are."

Vince took a slow drag of his Marlboro Light. "Yeah. You're right."

Andy turned to him. "So?"

"What do you mean, 'So'?"

"You said I was right. But what do you think?"

"It doesn't matter what I think. We got tumbled by queer-bashers. It happened and that's it. It's the risk you take."

Andy resumed looking out of the window. He looked to where the leopard's gaze was fixed. His face flushed red. "You've got a real fucking attitude problem."

"What?"

"Can't you even get a tiny bit worked up about this?"

"What's the point? You're just narked still because you got knocked on your arse. It reminds you you're just like everyone else."

"What?"

"This is what it's like when you live in a town. You take your chances. I've lived in bigger towns than this."

"Oh. Yeah. Mr Fucking Cosmopolitan. Just because he's been to Manchester a couple of times."

"Fuck off, Andy." Angrily Vince stubbed out his tab. "What do you mean, I've got an attitude problem?"

Andy burst out laughing and hugged his bruised ribs. Uncertainly Vince joined in. Then a dark silhouette swung into place in the doorframe. It set about unlocking the shop door.

"Fucking hell, it's Ethan Nesbit!" Andy whispered hoarsely. Suddenly he felt very stranded on the butterfly case. It seemed as if every stuffed beast in the shop had shifted its gaze to the door, hackles were invisibly raised and butterfly wings were astir beneath them. Keys rattled against the lock.

Vince froze. "Who?"

"He owns the shop." Andy drew his dressing gown in and tied it tighter as the door opened, admitting more of the bland light and revealing what to Vince looked like an ancient grotesque in a raincoat, balancing skilfully with one hand on the doorknob. The tip of his wooden leg was still on the pavement outside.

"What's been going on here, then?" rumbled the taxidermist.

The boy in the silk dressing gown gave him a shrug.

"We got stuffed."

THAT MORNING, TO MAKE HERSELF FEEL BETTER, JANE THREW OPEN THE washing machine and rammed in armfuls of dirty washing.

Already she felt guilty for her big night out. I'm not being a proper mother, she thought, as the engine throbbed and the first wave of escaped water began to spread across the lino. It was a thought brought on from the outside: I'm not doing my duty. It pressed like a cold flannel against her temples as she sat with the day's first cup of tea. The regular thud from the machine's motor kept pace with the pounding in her head. Like penance. She found she was staring at her Kevin Costner calendar as though it was the most interesting thing in the world.

Very soon she would have to walk across town to fetch Peter. Life would begin again in its old pattern. She could hardly wait. Her current novel waited face down on the table, split in thick halves, demanding attention. The insistent pulse of her daily routine itched on her skin, calling out, wanting to pull her from this inactivity, quell the depression.

Soon, subdued by the routine, she would be able to fall back into her book and find out what an awful time her characters were having. She hadn't created them, but they had been given to her to read about, to live among for a little while. On Tyneside they lived in the shadow of the docks in the days when there were still docks – days Jane imagined as always dark, morning, noon and night.

She hefted the rubbish from its plastic bin, opened the kitchen door and waded with it into the back garden. Getting rid of rubbish also made her feel better at times like this.

How many times like this had she seen? Quite a few, and it never stopped seeming that the nights she spent not caring, smashed out of her head, took place on another planet. A planet where her usual life was something to laugh at, something so narrow and silly it was incredibly funny. On nights like those it was all so difficult to believe. Everything became a mockery. Even time.

Especially time. Time was her enemy. It took so long. She threw grappling hooks at the future, one after another, hooking them on to significant events (Peter's holidays from playgroup, a night out, a clothes party, Christmas, Peter's birthday) and she would haul herself towards them. Often she would sit in the kitchen, finding herself counting minutes down from sixty in an effort to annihilate the time between now and then in interminable, easy calculations.

Nights like last night made all that into a joke. Those nights out flew by. They took all her counting, her scrimping and saving and pissed on them. Money was like time in that it was spread thinly out, taut through her waking moments. Then it snapped back like elastic when she got drunk. Time and money both vanish, she thought, when you catch a taxi home.

She thought again about what that taxi fare would have bought, what it might have been important for. She had to decide that it was a different sort of money. The money was a casualty of one of those nights. It didn't count.

Jane shuddered and pressed the rubbish down, shoulder-deep, in her new council wheelie bin. They would take it if it wasn't pressed right down. They made you buy your own plastic bags now, as well.

She straightened to see a tall figure in a dark coat scooting across the road. It was hurrying away from the block of flats at the end of Phoenix Court. Jane's eyes narrowed at the sight of carefully teased, bleached blonde hair, the slash of gold beneath the calf-length man's greatcoat. Jane opened her mouth to call out, but Liz had vanished, ducking into her own garden. Jane went back inside.

This was something out of the ordinary, at least.

It would do for later. Right now she wanted the ordinary. She went to have a bath, spurred on by the enthusiasm of the washing machine.

WHILE ANDY SAT THE OLD TAXIDERMIST DOWN IN THE BACK KITCHEN and saw to some tea, Vince trudged upstairs again. He decided he really had to get back into school. His first lesson of the day was at one fifteen. As far as they were concerned he was still full of germs, but he felt he was letting things slip. And now he had to go walking in with his puffy face and his purple patches of flesh. Let them talk, though. Obviously he was already getting on Andy's nerves.

The heads on the staircase walls studiously ignored him as he came down clutching shoes and coat. He hovered halfway, listening to the voices in the kitchen. The Axminster drew his attention and he stayed there, fascinated. He could never resist eavesdropping. In the voice of the old man downstairs there was a power that unnerved him. But as he boomed out staccato sentences in that tiny kitchen, it was not without a certain tenderness. Through every word he said he sounded sorry. Vince wondered what bad news was coming Andrew's way.

"Of course I don't mind you having friends to stay. I think it's healthy." Table legs scraped on the stone floor. Vince imagined them sitting awkwardly at the scarred Formica, balancing their mugs. Then he thought, Shit, it was probably the poor old bastard's leg scraping the floor.

Thoughts of physical pain, illness or debilitation always gave Vince the willies. His stomach folded in on itself with a roll of empathy.

"What's the visit in aid of then?" Andy was being quite rude. This bloke did own the place, after all.

"Are you sure you oughtn't phone the police?"

"Quite sure. They can't do anything."

"All the same..."

"Just forget it."

"You're your own man, Andrew."

"Yes, I am. Now why are you here?"

"Problems."

"Really?"

"I haven't opened the shop up in three months."

"I know. It's been nice and peaceful."

But Andy hated that peace. The night before last he had whispered fiercely to Vince that he detested living above a shop that was always shut. He said he wouldn't have minded a closed shop full of clothes or furniture. "But it's a shop of dead things."

Vince had laughed. "And that's not good for a healthy young imagination." He was trying to play down Andy's distress which, in the middle of that night, was quite real. It was as if he'd saved it up until the moment he knew Vince would come back. He could tell him he hated the way he was living now. And Vince thought it must be terrible, to work in that bar at night and come home alone to a dark shop, a shop empty apart from stuffed, mildewy bodies with black, glassy eyes. Imagine coming home to that threadbare, testy-looking leopard.

Ethan Nesbit sighted. "Business is down." The scraping noise came again. He must be shifting position, Vince thought. Getting a better purchase on the pitted floor as he prepares to deliver terrible news.

"Nobody wants taxidermy these days," he said. "You know, I used to have regular customers. People who had big houses with dark corners. They liked to fill them up with beasties that looked natural, ready to spring up at unwary visitors, or friendly-looking things, happy to be there.

"But customers go away. People die or they change their minds. Things that aren't stuffed aren't constant."

The taxidermist laughed at himself, at his own wit and wisdom.

Vince sat down on the stairs, listening harder.

"That's not true," Andy said. "Some of them fellers in the shop are starting to go off. It's the damp."

"Shit!" The old man's mug came down on the Formica with a sharp crack. 'Have you been putting the fire on regular like I said, to warm them through?'

"Course I have."

"Well," said Ethan bitterly. "The long and the short of it is that this place is finished with. Animals are dead and gone. You young people are wanting computer arcades, aren't you? Video shops and internetting, that's you lot."

Vince knew Andy too well. He could hear him shrug in response.

Then Andy said, "So you'll want me out, then?"

The old man didn't say anything.

"Uncle Ethan..."

Vince stopped himself from laughing. Uncle, he thought. That's why the rent's so cheap. It's not a sugar daddy, it's Uncle Ethan. Like something out of fucking Dickens.

"You'll want me out of the upstairs."

"When your parents died I said I'd watch out for you. Give you somewhere to live."

"You never adopted me. Anyway, I'm all grown up now, aren't I?"

Glumly the old man said, "Aye, but to chuck you out on the street... God knows what your little Nanna Jean will say when she hears."

"Maybe she can put me up."

"Haven't you heard? She's trying to get into the Sheltered."

"Not Nanna Jean. She wouldn't go into Sheltered."

"Aye, well. That's what she reckons."

Andy let out a slow breath. "Everyone's giving up the ghost."

By now Uncle Ethan sounded doubly apologetic. "You see, I need the money. It's time I cut my losses. I'm getting married, son. I'm giving up all the animals and I'm settling down. I want you to be happy for me. I want you to be my best man." The taxidermist couldn't keep the tremor of excitement out of his voice. In his mind the conversation had passed on to pleasanter things. There was a spring in his conversational stride that surprised both Andy and the hidden Vince. He sounded like a much younger man, just embarking on something. This vigour of his shamed the pair of them and made them feel sapped.

IT WAS NIRVANA IN THE SIXTH-FORM COMMON ROOM THIS MORNING AND that was the last thing Penny wanted to hear. She sat in her squashy chair and glared at everyone. This morning she had woken on the living-room carpet, rueful and stiff. She couldn't quite remember walking back from the road and the fields. Somehow she had got herself back after walking for hours. She arrived home in the dawn. Now she felt dirty and crusty and Kurt Cobain wasn't helping, bless him.

She was in torpor and what she wanted to be was organised, even prim, like the other girls who sat round now, eating their sandwiches early, from very small Tupperware dishes which they balanced on their knees. Nibbling crispbreads and considering their options. Penny wanted to shape up, suddenly.

She went to the window and stared out over the drab school fields. From way up here she could see the dark, forbidding trees down the Burn. She could see the grey ribbon of Burn Lane, connecting the Yellowhouse, Blackhouse and Redhouse estates to the town centre. I've got a whole panorama here, she thought, distractedly. She wondered if Liz was home yet, crawling back from wherever she had ended up with the bus driver. Surely they'd never shagged on board his Road Ranger.

"Penelope, I've been looking into those clerical courses for you."

"What?"

Her careers consultant was standing behind her, his pale podgy face in her personal space. "Last time you mentioned that you were interested in typing..."

Her heart sank. "No, I'm not."

His mouth opened, revealing very small teeth and a mouth full of saliva. His teeth were like a breakwater. Penny thought, No matter what, your teeth are always *wet*.

"I've put myself to a lot of effort on your behalf, young woman. How can you simply change your mind like this?"

"I never made it up in the first place." She looked him up and down She saw that he thought he was doing her a favour. "I never wanted to be a typist." He's doing what he thinks is a day's work, Penny thought. Messing about with all the things I want, trying to make my ambitions manageable. He's one of the people whose hands I'm in. Look at him! I'm better off doing stuff for myself. "I never said I wanted to be a typist,' she said. 'Oh, fuck it! She dropped her English file at his feet and fled to the toilets.

It was a windy day. The wind blew itself round the town-centre corners, it blew people into shops they didn't want to visit. The precinct was oddly silent as Jane arrived, though there were as many people as usual. Newton Aycliffe was a funny town, she thought, because people stopped and talked in the town centre. They danced an awkward quadrille and moved from group to group, spending ages, talking about nothing. When she went to other towns everyone seemed to go dashing about. Jane didn't think it was because people in Aycliffe were friendly. They didn't have anything to do, she thought.

At first the keening wind seemed to have killed the noise. Tossed it elsewhere, across the rooftops and over the clock tower, dropping it heavily into a field. But it hadn't. As she made careful, tiny footsteps under awnings, she realised that it wasn't sound the town was missing.

It was artificial light. Everything was dimmer. The shop signs, the windows...they were all dark and inscrutable like neglected fish tanks. Shit, she thought. Half-day closing. But it was only eleven o'clock. She went in the ladies' in the arcade and there she found Mary, who looked after the lavs, sitting in candlelight. Mary took great pride in her job, and you could find her sitting in her glass-fronted office very day, in her trackie bottoms, knitting and chatting to all her customers. She kept her lavs a treat. She was a reassuring presence, watching over her endless knitting for vandals or anything untoward. Today she was in her glass office surrounded by her twelve grandchildren. Boys and girls of all ages, all eating Greggs pasties and sausage rolls, unperturbed by where they were. Mary sat in the middle of them, proud, glowing in candlelight. It was like a holy picture, Jane thought when she walked in.

"All the leccy's off in the centre," Mary told Jane as she gave her change for the lock. "It's a disgrace. All the leccy's gone off in the wind." Mary repeated herself, Jane had discovered. It came of seeing too many people in one day, being obliged to make conversation with them all. When Jane sat on the lav, she heard Mary tell someone else, "It's a disgrace. Leaving us in the dark with no leccy."

When she went back out she noticed that some shops had resorted to candles, too. From the outside this gave their façades a Victorian glow. It was like going round Beamish, the open-air museum. Jane had hated it there when Peter's dad took her, when they were together. He'd made her go down into the pit with him. A real working pit and her afraid of heights. "But it's not heights," the ignorant bugger said. "It's underground. How's that heights?" And at the bottom Jane had passed out, which served him right. It was a wonder she hadn't lost the bairn.

The Spastics Society and the Gas Board looked inviting and curious, Olde Worlde. And Woollies! Woollies looked a treat! Oh, it was like something out of Scrooge. An air-raid shelter full of yellowing candles had been unearthed and they were stuck throughout the entire shop. No longer plastic and dirty white, it was graced with a dusky vitality.

She pushed in to see the glints of purple, gold, green of the pic-n-mix display. And, with a throbbing heart, she waited for the coast to be clear, and filled her coat pockets with humbugs and eclairs and blackcurrant limes. No surveillance cameras either. She felt about twelve. She looked at the wax congealing on the video counter, pooling on shelves and getting stuck in the silver tinsel they already on display. She looked at the hushed faces of the customers. They were acting as if they were in a cathedral. This is how shops used to be, she thought. Warily they all went up and down aisles, unsure of what lay hidden in corners. Usually they would bustle up and down, finding everything uniform, exposed. There was a gentle calm about Woollies this morning. And the absence of music, Jane thought. That helps, too.

It was getting late. She had to pick Peter up.

VINCE WAS HOPING HE COULD DUCK INTO THE STAFF ROOM AT LUNCHTIME and quietly go about his business. Get some coffee, set about marking. Keep his head down. But it was at this point that the PE teacher decided to acknowledge him.

That face coming across the room at him. That bloody monkey face! His pitiful strands of hair over skin the texture of an avocado. The man was avocado-shaped, in fact, in a too tight, unwashed tracksuit. Mrs Bell had made Vince smirk once by remarking that they should all complain about the PE staff wearing their tracksuits in the rest of the school. Teaching other subjects dressed like that! She thought it was awful. And she thought it was unwise, his blithely stomping about the place in his tight tracksuit bottoms, showing the plain impression, as she put it, of his genitalia. It wasn't right.

He came up to Vince and there was the smell of cheese-and-onion crisps on his breath. "Have you been in the wars, then?"

It took Vince right back. This bloke's face was always bearing down on him when he was in his early teens. Whether it was cross-country, swimming, rugby or the long jump, there was his bloody awful face coming into view and screaming at him to put some effort in. His face going scarlet. The other lads sniggering. Once he'd stood them all in a line and thrown a cricket ball at every one of them so they could catch it and get over their fear of hard balls. He'd taken Vince's glasses so they wouldn't get smashed and of course Vince couldn't see a thing. In protest Vince went from being hopeless to not trying at all. He simply wandered around the cross-country course down the Burn, twenty minutes behind everyone else, trudging through the black mud. And then he'd have this face screaming at him. And again, when everyone was showered and dressed and he showered alone, he'd have this face bellowing at him through the steam to hurry. To get out of his sight.

"Yeah," Vince said. "I've been in the wars." Under all his bruises he could feel himself colouring further.

There was a kerfuffle at the door as the careers master came in and caught sight of him. "There's someone wants you," he said. "Penny Robinson has locked herself in the sixth-form ladies' toilets and she wants to talk to you and no one else."

Vince turned to go, frowning.

"Well," said the PE teacher. "Isn't that the girl you were out having lunch with?"

"What?"

The careers master had turned to listen, too.

The PE teacher said, "You heard. Someone saw you out on the town and then catching the bus with one of the sixth-form girls."

"So?"

"One thing you have to learn," the PE teacher aid, "in this job. No matter who they are, no matter how much they're begging for it, no matter how much you want to give it to them, you have to stop yourself. Isn't that right?"

The careers master nodded. "Oh, yes."

"Right," Vince said.

He went to the sixth-form block and, with an air of unabashed curiosity, pushed his way into the ladies'.

"Pen?"

"I don't like being called Pen." She was in the furthest cubicle.

"Can I come in?"

"Did Mr Polaroid send you?"

"Yes, but I'm concerned as well."

The door opened, allowing him to slip into the little room to find Penny sitting on a cracked lid.

"Hiya, sweetheart."

She looked at him. "Do you know what we remind me of?" she asked.

"Go on."

"Some awful cheap version of one of them brat-pack films from the Eighties."

Vince grimaced. "You can be Molly Ringwald in *The Breakfast Club*."

"I feel more like Molly Sugden."

"Why don't you like being called Pen?"

"It's what Liz calls me sometimes."

"Oh."

Now she was staring at his bruises. "Jesus, what happened to your face?"

"Does it show up that badly? Can I borrow some foundation off you?" She knew she must have some. Her skin was still quite bad, lumpy and inflamed under the coat of foundation. She rummaged in her bag. He asked, "What's all this about?"

She stopped what she was doing for a moment. "Do you ever feel like you're bottom on the list of everyone's priorities?"

"All the time."

"I think that now and then and it scares me."

"It's best to assume it," he said. "And then, when suddenly you're not, when someone is thinking about you, really thinking about you, then that's a bonus."

"I supose you're right. Can I stay here until that happens?"

"'Fraid not, pet."

"What happened to you, anyway?"

"Queer-bashers."

She started to apply make-up to his bruises. He gasped at the coolness.

"They got me and Andy after the thing last night. It wasn't too bad."

"Is Andy all right?"

"He's fine now. A bit sore."

It was funny having his head in her hands like this as he talked. She felt his voice vibrate through the soft white skin of his throat. "How are things with you two?"

"Oh...well," he said. He wasn't at all sure what to say in school. "I'm not sure if we're sticking together. I don't know."

"I liked him. I thought he was nice."

"Really?"

"The little bit of him I saw, yeah."

"He was my first lover," Vince said. "Isn't there something sad in me going back to him? Isn't it just like coming home and working in my old school?"

The toilet in the next cubicle flushed. They heard someone step out, hastily wash their hands, and clip-clop out of the ladies'.

"Fuck!" Vince hissed. "It'll be round school in seconds: Mr Northspoon's a big fag."

"It was my fault."

"Never mind. Maybe it's best if I'm out at work."

"Yeah?"

He shrugged.

"Vince, my mam didn't come in last night."

"Is this what this is about? I saw her last night. She was in safe hands, I think."

Penny screwed the cap back on the tube of foundation. "Safe hands? You saw her with the bus driver, then?"

"Someone's told you? Yeah. She was having a whale of a time."

"Good."

"Ha'way, pet. Let's get out of the toilets."

"Honestly, when you go on about queer-bashers and all that–" She shuddered. "It makes you wonder if it's worth going out anywhere. Sometimes I think I'm scared of everything. The whole world. Even my mother's out on the prowl at night."

"You want to get on out there! Show them what you're made of!"

"Yeah?" She stood up from the loo and kissed him on the cheek, an unbruised, un-made-up part.

PETER HAS THE SWEETEST NATURE. THE SWEETEST BOY. ROSE THOUGHT the words over and over before Jane arrived late to collect him. He would grow to be a fine young man. A credit to his mother. Rose could see that now. She wasn't surprised that her daughter couldn't. Jane just didn't understand the things Rose understood about men. Jane hadn't held on to her own man, Brian, and Rose could see exactly why. Brian wanted a drinking buddy and, although Jane had never known it, that's what Rose became for him after he left her daughter. She took him in and saw him right. She despaired of her daughter's inadequate love. All these men wanted to feel they were sweet little kids, whatever they did. That was all Jane had had to do for Brian. He was a pig all right, Rose could see that. But a beguilingly rough pig, with a nasty temper and a passion she had taunted and brought to a head. She seduced him, bringing him running upstairs to her room, just days after walking out on Jane. He needed it, Rose needed it, and Jane need be none the wiser. Brian was walking out of their lives, he'd be gone soon, that was the way Rose looked at it, and she had been determined to fuck him. It was the one time, in her eyes, that it could have been respectable. She nursed and rocked his heavy fleshy body between her thighs, ran her hands through his thinning pale-yellow hair and told him he was pushing his fat, unwashed dick into his son's grandmother. And, funnily and pleasantly enough, he'd come back for more of the same over the years. She was fond of him. A sweet lad.

When Jane turned up, Rose was doing her ironing again. She told her that Peter had surpassed himself. There was nothing, no tantrums or doldrums, to report. He had gone to bed when Nanna said, eaten all his tea, played nicely and spent most of the evening talking with his new uncle Ethan, who was soon to be his new granda. That was the sweetest time of all last night, Rose thought. Ethan and Peter had talked about animals. Ethan knew all the animals and he promised to teach Peter how to talk to them.

"I'm like Dr Doolittle!" Ethan had cried. "Aren't I?" he asked Rose, who came in with bowls of her homemade broth.

"Oh, aye!" She smiled. "Dr Does-bloody-nowt." All night she was waiting on the pair of them hand and foot. But she was proud. It always made her feel good to be surrounded by men. She had always wanted five sons. That was her dream. And she got just Jane.

"Honest," Rose said, elbow-deep in ironing, pulling it out of her basked. "I can't see how you can complain. He's got the nicest nature I've ever seen in a bairn."

Jane's headache was seeping back. "When he's with me and it's just the two of us, he can be a right little shit sometimes." But then, turning to see what he was doing, her heart went out to him, and she felt bad for what she was saying. Peter was crayoning at the kitchen table, looking angelic. Jane imagined heaven must smell like this, of Radion and Comfort. "Fetch your things, pet," she told him. "He's good for you because you spoil him," she told her mother.

"What else are grandmothers for?" Rose grinned. "It's parents who get the rotten part. When you're a grandparent you have all the best jobs." Rose gave her daughter an appraising look. "So how was your night out?"

"All right, I suppose."

Peter came over to get his hair ruffled by Rose, Turtle rucksack slung carelessly over one shoulder. "Aah, lamb!" She smiled. As she kissed his face, her nose felt cold to him. "Any luck with finding him a new dad last night?"

Jane tutted. "Don't be daft. Come on, son."

"That's what he needs. That's how he'll calm down. A bit of stability."

"See you, Mam."

Rose stared over the sheets as she folded them, flapping her hefty arms like wings. "He'll have a granda soon. That'll do him good. He took to Ethan right well last night."

"For Christ's sake –"

"We've set a date. November the thirtieth."

Jane pushed Peter out into the garden. Once he was out of hearing range she hissed at her mother, "How can you look for stability from some old bloke with one leg?"

Rose just laughed in her face.

Jane took a long, slow walk around the streets, Peter docile at her side. As they passed the park he watched the skiving kids clambering on a huge metal spider crouched on the asphalt. She asked, "Nothing to say?" He shook his head, looking down, then gave her a shy smile.

"We'll go into the town centre, round the shops," she told him. "All the lights in the shops are off and it looks magical. It'll be like one of those adventures when you go back in time to the olden days. You like all that, don't you? Adventures?"

But the wind had dropped in time for the dinnertime rush. Town was noisy again and the electricity was back on. Peter looked at his mother as if to say she was a liar. We haven't travelled back in time at all, he was saying. We're still in the same rotten place.

Inside Woollies was bright and dirty again. She took him to the toys and bought him a Real Ghostbusters toy, one of those she'd meant to save till Christmas. It was only the price of another shared taxi fare. In the queue her heart raced because she remembered her pockets were full of stolen sweets.

LIKE A HERON IN A COBALT-BLUE TROUSER SUIT LIZ STRODE ACROSS THE filthy school field. She wished she had taken the time to walk the long way round. But she had dressed and done herself up in record time. She was worried. When she arrived home from Cliff's flat this morning there had been a note from Penny on the breakfast bar.

What are you playing at? I've been worried sick.
That daft Jane told me what happened.
Why didn't you phone?
Why now all of a sudden?

The mud was sucking at her silk slippers. She almost lost them. What am I doing, dressed like the mother of the bride, wading in mud? She looked up and cursed. The school seemed so far off. Oh, I wasn't made for nature, Liz thought. But she was determined.

The teachers and pupils outside the main entrance stopped to watch this elegantly dressed, if slightly muddy and distraught stranger slip past them and into Reception. She seemed to sail straight to where she was going. Once inside she rapped on the typing-pool window and commanded the secretary to find out where Penny would be now, and to take her there.

What worried Liz about the note from her daughter was its curtness. The absence of the following words, which beat a tattoo in her head as she followed the grim secretary to Penny's English class: *Mam, love, Penny.*

TEN

FOR A MOMENT THERE HAD BEEN LIGHTNESS AND AIR STREAMING IN through the windows. The day was turning out all right. Penny was back in Mrs Bell's yellow classroom and the conversation was easy and animated. They were having one of those lessons resembling a class chat, flipping casually through the first two hundred pages of their set texts, drawing up points, coming up with ideas. They had begun with a brainstorming session, and the board was full of words and phrases of different sizes and connotations, written by different hands. It was something Vince had learned from one of his seminar tutors at college and Mrs Bell was trying it out. Mrs Bell wasn't convinced; to her the board just looked a mess. But Vince was leading this session, getting involved and agitated whenever somebody made a point, waving his arms and drawing arrows between the nouns and adjectives on the board. This was one of those sessions on the set texts that they taught together and sometimes she had to hold back from taking over and also from shouting out her own ideas. She thought he was getting too abstract. Now and then she would look at the pupils' faces and they would appear confounded and cross. All except Penny, who seemed to be with him the whole way along. It was as if he couldn't do wrong in her eyes. Then he would seem to gather the others up again, with some glib joke at the expense of the book or the writer.

Mrs Bell thought that was all right up to a certain point, but you couldn't beat a proper close reading. Nothing like getting right in there and reading line by line, pulling it all to bits like remaking a bed. Vince was just walking round and round it. The startling image came to her that, teaching, Vince treated the book and its author like a patient in a sickbed. A begrudged sickbed and he was one of those young, obnoxious doctors showing off. Whereas she wanted to give the patient a good scrubbing and feed them soup and bring them flowers. Her attention was straying. The lesson wasn't moving fast enough. She would have to tell him.

The lesson was making Penny forget her dismal start to the day, but then there was a smart rap at the door and the secretary shoved her head in to ask if Penny could be excused for a few minutes. Immediately she knew what this meant. When she stepped outside, into the dimly lit cloakroom and corridor, the secretary turned on her heel and left, duty done. Liz was standing there at the mouth of the corridor, looking immaculate and helpless.

The walls were institution green, filled with reproduction Van Goghs. The atmosphere was just like the dense, seaweedy feeling in her dream about being in the caves. She was back in her diving suit.

"Hello," she said to Liz.

Liz was admiring the reproductions. They were badly printed, too bright, and jarred against Penny's nerves. She thought, this is how I dream, with volume and colour turned up too loud, like a telly that has to compete with the neighbours'. No wonder I can't sleep at night.

"I've been worried."

"That's why I came to see you. I thought you might be. Silly!" Liz avoided mentioning the note.

"So. What's happening, then?"

Liz took a deep breath. Her composure was cracking; Penny could tell by the fact that she was blinking more often than usual, plucking at her false nails. "I won't pull the wool over your eyes, Pen. I couldn't do that. So...I've invited him to dinner tonight. You can meet him."

Her daughter nodded slowly. Then, "What brought it on?"

"You've grown up. You can handle this now. It was an impulse thing. Like shopping. I felt the need."

"Like *shopping*?"

"I didn't mean that to sound...frivolous."

Penny didn't look convinced by this, but Liz was being honest. She wanted to say, but couldn't quite, that shopping was one of the most serious things she knew. Anyway, Penny knew that already about Liz. But here and now there seemed to be no proper context to say it, to talk about the anxiety Liz felt about shopping. How serious she felt when the mirrors in the shops caught at her attention, made her feel conscious or ashamed. How she felt the need always to buy something else, something she thought she needed. Penny should understand this compulsion of hers.

Penny said, "What if I don't want to meet him?"

"He's lovely. You will."

"Mam...you were careful, weren't you?"

"Absolutely. I'm not as stupid as I look. You can understand this, can't you?"

Penny was staring fixedly at the bed in one of the pictures. It was bowed under pressure. All the furniture in the Dutchman's colourful room was warped by the use of its owner.

"You want to bring us together to see how we react to each other. How we affect each other. That's what you do, isn't it? You bring people together for experiments."

"I've asked you to grow up very quickly, Penny. But I have to ask you for this one last thing."

You provoke, Penny thought. On purpose. The person Penny's father had become, the person he had wanted to be in order to be himself, not only partook of but also created life. It was his mothering urge.

Penny turned to look at her. The composure was really gone now, as startling as if the wig had slipped off. The mascara was running, the flesh tones patchy, fake. Under her Obsession there was the faintest tang of sweat.

"What last thing?" She was fascinated by this face in the process of deconstructing before her. It was between states and its tears could have been from exertion.

"That you accept this relationship. Accept that it is what I need now. That you will let go of that part of yourself that wants to keep me whole for ever."

"I'll accept anything." Penny smiled. "That's what I do. I accept anything."

"I want you to mean it."

"You sound like a soap opera."

"If I do, it's because I watch soaps. I don't read your kind of books. How would I say what I want to say...how would I say it in your language? The one you like?"

Penny blinked. "Just say it as you think it. That'll do, Mam."

"Well."

"I'll accept it. I'll meet your bus driver and I'll give my verdict. I'll give up my hold over you –"

"I don't want you to do that. You chose to stay with me. I'll never lose you."

"No. You won't."

"Your *real* mother –"

"She wanted me too. I know. I remember. But you made her redundant. I've had both in you. And I've been grateful." Penny smiled, tasting salt. "I needed to tell you that. Before we move on to the next thing, whatever happens next. I'm glad I chose you, back then."

Liz was hunting out tissues. "You were five. Christ, how can you know, when you're five? How could we have asked you to choose?" Her hands were shaking inside her handbag. "Life's never dull, is it?"

Penny gave her some toilet roll. "Yes, it is, but the bits that aren't tend to make up for the bits that are."

Gradually Liz drew herself back together and urged her daughter to go back to her lessons. Penny said, "Can you find your way back out of school?"

Liz looked around as if she had forgotten that was where they were. "You seem at home here already. In your new school."

"Do I?"

"I hate these places. I'm not used to being anywhere official and proper."

"I've got to get back," Penny said.

"All right, pet," Liz said. As she hurried out of the school building she was planning a meal and rehearsing introductions, only slightly self-conscious of her make-up smudges. Mr Polaroid bumped into her at the main entrance.

"Your daughter is being very difficult about this secretarial course business –"

"*Secretarial*?" Liz cried, quite her old self.

JANE LET HERSELF INTO FRAN'S KITCHEN. THERE WAS NO ONE ABOUT. She put the kettle on and watched Peter climb into his usual place at the pine bench. She couldn't shake the feeling that she could smell wee in the carpet. Then she remembered Fran's dodgy pipes under the sink. She couldn't get the council to come out.

It always struck Jane how funny other people's houses smelled. Visiting people, she would pick up the scent of old dinners, the smell of the people themselves. She always ended up wondering if people were clean enough, especially when they offered you something to eat. She'd thought that round Big Sue's house the other day. It was funny, too, after an hour or two somewhere, you stopped smelling their distinctive smell, as if you had yourself become part of it. And when you went home your own house would smell strange. Jane shook her head. Sometimes she thought she was obsessed with cleanliness.

Then Fran came in through the front door with Lyndsey and Jeff. Peter jumped off the bench and the kids greeted each other loudly, shouting out each other's names over and over, banging arms and blunt bodies.

"Oh. Morning, Jane. Kettle on?" They sat at the table.

"Tell them to be quiet. My head's coming back."

"I think it's still warm enough for them to play outside." Fran tightened up their anoraks and shooed them out. "Still feel rough?"

Jane nodded.

"Never mind." Fran's eyes were wide with a certain eagerness. She was brushing her wind-blown fringe away and ignoring the kettle as it gave out plumes of steam. "Nesta from next door has vanished."

"She's what?"

"They reckon she's been kidnapped."

"I'm flabbergasted!"

"Isn't it awful?" Despite herself, Fran started to laugh.

"Well..." Jane glanced backwards to see what the kids were up to. "At least you'll have your milk to yourself in the future."

Outside it was windy again. Lyndsey, Peter and Jeff were holding hands in a line, running around the tarmac play park, anoraks flapping as they tore into the wind, shrieking.

NOW ETHAN WAS TAKING THE BUS INTO AYCLIFFE AGAIN. HE WAS ALL over the place these days. But always going back to Rose, he reflected. That was home to him now, her cosy house in the old part of Aycliffe. He could sell up his old place and the shop in Darlington, and cut all his ties. They needed the money for the wedding and the cruise. The cruise! A lovely, long, luxurious word. It made him think of...what? Water the colour of forget-me-nots, as far as the eye could see, and flying fish zipping about and keeping pace with the prow of the vast ship. Taking a stroll at sunset. Bingo and go-go dancers and buffets with as much as you can eat. Stopping off in dusty, exotic bazaars and buying souvenirs for next to nothing. The thought of the cruise they were planning to take together was more exciting, almost, than the thought of the marriage itself. He could see them playing tennis on the deck, both in pristine, freshly pressed whites. And he had two legs in his.

He did feel bad about Andrew. Until this morning he hadn't given his nephew a great deal of thought in this. Now that he had seen him and gauged his reaction, the old man did have misgivings. Andrew looked so browbeaten. There was no zest in him, no desire to go out and challenge the world. Bless him, though, he'd lost his parents when he was, what? Eight? And God alone knew what that had done to him. Brought up by Ethan's mother Jean and then, latterly, sort of looked after by himself. It's a wonder the poor lad could function at all. He was always surrounded by old people, Ethan could see that now, and he wondered if they had done him damage, trying to get involved in his life. Well, anyway, he'd be looking after himself now. And he had friends. That bloke there this morning, he was a friend. It wasn't as if he had no one his own age.

No more fretting, Ethan told himself as the bus came into the town centre. You sound like an old woman.

Soon he was off the bus and walking slowly, doggedly, down the few streets to the house of his intended. Her front windows were fogged with the steam from her ironing. He stood by the garden gate and serenaded her with 'Love is in the Air'. His voice was booming and off-key and people on the main road stopped to look. Ethan couldn't care less. He sang at the top of his voice with his arms spread out wide.

Rose wiped the condensation away with a tea towel. She saw him and mouthed, "Silly bugger!" at him across the grass, grinning delightedly.

It's ridiculous, really, Ethan thought as she came out, stamping her winter boots on and fastening her furry coat. It's only about two hours since we last saw each other. What's making us carry on like this? She came up and linked arms with him. "Ha'way there, Captain Birdseye," she said. "Let's get into town."

"You mean Long John Silver," Ethan said. "He was the one with one leg."

"Who was Captain Birdseye then?"

Ethan frowned. "Wasn't that Burt Lancaster?"

Suddenly she laughed. "I'll tell you what I'm thinking of. Fish fingers!"

"Oh."

"Ha'way, Captain Birdseye!" she cackled, and led him into the main street. All the way down the road she tempered her usual healthy stride and brought herself down to his pace. He struggled manfully to wield his wooden leg faster for her. Together they were keeping pretty good time.

SEEMINGLY OVERNIGHT THE BIG SUPERMARKET IN TOWN HAD CHANGED hands. Cardboard signs swung from the ceiling, yellow spots on red backgrounds. Liz was confused when she walked in. Everything was in different aisles, just as she had learned her way round. At least the delicatessen was in the same place, its tiled walls covered in yellow and red posters. The woman serving on was in a new red and yellow uniform, scowling with her tongs held out. "Giving me bloody migraine, all those spots," she said. A tannoy voice announced, "Welcome to Yellow Spot!"

Liz shuddered and concentrated on shopping. She would dish everything up with expansive gestures, be gregarious, spreading good will as she went, letting the wine flow like busted guttering. It was to be a family meal. The vegetables here were rubbish. Where were the fresh herbs?

While she took out her chequebook in the queue, she felt everyone was peering into her trolley. At the last minute she plucked a cheap CD off the display by the tills. It was a Burt Bacharach compilation, all his best songs played by the Boston Pops Orchestra. In her haste Liz had assumed they were hits by the original artists. Perfect for tonight, she thought.

"I SAW HER THIS MORNING," JANE WAS SAYING. "SNEAKING BACK FROM somewhere. His place, I suppose. The bus driver's. Wherever he lives."

"Fancy her leaving Penny all night like that!"

"No sense of responsibility. And she looked awful, too. Hadn't done her hair properly or anything. Had a massive duffel coat on. His, I suppose."

"That's passion for you."

Jane frowned. "I think that hair of hers is a wig."

"Do you?" Fran mused, playing with her own.

ROSE HAD MADE HER OWN LIFE. UNLIKE MOST FAIRY-TALE PRINCESSES she had had to carve out her own niche in the world. This didn't stop her thinking of herself as a princess. She shared her birthday with the Queen. When her Prince Charming had at last appeared, slobbery and drunk at the Labour Club one night in late spring, she had accepted him belatedly as her reward. He clung to her under the club's new glitter ball as they danced, pivoted to one spot by his legs slowly unscrewing itself as they revolved, love in their eyes.

Until then, Rose had lived a life of hardships. Of early deaths, single parenting, skivvying after others, one-night stands, the lot. And she had relished every minute of it. It was the same kind of relish she felt once when she lost a ring in the swing bin and found it again by tipping everything on to the lino and rummaging through every particle of filth. She picked through the grime and got rid of it, systematically, finding her treasure, tarnished and safe, then scrubbed her skin red raw under the hot tap afterwards. Jane had picked up the same habits. Mother and daughter spent their lives purging themselves under hot taps. They owed a lot to their immersion heaters.

Now Rose had decided it was time to chuck in the tea towel. Someone else could support her from now on. No more faked fiancés, no more soldiering on. At last it was time for the big white wedding and the trip around the world. She wanted a cruise that would never end. She wanted a big brassy tart of a finale to all those years spent scrubbing.

She beamed at Ethan as he trundled along beside her. They were circumnavigating the boating lake. It was in two tiers, connected by mechanical waterfalls. Both lakes a dull silver, ruffled by wind. Ragged willows ranged their edges and three banana-yellow kayaks transported children back and forth.

She thought about a photo of the same scene, taken for the town's official postcard in the seventies. There were still a faded handful left on sale in the newsagents in town. In the photo everyone was wearing tight nylon turtlenecks and long hair that needed brushing. Perhaps the card would be reprinted soon – wasn't that look coming back? If she closed her eyes she could smell lake water dried into denim flares. And what was it Jane had had a craze for that summer? A kind of lolly without a stick. A big hunk of flavoured ice in a packet. She had eaten seven in a day once and given herself the runs.

Rose remembered the photo because she was in it. Twenty years younger, in an orange and blue minidress, helping a plump Jane into one of those banana boats. The postcard was framed on her wall. Mother and daughter had been employed to promote the town. Come to our town, their beaming faces said. Rose felt that she and Jane had done their bit, had signalled people to bring their health, wealth and happiness to the burgeoning new town. And people came. She liked to think that their brave effort, single-parented and self-sufficient, a happy park outing one Saturday in the mid-seventies, had stood for something. Had, in some small way, helped. People came and, she hopped, they had their happy Saturdays too.

Happy Saturdays on your own with a kid took a lot of effort. Teachers must find that too, thirty times over. Rose had a lot of respect for teachers, but she had never had the brains to be one or really talk to one. Teachers, though, could wash their hands. Love, obligation, and the disapproving eyes of everybody else didn't come into it. Teachers were doing a career. Single parents were doing a life sentence.

Rose still worried about Jane. She had trained her to full self-sufficiency, trained her too well, and now Jane showed no inclination to end her solitary confinement. She wouldn't stir herself to seek out a Prince Charming. She never thought of herself as a princess. But at least she still went out. That was something.

"Me and you," she smiled down at Ethan."We'll set an example to our Jane and all the other young'uns." His face creased in pleasure, hanging on to her arm and every word. "We'll show them they can't do without marriage and a family and proper home, no matter what." She sighed expansively, crushing his hand in hers.

Following the Burnside path lined with poplars, they passed by the junior school Jane had attended. The grass was long and rank, full of the bright purple tails of foxgloves and those fleshy, pink flowers that stood taller than Rose herself. Sometimes the Burn was like a wilderness. They should do something about cleaning it up, she thought. And she certainly wouldn't come down here without her escort.

At last they came to the town centre. They made straight for the café, where the waiter looked cross and flustered again. He had a stub of pencil behind one ear and a Silk Cut behind the other. Rose asked if the ladies were in yet. The boy rolled his eyes and led them to the table at the back. There, the pensioners who edited the free local paper were waiting for the happy couple, their yellow legal pads open on the gritty tablecloth. Love had been found locally again, among their own. Rose and Ethan deserved to be publicised as an example. Cilla Black should turn up, really, singing something. Rose was leading the way forward, the town's figurehead and inspiration once more.

Once she sat down, her coat over her knees, sipping tea, Rose found herself warming to the idea of being interviewed. She told them that the secret of making a relationship tick was never going to bed not talking. Ethan and the lady reporters beamed. Then they told them to pull in closer, they were going to take their picture.

FOR FRAN THERE WAS A CERTAIN CUT-OFF POINT AT WHICH ANOTHER CUP of tea would just taste of so much hot water with a dribble of milk in it. But Jane never seemed to mind.

There was a Battenburg cake on the table, waiting for the kids and teatime, cut into eight irregular slices. Fran urged one on Jane. She took one, then another and another, at five-minutes intervals, talking as she did so and hardly aware of what she was eating. Her fingers went picking automatically over the greasy yellow crumbs. Fran had a rush of protectiveness for her kids. Their cake, she thought. I'll never do enough for them. They deserve more because they're mine. She felt a sudden hatred of Jane, smacking her pale lips, but quelled it.

"So Nesta's really missing? How do you know?"

Fran sighed. The novelty had worn off her piece of news. Jane would talk things to death and gossip with her became less fun as the hours went by. It was like Aladdin's lamp rubbed too hard, too often. "Well, first of all she never came round for milk this morning. Then I saw that gormless husband of hers, Tony, taking their Vicki to school."

"Poor kid! They'll have her crackers as well."

"After that he came here to ask if I'd seen his wife. He said it like that – 'Have you seen my wife?' – as if I'd shoved her under the settee." Fran thought that Jane wouldn't find the whole thing as funny if she had dealt with Tony at that point. He was in his blue, snorkel-hooded anorak, looking red in the face, and his eyes looked weepy, though that might just have been the cold. He really wanted Nesta to be hiding out at Fran's house. Fran thought at that moment, He really loves her. We spend so long laughing at them or saying they're daft and drinking cider all the time, we don't really think about that. A few hours apart from dozy, lumpy, obnoxious Nesta and Tony was pining away. He was banging on doors belonging to people he was usually too shy to talk to.

"He's probably shoved her under the settee himself and forgotten. Have you seen their manky settee?"

"He looked really worried."

"I think he's got a look of that Fred West."

"Oh, don't say that, Jane. That's awful!"

"She's on pills, isn't she?"

"They're bringing her off them again."

"Don't you think we should pop round, see if she's back?"

"I'll wait till he brings Vicki back at hometime. I'll ask then. I've got my own life to get on with." This was aimed pointedly at Jane. "I can't go worrying about neighbours all the time."

"There goes Liz." Jane stood and went to the window, closing the blinds slightly to hide herself. "Back with all her shopping. She's got a French stick. I bet she'll be entertaining this evening."

Fran joined her. "Off the bus."

"She'll be getting free fares now," Jane muttered. "You know, she's not as attractive as I thought at first."

"She's glamorous," Fran said. They watched her vanish indoors, the light go on. Fran thought about pulling the kids in since it was starting to get dark. "I saw that straight away when we first met her in the Copper Kettle. She's definitely got something about her. Charisma. She's got something about her that you don't see very often."

Jane swivelled the blinds open again, narrowing her eyes to look at Peter, who was up a climbing frame. "He's showing off for the girls. Like his father. Yeah, there's something about her. But not just glamour or charisma. I'm not sure what it is, but it's something else."

"WHAT NOW THEN?" PENNY ASKED AS THE SCHOOL STARTED TO FILL UP with the smell of disinfectant. The cleaners emerged in their blue coveralls for the end of the day. Their chemical smell masked the fug of dirty hair and sweat. 'What are you doing tonight?'

"I'm going home to Daddy Dearest," Vince replied, cramming his Victorian novel into an overcoat pocket. "Another nightmare."

"Do you fight much?"

"Oh, you know. Two men together." He shrugged.

"Why is it I know so many one-parent families?" Penny asked. She asked this as they came, last of all, down the cement staircase and pushed through the airlock doors at the bottom. "Where do we all come from?"

"I think it's more of a case of where we all go to. And it's usually places like this. That's why." He pulled up his coat collar, shivering under the darkness of this part of school.

She considered this as they passed the staff-room rose bushes, following the crazy paving that hadn't started out that way. "Sometimes I wish I knew some normal people."

"Yeah," he said with a harsh laugh. "Right."

"You know what I mean."

"When you get to college you'll meet people there more normal than you'll ever meet. More space cadets too. And everything in between." He sniffed appreciatively at the teatime sky.

Penny asked, "Is that what it was like for you?"

He smiled. "Oh, yes." They were standing by the incinerator at the edge of the field.

She studied his face. His bruises were showing up again, and there was something else there. He looked flushed. "Something's happened this afternoon, hasn't it?"

"It's nothing really."

"Tell me."

He looked at her and smiled. Penny looked fierce and...loyal. He realised he trusted her. "Oh, in the staff room, as I was leaving just now, Melanie Bell had a little word with me."

"Is that what she's called, Melanie?" Penny asked.

A whole gang of fifth-year boys were coming past, lighting cigarettes, ripping off their ties, their shirts untucked and hair mussed. They jeered at Penny and Vince standing together by the incinerator. One of them, the tallest, called out loudly, "Queer bastard!" The others were straight on to this. There was a spate of mumbling and hissing and then a ragged, deep-throated chant of "Queer bastard, queer bastard!" until they were gone.

Vince's face had drained. "That's what she wanted to talk about."

"Oh, God!"

'The lass in the toilets who overheard us talking about Andy is seeing one of the fifth-year lads. Now it's everywhere. Today's news.'

"What was Mrs Bell saying about it? You're not gonna get the sack?"

Vince smiled ruefully. "No, she was really good. She talked about the implications of being out at school. She was shit-hot, actually."

"Good."

"She wanted to make sure I knew what I was taking on, being out here. I said I thought it was important. She wanted to remind me what our school was like. And she was good, you know. She remembered what a rotten time I had when I was going through this school myself. When the kids ganged up on me without really knowing why. She said, don't be surprised if it's worse now. Even worse. She said, don't think that being grown-up makes you any more brave."

Penny was fishing in her bag for her own cigarettes. She lit them one each. Vince didn't want to tell Penny the rest of it. At that point the PE teacher had loped into the staff room, leering at him. He had just left the boys' shower block after taking the fifth-years for rugby. In the showers he had caught up with the gossip. He called across to Mrs Bell and Vince, where they were standing, "You can forget what I said before, when I warned you about hanging around the lasses you taught. No one's gonna worry about you doing anything with them, are they?"

Melanie Bell bridled. "Are you talking to me, Mr Ariel?"

His eyebrows knotted. "No, Mrs Bell. I'm talking to him. Your little mate."

"Perhaps it would be better not to shout across the room," she said. "You aren't out on your fields now."

"It's a staff room. It's after four o'clock. I can do what I want in here."

"You can't harass other members of staff."

"Harass!" He laughed and looked around for support. Beside him was the other, older PE teacher, who was deaf. "Was I harassing you?" he asked Vince.

Vince just wanted to get away from there. It was too much like being fourteen. But to see him looking so bluff and aggrieved, shouting his mouth off, made him stop and say, "No, you aren't harassing me. You're threatening to. And I'll warn you now. If I start getting hassle from you, if I get any more hassle from you, I'll fucking report it. But before that, I'll fucking deck you."

And that had been that. The PE teacher snorted and started to pack his Adidas bag, slinging piles of first-year maths books in with his dirty boots and towel. He stomped out past Vince and Mrs Bell and mumbled under his breath, loud enough for the room to hear, "Arse bandit."

Mrs Bell looked up at Vince. "You see? That's what you'll have to contend with. Pigs like that."

Vince shrugged. "He's like that anyway."

Penny looked at him now. He looked terrible. "Don't worry about it. People will be all right. It's not like you've made a mistake or anything. I don't think you had any choice about coming out."

"What do you mean?"

"There were rumours going about anyway."

He shrugged. "Ah, well."

"They can't do anything to you."

"No. But sometimes it feels as if people can cut you down to size with just a few words."

"Yeah," she said. "I've got to get home and meet this bus driver my mam is seeing."

"He's coming round, is he?"

"That's what she came to school to tell me."

Vince shook his head and whistled. "She's a right one, your mam."

"You can say that again."

Then they said goodbye and turned to leave each other. He turned back to give her a swift hug and Penny lurched awkwardly into it, as if she wasn't comfortable with people holding her. Walking away, Vince felt sixteen again, walking home on the slippery school field, fumbling embraces with girls.

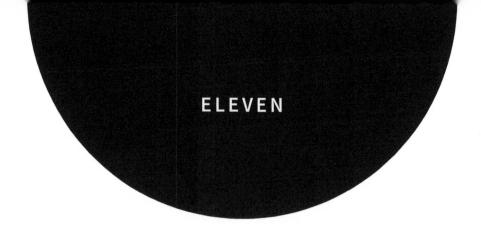

ELEVEN

VINCE'S DAD OFTEN CAME HOME WITH INJURIES. HE WORKED IN A FACTORY
on machines with heavy, grinding parts. Something like that. Vince never
asked about the particulars. For as long as he could remember his dad had
been coming home sporting bandages, sticking plasters, even slings. It was
part and parcel of the job.

Further down school Vince had detested metalwork. He fell behind
the rest of his class, keeping his specially bought, oatmeal-colour apron
spotlessly clean, avoiding the machines. He had seen enough industrial
injuries.

His father slowly came to accept that he was not the sort of boy who
tinkered with metal machine parts. In a way he was pleased. It would keep
him out of trouble.

Vince let himself into the kitchen, finding his father at the cooker, in
shirtsleeves, stirring a pan of baked beans. Before looking at him, Vince's
father bent his neck to light a cigarette on the ring. Vince stared at the
smouldering tobacco flakes left behind.

"What's happened to your face?"

"Someone decided to have a go at me." The make-up must have rubbed away. There's none to replace it with in this house.

"Who? Have you phoned the coppers?"

"No." Vince made his way up the narrow staircase. The house was very small, its walls yellow with ingrained fumes and covered with ancient LP covers, stuck up with drawing pins. The carpet on the stairs was full of swirling blue and purple shapes. To Vince, the carpet colours and the LP covers meant home, though he would never wear the colours or play the records.

A night at home. Here we go. Should've brought Andy back. He clicked on his room's light, across the landing. Ha! What would Dad make of Andy? A lathe operator most likely. Ask him if he's ever considered the possibility. Andy might be interested too. Vince could see him working at a lathe, working intently, his mind on nothing in particular but bringing two surfaces together. To grind them into powder. Andy's scary eyes glaring at the spinning blades, happy forever more. He mustn't let Dad and Andy meet. Andy was too susceptible. He could turn into anything, whenever anyone asked him to. This facility scared Vince, and it made him jealous. Now that he thought about it, it was with Andy that he felt most wooden and intractable.

Vince's room was large and very bare. Its walls and floor were a searing white. The expanse contained a single mattress sprawled messily in the centre, out of kilter with the right angles of the room. Vince's bed looked as if it had been sailing under its own steam from one side of the room to the other.

One wall had two mirrored doors, walk-in cupboards where Vince stored all his things. He couldn't bear to look at them all at the same time. Clothes, books, paintbrushes, were only useful when they were useful. Besides, he hadn't really unpacked since moving back here in August. When he left Lancaster he loaded the tiny hire van, crammed it all in, and drove across the mountains. When he got back to Aycliffe he had just shoved everything in the cupboards. He didn't want to see his things out here. They belonged in the house by the canal in Lancaster. There, everything had been perfect. He wanted everything still in boxes so he could leave at a moment's notice.

He closed the door and sat on the mattress, admiring his collection of open air and space.

JANE WAS GONE. IT WAS PETER'S TEATIME. FRAN'S OWN KIDS WERE IN THE front room with children's BBC. They were biding their time till *Neighbours* came on. Today was special, there was a wedding.

Fran busied herself hacking vegetables in the kitchen. She nicked her thumb with the potato knife. For a moment she glared at the white slit just above her knuckle, defying the blood to come. Then she started worrying that it wouldn't come at all: 'I'm turning into a potato!' So she was glad when the glistening line of red sprang up, flooded over and dribbled on to stainless steel. She held her hand under the tap, watching it sluice away. It kept bleeding.

When the knock at the back door come, she had to twist awkwardly to open it. Nesta's daughter Vicki stood there, blinking in the light from the kitchen. Even though it was freezing she was in a thin cotton dress. Her hair was matted with grease, plastered across her pudgy, mottled face. She wouldn't even look at Fran as she asked, 'Is my mam here yet?'

Fran shook her hand dry and turned off the tap. She let her full concentration fall on Vicki, seeing her grey socks rolled down, her bruised, skinny legs. "I haven't seen her all day, pet. Is she still not home?"

Vicki looked at her. Beads of blood poked out of the flap on Fran's thumb. They merged and began to trickle again. Vicki never noticed. She had a glazed expression. She was supposed to be deaf, but if you offered her sweets she was quick enough on the uptake.

"Has she still not come home?" Fran asked more slowly.

"My dad says, have you seen her today?"

"I haven't seen her at all. Since yesterday."

"My dad says..." Vicki's voice faded away.

"Tell your dad to come round here. Have you had your tea yet?"

Vicki blinked.

"Have you had anything to eat since you've been back from school?"

She shook her head.

Fran shoved her hand back into the sink. "Get yourself back home, get your dad to feed you, then tell him to come here himself, and we'll see about your mam. I'm sure she'll be back by the time you've had your tea."

She turned on the tap again. Vicki refused to budge.

"All right, pet?"

At last the words appeared to reach her, and Vicki nodded quickly, turned, and ran out of the garden. Fran swore as her thumb began to hurt, a long throbbing pain. They're having oven chips, she decided. Bugger the taties.

VINCE SLUNG HIS JACKET ACROSS THE WHITE WOODEN FLOOR. HE WAS pleased with the effect of the purple on white.

Stretching out on the mattress, he reacquainted himself with his ceiling. Moving the bed about in the empty room threw the ceiling into different shapes, a fresh angle each day. It gave him the feeling of rotating very, very slowly. Vince didn't like people who moved too fast and he hated people who didn't move at all.

At the back of his mind was the impulse to think over the scene in the staff room. He ought to be teasing out implications, rationalising, making plans. But it was too awful. He hated doing those things at the best of times. He supposed he would just muddle through. Fucking muddle. All he ever did. And improvise when it came to the point, when a crisis loomed or somebody said something. So of course there was no game plan, he would be reliant simply upon the force of his own personality. I always find myself living on my nerves like this, he thought. It isn't very professional.

And then he wondered if he would be forced to punch the PE teacher.

He laughed at himself. What with being jumped on in the street last night and the hassle at school today, he felt he was in a documentary about something.

Oh, but I'm too arch, he thought. I wish I could get properly worked up and earnest about something. But he had got worked up in the staff room. He had very nearly flown off the handle. He had always assumed that the moment he lost control, that was the moment that would work like a charm and make him, like Pinocchio, into a real boy. A real boy like Andy.

One hand connected with something alien to his bed. A poster tube.

There was a brisk knock and then his dad was bringing in one of his

mugs of sugary tea. Weeks ago Vince had asked him to wait longer before
barging in, that he could be doing anything, but his father always forgot. It
was as if they lived in a garage or a workshop.

"Oh, I got you something today. A present to cheer your room up."
Vivid in his scarlet waistcoat, his father was frowning at the bare walls.

"What is it?" Vince wasn't used to getting things. He unsheathed
and unrolled the poster. Looking down at it, he couldn't think what to
say. It was tasteful. A black and white photograph, quite unlike his dad's
taste, which tended towards things that looked like Warhol or Jeff Koons,
though he'd never have known who they were. What was more unlike his
dad's taste was that it was a picture of a nearly naked man, shielding his
face and standing by a bath. An Athena poster. He must have been out
of town to get it. Vince stared at the grainy silvery grey flesh of the solid
thighs. There was a peekaboo tuft of pubic hair over his towel and the
weighty impression of a partial erection under it.

"What's this for?"

"I thought you'd like it." His father wouldn't look at it.

Vince was appalled. "I don't like posters," was all he could say. He
kept thinking, what's he playing at?

"It's what you like though, isn't it? That sort of thing?"

Vince glanced up sharply to read his expression, but his father was
looking away through the window.

"Men with all their bits on display? Is that what you're saying?"

His father's averted gaze flinched slightly.

Vince threw the tube after his jacket. "Is this some kind of sick joke?"

It wasn't meant to be like this. No disappointed, vengeful father ever
did things like this. When he found Vince, at the age of eleven, smoking
by the garages, he gave him a packet of twenty and tried to sicken him by
making him smoke one after another until they were all gone. Vince had
thanked him and done just that. He'd had a headache afterwards and a
craving in the morning.

This could be the same shock tactic. But the poster was too...well,
tasteful, although tacky in the way that tasteful things from Athena are,
and his father's whole manner was cowed, submissive.

"I've been reading some of the books you've read."

"You've been going through my things?"

"The books you've left lying about downstairs..."

"And?"

"Well, that Maurice bloke, and..."

"What are you trying to say?"

"I know, son. I know what you're going through."

"Been through, Dad. You missed it."

His father looked at him, pained. "I'm trying. Bloody hard."

"Pictures of this feller getting into a bath aren't going to make it any easier. What's the matter with you?"

His father fiddled anxiously with his string tie, jamming the metal wings right under his thick chin.

Vince stood up and kicked the mattress into a new position. "You're supposed to be furious." He looked at him. You're supposed to threaten me with death, chuck me out, he thought, finally break down and tell me about all the sacrifices you've made for me. Plead with me eventually to mend my ways and find a nice girlfriend. You're supposed to be my father, for God's sake, wanting grandchildren, a daughter-in-law. "You're not meant to be buying me dirty pictures."

"It's not a dirty picture."

Vince had once found his father's stash of 1950s pornography in the attic. Jazz mags, the lads had called them at school. The colours were very bright. Very blue skies, very orange skin. Vince had wondered why the Fifties were so colourful, the Sixties so black and white. "Not by your standards it's not."

"What's that mean?"

"Nothing."

"I threw them all out. After you found them."

"No, you didn't."

"All right, I sold them."

"And bought my Christmas present with the proceeds. How would you like to have a bike bought with profits from dirty magazines?"

"I've tried so hard for you. I've made so many sacrifices –"

"I knew we'd get to that. Even though you're trying to be so bloody liberal."

His father turned to go.

"Is this the only way you can deal with it? Pretend that I'm still like you? Why didn't you talk to me?"

He followed his father on to the dark landing. He found him slumped against the wall, forehead resting on Gene Pitney, who was grinning. "I just wanted to understand."

"But it's not the same, Dad. Not the same."

His father looked up. "Isn't it?"

DINNER WAS ALMOST FINISHED WHEN THE KITCHEN DOOR FLEW OPEN, and Fran and the kids were treated to the sight of Frank, home from work and already drunk. Gary stood a little way behind in a similar state, and smiling inanely in his snorkel hood. Fran went to the oven, where Frank's tea had spent the last half-hour coagulating.

"What was the excuse for celebration tonight?" she asked. The kids kept quiet, unsure.

He made to take the plate but she pulled it away. He'd burn himself. "Consoling Gary."

This forced Fran to acknowledge the army man. She was reluctant after the summer holiday street-fighting. "What's the matter with Gary?"

He stood where he was on the doorstep, face dark inside the furred hood, teetering slightly. "She's left me."

"Oh. Another one." Fran put the plate down. The heat was scorching through her damp tea towel. "I'm sorry to hear that."

"I threw her out. She took the kid. She was too weak."

"Frank, come and get your tea." All the heat of the kitchen was vanishing out the door. Into the army man's snorkel hood, Fran thought grimly, and wished he would go. Frank had his head in the fridge.

"Aren't there any cans left?"

Gary said, "She couldn't hack married life. Married life's about being stuck in the same house together sometimes twenty-four hours a day and surviving. No matter what happens. It's not about breaking down. That's weak."

"I'd give you a can if we had one," Frank apologised.

"No. I'd better go home."

There's male bonding for you, Fran sneered. Only a little while ago they were threatening each other with axes in the street. Gary stood a moment, as if regaining his bearings, and turned to leave. At the garden gate he was startled in the dark, yelling, "Who the fuck's that?"

There was a quick wet crash, the kids giggled and Fran groaned.

"It's me," Tony gasped, appearing in the doorway. "I've smashed a bottle of milk. Here's two more, to pay you back. I never knew she'd been taking them off you." Fran automatically took the bottles. Tony stood frozen, mouth open, apparently fascinated by the Elastoplast on Fran's thumb. He asked, "Have you seen her yet?" The streetlight made his thickly curled hair look blue, the same blue as his anorak.

"Have you fed your Vicki?"

"She's had *Lion King* pasta shapes. Where's Nesta?"

"I don't know."

Tony began to look very scared. Fran pulled him into the kitchen, still with an eye on Gary the army man making his unsteady way up the street. He was singing 'Respectable' by Mel and Kim.

"I think the police ought to know."

Tony looked sick. "Is it that bad, do you think?"

"You've got two bairns, one of them not out of nappies. You can't go out searching the streets while you've got them to see to. I'll phone the coppers and you can sit with Vicki and the baby. I'll come and tell you what's happening."

As Fran ushered Tony out, Frank sat down heavily at the head of the table. He eyed his kids as they resumed their meal, their chips cooled by the outside air.

"All the women are going," he told them. "They're all leaving the street. You lot keep hold of your mam."

Fran paused on her way to the phone. "I'm not going anywhere, am I?"

CLIFF WAS SLIDING ON A WHITE SHIRT, NEVER WORN. IT HAD HUNG ALONE in the bedroom of his small flat, waiting for tonight.

He shivered, listening to its creases unfold, rumpling closer to his body's shape. Like the shadows of clouds, goose bumps appeared and faded on his ruddy flesh.

Matching jacket and trousers. His interview suit. His facing-the-public suit. The thin black tie, draped around his neck, down his chest, alive of its own accord as he pulled it on before the mirror. Music played in the next room. The Human League, 'Don't You Want Me?' This kind of excitement always sent him back to the music from his teens. Music on the radio, from the time of hanging around the streets in gangs.

Dressing, he made slow but steady progress. He was taking his time. Making sure that all the bits were right, especially for dinner with Liz.

VINCE'S FATHER ATE BOTH PLATEFULS OF FISH FINGERS, BEANS AND OVEN chips, by himself in the kitchen, looking out at the back yard. He had played *Gene Pitney's Sixteen Greatest* through three times over. Vince was upstairs, adrift on his mattress and refusing to speak.

The flesh beneath the grilled orange crusts was, in places, an unhealthy grey. Cheap fish fingers. He felt sick. What was it Vince wanted him to cook. Pasta, rice, foreign things, but apparently healthy and economical. Vince's father had been stung by the suggestion. What's wrong with fish fingers? Or with mince pies from the bakery? It's what I brought you up on. Remember the pieces of string we found in a pie once? You said it's what they had strangled the cow with.

So the poster had been a bad idea. What next? Maybe he would come round. Maybe it would be up on his wall tomorrow morning. I'll check, he decided. Surely it was the same as an ordinary lad having a picture up of some tart with her baps out? What was wrong with that? It was healthy. Only appetite. To him Vince was just the same, only the other way round. Vince didn't have to have such a different life.

Vince himself didn't see that yet. He wanted to seem queer.

There would be no grandchildren, though. Never mind. He went to wash the dishes.

Grandchildren made you old. Teddy boys can't be old. You can't be an old rebel. You can't have a leather jacket with a grey quiff. Distressed leather, fine; distressed hair is another thing altogether.

But a house of bachelors, washing two dirty plates by themselves. No noise except Gene Pitney.

And now, the noise of pebbles against glass. Thrown from the field, out of the darkness. A swift ricochet and into the grass. Someone was out there, throwing stones at Vince's window. The floorboards creaked upstairs. Vince would be craning his neck out the window. His father did the same. He saw a dark figure; Prussian blue, fists clenched, looking up.

"Vince!" he heard, cautiously hissed by a male voice.

LEAVING EVERYTHING SIMMERING, LIZ HAD RUSHED UPSTAIRS FOR LAST-minute adjustments to herself. Penny went to oversee the pasta, which she found clagged together, bubbling in a sickly yellow froth. Liz was a careless and extravagant cook. Penny set about separating pasta twirls with a wooden spatula.

The dining room was aglow with golden candles and sprays of plastic tiger lilies in blue glass vases. Liz had reappeared, standing ready, arms draped on a chairback. The scene had taken on the gaudiness of a Pre-Raphaelite painting. The wine they had drunk already was making Penny lose her appetite.

"Open another one." Her mother passed a bottle. She couldn't deal with the cork herself because of her nails. Penny went to the kitchen sink; she might spill red wine everywhere. Her nerves were shot. Liz busied herself, easing the soundtrack of *Saturday Night Fever* from its worn sleeve.

"I'VE BEEN MADE HOMELESS. CAN I STAY HERE?"

It wasn't certain whether Andy was asking Vince or Vince's father. One was frozen on the stairs, the other was holding the back door.

Andy was in his leather jacket, carrying his rucksack. He looked whiter than ever, fading away beneath the unshaded kitchen light. His eyes roved hungrily around the room.

"He's your friend, Vince?" Vince nodded. His father asked, "Who threw you out?"

"My uncle. Because he's getting married."

"That's hard luck. You'd better close the door."

Vince took a hesitant step downstairs. "You're letting him stay?"

OUT OF HIS BLUE NYLON UNIFORM THE BUS DRIVER LOOKED STRANGE TO Penny. He was grinning hugely, a vision in the steamy kitchen, a bunch of roses in either hand. Liz stepped forward and kissed the bus driver's cheek. "Hello."

I hope she's shaved properly, Penny thought. Of course she has.

This was the crucial moment for Liz. This was the moment by which she could gauge the future. It was the moment when something new becomes something current and ongoing.

Penny recalled one of the late-night washing-machine conversations, years ago. Her father sitting in a kimono, clean-shaven and with his hair cut short. He was telling her about one-night stands and lasting relationships.

"A first meeting, first-night sex, is something that seems to happen outside of time. The mental life is suspended, no matter how lucid and unphysical you may be. Thinking about consequences is for the future. You've been rendered exempt from time. The next morning, waking together, may still be like that. But it is too early to be sure. It is not until the moment that the love returns" (*This moment,* Penny was thinking) "or when you return to the lover, that you may begin to see how things will end up.

"Does he smile? Does she look happy to see you again? Are you content to return to the present together? To pick up the everyday strands at once and in the same place, start to wind them together into a tangle of both? Can you tell?"

Liz beamed. "I'm so pleased you could come."

"I *CAN'T,*" ANDY WHISPERED, CORPSING WITH LAUGHTER. HE WAS CRUSHING his jacket into the mattress with his back, squirming as Vince unpicked his fly buttons with his teeth. "Not with your old man downstairs."

Vince drew back, palms pressed down like the Sphinx, pinning Andy to the bed. "He's probably listening in." Thoughtfully and tenderly, he took Andy into his mouth for a while, nuzzling shoulders under the backs of Andy's legs, feeling the thighs relax and tense, of one movement now. He loved the feel of the end of someone's cock in his mouth. The oxymoronic thrill of it: something so tender and yet determined. It was the most intimate thing Vince knew. They had hardly exchanged two sentences tonight and here they were.

He paused at a well-known point, recognising the spasm. The lull before crisis. "Well, I can. And so can you."

And he proved it.

Andy had come home.

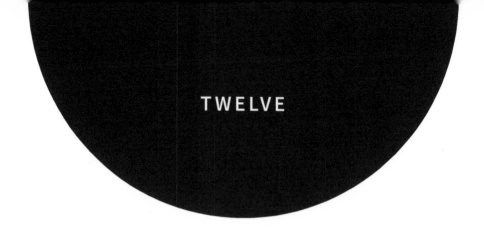

TWELVE

PENNY LOOKED DOWN AT THE RUINED REMAINS. THEY HAD BEEN TALKING for so long that the leftover garlic bread was hardening. Almost an hour ago the music had petered out without anyone getting up to change it. Their conversation had carried them through. It had been endless, seamless. Cliff never stopped.

Liz held her wineglass carefully, watching him talk, content not to break in. The night had been hers also. She had been full of energy. Penny wondered whether she was on something. She kept jumping up as if pulled on wires for more wine, more food.

Just after one, Penny shook herself free of the scene. She looked at the rumpled tablecloth, the crumbs, the scattered cutlery, and thought over this talk – the relaxed tone, the loud vigour of their mutual epiphanies, and the starchy friendliness of the evening's start. She was keeping it all in mind. Saving the implications for later.

"I'll have to go to bed."

They looked at her. She liked the bus driver. He had done everything he could to make her like him. So she did.

"Thanks for your company," he said.

"That's all right," she returned.

Liz grinned at her and Penny made her way out into the hallway, securing the door behind her. Naturally she stood to listen.

Nothing at first. Liz and Cliff were evidently wrestling with the weight of each other's undivided attention. Then the odd murmur, their conversation was picking up again. Penny caught, "...a lovely girl. You've done amazingly well, bringing her up on your own." She groaned and headed off up the stairs.

Cliff's voice sounded more distinctly. Yet she could not be sure whether she had heard correctly, so she sat perfectly still on the middle stair and listened hard just to make sure.

"I've been following you around. You know that, don't you?"

As if he was enacting a scene in a play, weighing down his words so that everyone could follow.

"Have you?" Liz wasn't playing this particular game. She was still indistinct, slurred, playful. Penny thought, when people turn serious they have to pretend they're in a TV play if they want to come across as real. Cliff was suddenly intent, almost hammy.

"Ever since the day you moved in."

"Oh." There was the clinking of glass, the thud of an empty bottle.

There was that dusty smell of carpet, poking itself right up Penny's nose, and the tough, fibrous feel of it, harsh down her side as she leaned across the stair. She put her forehead on the next step up and closed her eyes.

So that's all right, then. He's in there pleading his troth. Liz will be pleased.

How can the room, she thought, spin round like this, when my eyes are shut? All the darkness available to her was oscillating. She shifted her head and everything began a sideways slide. It was as if a plug had been pulled in one corner of her brain and the fluid had begun to roar away, leaving her parched and sick. Then the darkness was clearing in bleeding patches of purple.

"You want to stay, don't you?"

At least the conversation was gentle. There was no fighting, no raised voices. Penny's memories of sitting on the middle stair in the early hours all had to do with fighting going on. Flinching at the sounds of breaking glass, praying that there would be no injuries, though there always were.

"Yes, I want to stay. I don't want to go now."

Staying.

People can't be relied upon. People leave, people go and you can't stop them. They expend themselves in your life and they have to go. Penny knew this. For her, life seemed to be about the very act of relinquishing. She had let Liz go, freed the constraints and waved goodbye in the school corridor. But did such acts necessarily involve separation, separateness, never seeing again?

The patches of purple in her darkness lightened to a view of violet snow, crusting the brickwork of the cathedral and castle in Durham. A scene plucked from her childhood, the winter sky that turned the snow purple on the night her mam gave her back to her dad.

Penny was five. She stood on the bridge alone with the searing cold. She was fascinated by the buildings looming above, over the river. Their tops surmounted high embankments formed by blackened trees. All the buildings were chocolate brown, ancient and edible. She stood in the middle of the bridge, her footsteps in either direction now lost.

Two cars faced each other across the bridge. Their separate headlight beams shone across the slush and refused to meet, to illuminate Penny.

Mam in one, Dad in the other. Mam had left her, swished away in her long brown coat, back to her own car. Dad was coming out of his, hurrying towards her, urging his daughter into the safety of his car, where it smelled of cigarettes and Bob Dylan was playing. Penny at the age of five watched this bearded father in his patched jeans and headband with interest and hindsight.

He approached her with a smile. "Let's get fish and chips. You must be starving."

"No, Liz," she was bursting to say. "You've only just cooked a lovely meal for me and the bus driver."

And that shifted the dream's tone. Her father frowned under the lemony streetlight, his beard softened and vanished. His features darkened and became harder, pricked out in eyeliner, lipstick, blusher. His hair sprang out into well-tinted curls and his body actually changed shape. He grew aware, almost painfully aware of each nuance his movements took on. He moved with grace and it seemed to cost him dearly. He was starting to act as if the eyes of the world were watching each fragment of his body. His heavy man's clothes were falling away. He was in his gold lamé, skin-tight and shimmering across the snow, a hot knife through butter.

Ravishing, Penny thought. Yet when you were close enough to see the eyes you could count the cost of the scrutiny he suspected. From nowhere he produced a black scarf, calmly wrapping it about his throat. To make it look more tender, more vulnerable, make it seem as if there was not an Adam's apple there.

Each sinuous movement was a dead giveaway. He hung his head and stared down at himself. Penny watched her father in a dream become a mother, and worry that the world might glimpse the impression of his cock through what he liked to wear.

But this dream came up to date. Cliff appeared, hiding part of Liz's body with his own, in an embrace acknowledging and discreetly accommodating everything of which Liz might be ashamed. Cliff tugged her away and they went to the Hillman Imp, driving off and leaving the bridge one-sided.

Something caught in her throat. Penny sensed one side of herself sinking again, balance gone. She looked for escape to the other side of the bridge, where the mother, the original mother, had gone, but had left her car standing abandoned. Penny had the keys in her hand. It meant mobility, that she must have money of her own, now, in this dream, this new life. She wouldn't be stuck forever on this bridge. Keys, money, cars, all of these could rescue her from the mid-point in ways that people could not.

She started to walk towards her mother's empty car, but her resolve was thrown off balance by her heart missing a beat. Something moved across the bridge before. Little creatures, cackling and sniggering, running and hopping through the wet snow. They flung themselves into it up to their fragile necks, stopping Penny in her tracks for fear of treading on them. A constant stream of gleeful animals, scampering out of the brickwork, holding her up.

What were they up to? Freed from the cracks in the stone, what were these miniature buffalo, ibexes, antelopes doing?

Like ants they worked together. They hoisted their loads (What are they carrying? Penny wondered, squinting) and as one they negotiated familiar burdens over snow.

Round, dark shapes were bundled on their shoulders. Apples. Lots of apples. The little creatures carried apples and laid them down at Penny's feet.

"APPARENTLY SHE WAS AT THE RIVERSIDE INSTITUTE FOR DEPRESSION." Fran shrugged. "I never knew that before. So the police are quite worried about her. At least they're taking it more seriously."

Jane sat opposite her, by the television set, with the last weather report of the night casting a blue gloom. Peter was in his pyjamas, glad to be up this late. He was showing Vicki how his *Ghostbusters* toys worked. Vicki was still in her coat, a carrier bag of clothes, hastily packed, beside her.

"I'm sorry about this, Jane. We haven't got the room at ours for Vicki as well. I'm going to be up all night with the baby."

Jane was altogether bewildered. "That's fine." She wasn't used to having people in her living room, especially at this time of night. "What's her stupid bloody husband doing?"

"He's going off his head. Out looking for her, on the streets."

"Jesus!"

"I had no idea she was on so much treatment. It explains a lot." Fran caught Vicki looking at her, faintly puzzled. She's not deaf, Fran thought.

"It does." Jane yawned. "So anything might have happened."

"They think she may just have wandered off. They said she may just wander back again. It happens."

"We'll have to see."

"I'll let you all get to bed. Thanks for taking Vicki on. Like I say, we've got a completely full house. She's got the stuff she needs. The police are coming round in the morning...statements and that..."

Jane quietly led Fran to the door. They were shaking their heads at each other in unspoken bemusement. They both knew that something, possibly something awful, might have happened to Nesta. Saying it aloud would make it seem closer. They also knew that she might simply have wandered off. That possibility seemed worse, somehow.

"LOOK AT THIS."

They laughed when they found Penny asleep halfway up the stairs. Liz took her ankles, Cliff her head and shoulders, and together they carried her upstairs, into her room, and arranged her on the bed. It didn't disturb her in the slightest. There was the faintest of smiles on her face.

"God knows what she's dreaming about," Liz said.

They were relieved to have Penny to take upstairs. It got them both up there, the heart of the domestic home, without embarrassment. Cliff was staying. Liz showed him her bedroom and he smiled. She left him like that and went to the bathroom.

CATCHING HIS JEANS ON BARBED WIRE, HE FELT RATHER THAN HEARD THE rip. As he bent to free his leg, the undergrowth seemed to uncoil itself, move in on him. The vegetation glistened like oil in the darkness.

"Nesta!" he hissed, with a sob.

His palms were full of crumbling earth, reeking of petrol as did all the earth by the Burn. Cars on the road above him moved past. Tony made for the concrete bridge beneath the road and called out "Nesta!" again for the benefit of the echo.

He watched the play of moonlight on the stream, stared at the graffiti on the underpass wall, which appeared brown in this light. He couldn't read, so it wasn't a clue he was looking for. Tony crouched down and sat on the path, his back to the wall, finding himself damp in a puddle. Piss, by the smell of it.

Looking down for a dry patch of concrete, he found Nesta's heirloom Victorian locket. It had been her foster mother's. His heart beating, he flipped the locket open and saw Nesta's pictures of Noele Gordon and Pat Phoenix inside. They had been cut out of the TV Times a number of years ago, and pasted into the locket's open shell with nail varnish. He had found a clue.

LIZ STOOD VERY STILL, GAZING INTO THE HALF-LENGTH BATHROOM mirror. Her shoulders sat square in the frame, as in a formal portrait. She was face on, unblinking; unabashed like a tailor's dummy.

Cliff was poised behind, his chest just touching her shoulder blades, the rest of him bracing her weight, as if she were about to snap and fall.

"You and your obsessional nature!" Liz smiled, and watched her lips work. "Fancy following me into the bathroom. Is my toilette so fascinating?" The harsh lighting rendered her make-up shiny, and showed the cracks in the tiles. Cliff's warm face appeared on her shoulder. He nudged her Adam's apple with his nose, making her gulp. She took a tissue from the box on the cistern and started to wipe her make-up off.

He watched her very carefully as she wore through the layers with daubs of cold cream. Finished, she looked the same, only paler. The bottom half of her face was cast in a bluish shadow. Liz reached for a long-handled, bright gold razor on the windowsill.

"I'll do it," the bus driver said. She thought about complaining as he took the shining blade from her, applied lather to her face, covering up the shadow, but she stopped herself.

"I was never any good at shaving," she said as he began to carve into the soap with deft movements. "Nobody ever taught me properly."

His face was intent as he worked, moving delicately but surely about her. He eased back her head to expose her throat and she felt her breath catch, hearing the rasp of the blade. At one point it struck with an audible nick. She saw the alarm in his eyes.

Liz stared at the bright line of blood darkening in her reflection. "Shit!" She made a grab for more tissues, holding her head still.

Cliff darted forwards with his tongue, and licked away the first drops that had formed. He grinned, smearing his teeth with her blood.

"The biggest taboo, these days," he said.

"Stupid! You should be more careful." She held damp tissue to the cut, alone with the pulse of blood in her neck, feeding into her own consoling hand. Cliff went back to holding her from behind, dropping the razor with a heavy clatter into the sink.

They stood for a while, until the bleeding stopped. He unzipped her dress and began to peel back the shoulders, gently undid the bra and helped her let the falsies fall with dignity on to the heap that her discarded dress had made.

"What I always wanted, really. People like you are so hard to find. You'd be perfect as either a man or a woman. But what I really wanted, you are. A woman with a prick."

He's nice, but maybe a bit shallow, Liz thought in order to distract her attention from the mirror image. The narrow man's chest with its hair and wiry muscles. And the shock of her wig on that body, the face now androgynous and beautiful. Flowing and abundant false hair on a stringy, underdeveloped body.

Until now she had avoided seeing this combination, woman's head on a man's body. Usually, the wig came off first, then make-up, and then she was just a man in a dress. That was all right, a standard figure of fun. But with her wig still on and the clothes on the floor, she was a woman inside a man's body. She looked at herself as she was now, standing in her Marks and Spencer's knickers with the shaft of her stiffened penis strapped by the elastic to her stomach.

With his index finger Cliff traced the shape of her nipples, the cool tip making her shiver. He cupped his hand around the smoothness of a pectoral. "You're a woman, aren't you? But you've got all different things..." His other hand reached to the end of her cock where a glistening droplet was forming. "But you're really all woman."

She thought, I'm content to let him say this to me. He's defining me absolutely and I'm quite content to let him. What does that say about my current state of mind?

But I can be anything. It's a political thing, a personal choice. I am determined to be what I want. Yet at his touch I harden and seal. If he says I am a woman, a woman with a prick that he wants to marry, then I seem happy to be that. Why do I do that? How can I let him?

But his jaw was resting heavily on her shoulder, one palm grinding gently into her chest as he moved his own body against her from behind, making her follow his rhythm. She fell into it, pulled by the arc of tension across her chest and drawn out on the raw, choking bliss as he fingered her cock. His fist closing over the apple-red flesh, drawing reluctantly away, fingertips playing over it, a beautiful but sullen tropical plant, almost about to flower.

He of course had his own erection ground into her buttocks and the sensation was almost shocking to her.

"I don't want you to fuck me," Liz said. And her voice was dry and lower. "I want us to come together, face to face. Both of us held together, in each other's hands. That's safest and it's equal. It makes us one, in a way. Like grafting stems in a nursery."

"Like last night?" he asked. "But that was just the first time. It wasn't really sex. Just messing about. Just wanking each other off."

She halted each responsive gesture. "No, it wasn't. That's childish. We're all wankers, aren't we? It shouldn't be a term of abuse."

He shrugged. She went on, helping him to remove her knickers.

"We oughtn't to feel the need to ape the usual cut-and-thrust. Not if we don't want."

Looking confused, he took her face in his hands. "I'm just trying to say I want you. I do. I do. But how do I want you? All I can say is that I want to fuck you – and I do. But what else is there? What else do I know?"

"We'll learn together. It's never too late, honestly. Last night is a wonderful starting point. Don't you think?"

She unbuttoned his shirt, drew him tighter to her. Her cock rested nose-first against his midriff and had to be moved as she unzipped and released him. Then one cock met its companion; they nudged against each other familiarly, rasping as their owners collided and fastened this hardness between their bodies. ·

THIRTEEN

IT WAS RAINING EVERYWHERE. LAST NIGHT THEY HAD FORGOTTEN TO pull the blinds and the water ran in sheets down exposed glass. Grey waves of light rolled through the room, and Andy woke to find the world television-grey and uninviting.

He woke Vince up. "It's twenty past eight."

Vince turned over with a groan to find Andy staring pensively at the window.

"Today is the day I sort my life out."

"It is?" Vince was listening for sounds from his father. He recognised the bass line from 'The Man Who Shot Liberty Valance' somewhere below.

"I have to find out where I'm going to live."

"It's not a good day to do that on. You should never be decisive on rainy days. It's a chemical thing. You need sunshine and happy thoughts, you do."

"You're cheerful this morning."

"I had a visitor last night. Of course I'm cheerful." Vince was quite genuinely pleased and surprised by himself. He rested his head on one palm, speaking from the throat in chalky early-morning tones, the sound raw in the room.

"Well, bless you for that, anyway."

"So what are you going to do?"

"Sort some stuff out. Loose ends. I'm going to see my good old uncle Ethan. My benefactor. See if he feels at all responsible for my wellbeing."

"Back to Darlington then?"

"He's here in Aycliffe. With that old woman of his. Somewhere near the boating lake, the address is. Will you give me directions?"

"Yeah, course." Vince sat up and found he was in his T-shirt and nothing else. There were socks poking out of the pillows and clothes all over the floor. It had been one of those nights. "Look, I'll come with you."

Andy shook his head as if he'd already thought about this. "I've got to do this just by myself. It's embarrassing."

"What can you possibly be embarrassed with me about?"

"I mean, I'm sick of getting dependent on people. I want to sort my own life out now."

"Right." It had been on Vince's mind to suggest they find somewhere together. That they think about moving in together. As he watched Andy haul himself up off the mattress he considered the glorious, erotic charge of such a thing. His stuff was ready and packed to go. He could imagine unloading all his belongings in a shared space with Andy and it was a sexy thought. The promise of domestic ease. It was like opening out.

"I never want to depend on anyone again," Andy was saying.

FOR THE SAKE OF EASINESS AND QUICKNESS JANE WOULD TAKE HER morning bath with Peter. It made him seem more like a baby. This morning, though, she took her own briefly and alone, scalding herself lobster pink. Then she filled it again and put Peter and Vicki in together. They looked suspiciously at one another.

Vicki said she got a bath each Sunday night. Jane cut her protestations dead, shoved her in and took the dirty clothes downstairs with the rest of the linen. She jammed them all into the washing machine. Although other people's dirt made her uneasy, her routines went on this morning regardless. When she brought in the milk she saw that there was already a police car parked outside Fran's house.

Vicki watched her dry Peter first. She exhibited a frank interest and Peter was babbling to show off. Jane sat on the toilet lid while Peter went on about *Baywatch*, his favourite programme, where people were always in the bath, or was it the sea, and there might be sharks and they might get eaten.

"My mam's not coming back, is she?" asked Vicki, rubbing a heavy sponge into her hair. Her hair was tangled in clumps, with a few wiry strands sticking stubbornly up. She had been washing it herself with soap.

"She'll be back before you know it."

The question disturbed Jane. How was she supposed to cope with this? Just give her the usual day, packing Peter off to playschool, going off to town. She couldn't do this sort of thing. All of a sudden her usual life seemed something unrecoverable and ideal.

"I don't mind about it. I know that she's gone."

"She'll be back." Jane was tugging hard at Peter's T-shirt. It was trapped over his head and he was squealing. She could feel the nylon fabric shriek and glisten with static under her fingernails.

Vicki sighed and said, "She's gone off with the Dog Man. She said she would."

"She what?" Peter gave a louder shout and Jane slapped him to shut him up. His head came out of the T-shirt with a quivering lip and teary eyes. "What did you say?"

"She said, one of these days. With the Dog Man."

"THERE'S NO ANSWER NEXT DOOR. ARE YOU THE NEIGHBOUR THAT'S BEEN helping?"

Detective Inspector Collins stood at Fran's back door, rain sparkling off her black waterproof jacket. Fran, who hadn't slept a wink, let her into the kitchen. She was worried about Frank, left in charge of bathing the baby upstairs. The baby had been filthy, tattooed with dirt.

"Nesta's husband Tony should be in. Have a seat." At least the kids were out of the way. The two eldest had gone off to school with no problems this morning, taking Lyndsey to playschool on their way; little Jeff was upstairs supervising the baby's bath. Leaving Fran to deal with the police.

Detective Inspector Collins took off her hat to reveal almost white hair, cut short like a schoolboy's. She was about forty, angularly attractive with hard intelligent eyes. Straight away Fran felt as if she was being sized up and judged.

Collins said, 'He isn't there now. I spent a full five minutes shouting through his letterbox.'

Fran rubbed her eyes, put the kettle on, and came to sit down. "He was going out last night to look for her himself."

"So he knows where she might have gone?" The policewoman was looking annoyed. "Has he got some idea of her whereabouts that he hasn't reported?"

"No, he just went out to look by himself. Nowhere in particular."

"Ah."

"Tea?"

"No, thank you. I managed to see through their windows." Fran could imagine what the officer had seen: lino in the living room yellow newspaper and drink cans; in the garden a mould-encrusted three-piece suite, parts of a rusting motorbike scattered; more on the kitchen floor. "As a neighbour, would you say that you thought the family had problems?"

Cagily Fran replied, "Who hasn't?"

"It might be worth getting in touch with social services. Whether or not the mother is found or returns of her own accord. You said yourself that you had to take the children off the father's hands last night."

"He's...well, not simple, exactly..."

"But you wouldn't trust him to look after two young children?"

"He's upset at the moment. He has other things to think about."

"Well, I'll talk to this...Tony, when he comes back. For the moment I could do with a statement from you."

She started to take down various particular, writing in a cramped style in a tiny leather notebook. The radio in her top jacket pocket kept crackling and bursting into harsh messages, filling the rain-darkened room with alien chatter, bringing an outer world into Fran's house. She found that she resented this. She stole a glance at the kitchen clock. Frank would be clumsily attempting to dress the baby. Jeff would be watching with horrified fascination, glad to be grown up.

"And so when was the last time you yourself saw Nesta Dixon?"

"I..." The question caught her out. Fran had no idea. Yet when one of the kids lost something, hair clips, crayons, the first thing she would ask, without even think it, was always, 'Where did you see it last? Where did you leave it?' As if things were always put down with tags, mental notes attached, and Fran herself moved through life tugged by strings of association connected to all her accoutrements. But that was being a mother. Yet get tied down. Of course, she couldn't remember everything, and much of her daily grief stemmed from her apprehension that she needed to. There were only so many things that she could keep in mind and Nesta wasn't one of them.

Then up rose a sense of guilt. At having shouted, recently, brutally, at poor, vanished Nesta. It hit Fran plainly and her shame was all too evident on her face. The last time Fran had seen Nesta Dixon was when she threw her out of her kitchen. Over the milk upset, the cigarette-burned jacket. Had the silly cow topped herself because they never asked her to come on the girls' night out?

She had been going to the Riverside for depression. Who knows how badly she might have taken it?

"I saw her two days ago...exactly. We...argued. Well, I'd given her some stick for scrounging. Not scrounging exactly. Just a few bottles of milk."

"They were badly off, as a family?"

"Who isn't?"

"You aren't making it any easier by making these generalisations. I'm asking whether the Dixons specifically were hard up, whether they were a problem family."

"How can you tell? What does that mean?"

The walkie-talkie gave a shriek and the policewoman was forced to reply. As she spoke she kept her eyes on Fran. How can she understand that thing? Fran wondered. It sounded like static to her, with only odd words emerging: 'vagrancy', 'station', 'ma'am'. The policewoman snapped the radio off.

"Tony Dixon is down at the station. He was picked up last night for vagrancy, sleeping under the Burn Lane bridge." Collins stood up, sighing heavily. "Some family! Not what you would really call a nice one."

Fran held her door open. "I wouldn't call them what you called them, either. I don't know, maybe families aren't very nice. Goodbye. Let me know what happens."

"We will."

ROSE HAD MADE THEM BOTH A CUP OF TEA. SHE BROUGHT IT UP TO HAVE in bed. They were having a lie-in. Old people should take it easy, she said, laughing. She patted Ethan's stump fondly and listened to him talk. The rain drummed at the window, making the floral pattern of her drawn curtains shift.

"I knew a poet once. A lad in Germany, just after the war."

"Did you, love?" She slurped her tea, fingering the gnarled mauve flesh rounding off his knee. She was becoming quite attached to this truncated limb. Everything was just right. Even the tea was perfect. She wished she had brought the pot.

"This lad's poems were good. I wonder what he made of himself."

"I used to read poems."

"He used to tell me that a poet is there to keep things alive. Like I say, this was just after the war. Keeping things alive was something we used to talk about a lot." He had shown Rose the photo of him and the lads, holding up the worn Nazi flag in a cobbled street. They had torn it down, they were grinning, guns relaxed on their shoulders. One of them, Rose thought dreamily, had been a poet.

Ethan continued, "He said a poet lives in this world to experience things, not think things. Just take things in, like bombs going off, falling in love, bread baking and things getting born. His poems kept them alive, all them things. I never saw him after we were demobbed. But I remember what he said then and I agreed. I could never write a poem, but I could keep things alive."

"It'd be nice if you wrote me a nice love poem."

"I learned about taxidermy. I'd keep things in their real forms, before death hit them. It was my little bit."

"There's someone at the door." Rose inched forward on the bed, listening hard. "The letterbox is rattling." She got up and pulled on her dressing gown, a startling red. "I'll go. You finish your tea." Before leaving the room she bent to give his leg an affectionate peck. Ethan was far away.

FRAN WAS PUZZLED. "WHAT'S A DOG MAN?"

"God knows," said Jane. They were standing by the bus shelter, Fran holding the baby. "I thought I'd better mention it."

"I don't know whether we should listen to anything that bairn says. Bless her deprived heart and all that, but –"

"I've left her at playschool. She should have gone to her real school but we were late. She seems happy enough back with the young 'uns."

"That copper was on about getting social services in."

"Might be for the best."

"How can you say that? You know what'll happen."

Jane shrugged. "We don't want to be left with her rotten kids, do we? We've got our own, haven't we? It's bound to happen sooner or later, anyway."

"We'll just have to see. She might turn up yet."

"I'm just off to buy more beefburgers. I don't think that Vicki's been fed in her life. She was up all night wolfing custard creams."

THIS TIME LIZ HAD LEFT A NOTE FOR PENNY. IT WAS WAITING FOR HER when she came downstairs, late, at nine thirty. When she walked into the front room she knew something was up because the stereo wasn't on, there were no curling tongs left lying around, and no one swirling around the place in her housecoat, full of the joys of spring.

> Penny dear,
> I've already gone. I've gone to look at a bus station.
> Cliff insisted.
> Aren't you late for school?

LIZ WAS SITTING ON A WOODEN BENCH, ONE ARM FLUNG ALONG THE BACK and legs crossed. She picked idly at a scab of hardened chewing gum with her nails.

She was smoking heavily to cut out the greasy diesel fumes. Everywhere there was the sound of groaning machinery, chain-smokers walking, the early birds lurching into the depot with pneumatic squeals.

But she liked this place. Plenty was happening. She was glad, too, that Cliff had brought her at the crack of dawn.

She watched him running about, from the frosted-windowed staff room to the buses, greeting other men in blue nylon trousers, jumping on and off buses, opening their rubber-hinged doors with a proprietorial air, patting the bonnets of others as he passed. He was showing off, but she would let him, for this morning.

He came up to her, grinning. "They all want to meet you. They've all seen you sitting here. Everyone wants to know who you are."

"The buses?"

"The blokes. I've told them you're with me."

He hasn't got much of a sense of humour, Liz thought. Bless him!

He led her to the staff room. Inside someone was whistling 'Love Is a Many-Splendoured Thing'. The first line only, over and over again. Around a Formica table scattered with fag packets and timetables, six men were having an argument about *Daktari*. What was the lion's name; Florence or Elsa?

"It was Clarence," Liz told them. "Clarence the Cross-eyed Lion."

They all looked at her.

"This," Cliff said, "is the woman I love."

ROSE GAVE ETHAN A HAND TO GET HIS LEG BACK ON. SHE WAS GETTING the hang of it now. He fumbled dressing, asking all the while why Andy was here. His tetchiness and his slowness took Rose by surprise. This is how he'll be when he's old, she thought. An invalid. His novelty might soon wear off. She hoped not.

"He didn't say. He looks upset, mind." Rose stood by the doorway. "He doesn't look anything like you, you know. For a relative."

Downstairs they found him watching *This Morning*.'

"Now then, Andrew. What's all this about?"

Andy was keeping his eyes downcast, on Richard and Judy doing the phone-in. Richard had just asked some poor woman if her problem was that she was too dry. "They're discussing women's health problems," he said.

"What did you have to see me about so urgently?" His uncle's voice was full of that menacing power again. Andy turned to look at him.

"We have to talk about where I'm going to live." And suddenly he looked helpless. "I don't know what to do."

Ethan sat down heavily on Rose's overstuffed sofa. He could manage that now without looking. He's settling in, Rose thought, and took herself off to make some fresh tea.

Jane was coming up the garden path, looking harassed.

"What's the matter?" Rose asked, head out of the window, afterglow dissipating in the wet breeze. Jane stomped into the kitchen, slamming the door.

"I've been turned into a bloody nursemaid, that's what!"

"Who by? What's –"

"That Nesta woman round the corner's done a bunk, and –" Jane stopped and listened. Two male voices could be heard clearly from the living room. Two male voices and, in the background, agony aunt Denise Robertson.

"What's going on here?" Jane asked.

THEY LET LIZ RIDE FOR FREE THAT DAY. "I FEEL LIKE AN OLD-AGE pensioner," she said with a grin, standing next to Cliff. All his loose change was jangling in the dispenser at his side. "A pensioner with an everlasting bus pass and no desire to get off."

The countryside outside Darlington, muggy and olive green, went swirling by. Their bus was as yet empty.

"You'll never be a pensioner," Cliff insisted with his eyes on the road. "I can't actually picture you being old."

She considered. "No. Neither can I."

They pulled into a little village, an up-market village featuring a suitably picturesque ginger pony in a tiny field. The bus began to fill.

"I haven't asked where we're going yet," she observed over the top of somebody's headscarf.

"The Metro Centre. Straight up the motorway." He slammed his palm down on the dashboard and Radio Two burst out of every speaker. "God, I love the motorway."

Liz grasped her handrail and tottered expertly on her heels, buffeted by the acceleration. Cliff's glossy black head was inching nearer to the steering wheel, his elbows flexing out like wings. Pensioners went scuttling for their seats.

"Yeah – straight up the motorway and then an afternoon spent with you."

"An afternoon?" she asked. A bus driver's lot was beginning to sound like quite a cushy number.

"Important business. We're going shopping."

They hurtled north, into the driving rain.

DETECTIVE INSPECTOR COLLINS WAITED FOR TONY TO HAUL HIMSELF OUT of her car. He had a bit of a bother doing this, because he was cupping something precious in both palms. Collins grunted as she locked her car behind him and firmly led the way to Fran's house.

Fran was waiting. She was wondering what she should say about the Dog Man, and whether such a thing was worth mentioning. Tony was following the policewoman, head bowed. Collins seemed impervious to the rain, eyes hard, face clenched like a fist. You could chop sticks on that face of hers, Fran thought. Honestly, it's like being in one of them Ruth Rendells.

"I've brought him back to you," Collins said coldly. "We can't get any sense out of him. Ask him what he was up to last night." Her walkie-talkie was fizzing dangerously in the wet.

"Well, Tony?" Fran asked, and felt sorry for him. His curls were pressed down damply to his forehead. He looked like Benny off *Crossroads*.

Fran was struck by another thought. "Have you dropped the vagrancy charges?"

Collins nodded. "He is clearly very upset and disturbed."

Uninvited, she sat down. "How are his children?"

"The baby's having a nap. I gave the other one to my friend Jane." Fran looked at Tony. "What's he got in his hands?"

"He won't tell us. I presume it is something belonging to his wife."

He looked up sharply. "It's her locket. Her mother's locket." Tony held it up so that it glittered in the steamy kitchen. The two tiny photos, shiny and hard as thumbnails, dangled between his plump, red hands. "Pictures of Meg Mortimer and Elsie Tanner. She always wore this. Strong women, she said."

Fran grabbed his wrist. "Did you find it, Tony? Did you find this last night?"

He nodded. "Under the bridge. When I went looking. I found it in the light." His face crumpled. "She left it behind for me."

Detective Inspector Collins was already speaking into her radio.

PENNY OPENED ANOTHER PACKET OF BISCUITS. THE FIRST TWO WERE cracked, so she ate them quickly in the kitchen, put the rest of the packet on the tray with the mugs of coffee, took a deep breath, and carried the whole lot into the living room where Jane was staring blankly at *This Morning*. Judy and Richard were talking about keeping warm this winter.

Penny wasn't going to school this morning. She was having a quiet day.

"I thought I'd come and see Liz. I needed someone to talk to. I couldn't get any sense out of my mother."

Penny nudged the biscuits at her, nearly choking on her own crumbs. "So what's it all about then. You said something about a dog man."

"Vicki said her mum's been taken by the dog man."

"Right."

"I think the world's gone mad."

Penny didn't want to even think about madness. This morning she had woken up with the distinct impression that she had dreamed of driving a tank, crushing everything in her path. Her foot clamped on the accelerator (did tanks *have* accelerator pedals?) had been wearing a sandal. She woke with cramp.

"And my mother's too busy with her peg-leg boyfriend and, would you believe it, his wet nephew, who's a you-know-what if ever there was one –"

"So your mother's not interested?"

"She's wound up in her wedding plans. Oh, she was very concerned about Nesta's vanishing and the wellbeing of the poor orphans left behind. But what about me being stuck with her brats?"

"What do you think a dog man can be, then?" Penny was pushing idly at different avenues of conversation, urging Jane here and there because she was bored with her. Jane consented to be shoved, her voice quavering.

"You can't listen to everything that kid says. I'll have to go and pick her up soon. And Peter. God, I hope I'm not neglecting him over this!"

She dunked a chocolate biscuit in her coffee, held it there a moment too long, and it sank without a trace.

HE LAY AROUND FOR A WHILE THAT MORNING, HAVING FOND MEMORIES. Andy had gone, purposeful and independent, striding across town to sort his life out. He'd used all the hot water in the tank, too. Vince heard his dad going in some time after him and cursing. Vince lay low.

It was the weekend. It was like weekends when he was a child: dismal, nagged by dread. He realised that he hated the idea of the next week. It was too familiar a feeling. The dread came back like an older, more intimate friend than Andy. Once his dad had told him that, of course, everyone hated the week ahead. Everyone hated work. But they had to do it. It was grown up. It was responsibility. The problem with Vince was that he expected to love what he was doing. He thought he was so bloody different. As if he deserved something. And at that point, leaving school, Vince had been told in no uncertain terms by his father: "You are just like everyone else. Get your act together and believe it." Vince was shocked. Really shocked. He knew his dad thought like this, but at the same time to hear it put into words was crushing. Especially the night before he caught the bright pink Primrose coach to Lancaster for the first time. His dad was trying to make him feel just as good as everyone else, as good as all the new people he'd meet. But Vince didn't want that at all. One of the last things his mam had said to him, maybe the last thing ever as she went, kissing him and shouldering her handbag, was: "You are like no one else in the world. You're more special. And you never have to do anything you don't want." His dad had never heard this, but Vince had nursed her words to him like a parting gift. It was only rarely he thought they'd done more harm than good.

The fond memories he dredged up were to counteract the anxiety. He thought about broaching the idea of living together with Andy and this led to remembering the weeks they had spent together when they could. A week in Stratford once, and one in Windermere. They'd grown tetchy and difficult with each other. Vince had slept through and laughed about Andy electrocuting himself in the middle of the night, spilling a cup of cold tea on a beside lamp. "I went off with a bloody bang and you never noticed!" Andy complained. And then, one night after *Macbeth* in Stratford, Vince woke in their bed-and-breakfast room, straddling Andy and hitting him with a shoe.

Sometimes, looking back, Vince thought there were distinct and fundamental reasons for their not being together. A deep animosity would occasionally surface; he wondered what it was about. What did he resent about Andy? Surely the fact that he found things so simple, so clear cut. There was a sentimental streak through Andy that laid him wide open. Together they lay awake late one night, watching Andy's favourite film, *Escape from the Planet of the Apes*. At the end Vince turned his head on the pillow, looked at Andy and there were tears soaking his face. "But she chucked her baby in the water! The FBI killed the baby!" Andy cried. "It's terrible!"

Vince had to hug him. He shuddered under the blankets.

"It's just too sad! They were so nice and trusting!"

Vince kept thinking, but didn't say, it's only about apes. Not even that, it's people dressed up as apes. He kept quiet, though. Now, *Terms of Endearment*, there was a sad film. *Who Will Love My Children?* too. That knotted him up inside just thinking about it. And Andy got worked up about monkeys.

He thought about getting up. He slithered over to look at the clock and it was almost lunchtime. He stood and slid open the mirrored cupboard door. A nip of gin. It was early but he was allowed to be decadent on a Saturday. He lay back down with a second glass of gin. He stared at the little colourful jar that sat beside the gin bottle. It was the purple bottle he'd nicked from the taxidermist's shop. He imagined it had a genie in. A small whiff of magic. Brimstone and treacle. Or a Blue Fairy.

What he really wanted was to wake up with Andy again, now. He wished he hadn't dashed away. He wanted to make love with him now, more slowly and tenderly than they had yet managed during this reunion of theirs. He wondered why it was always so rushed and intent these days. Brusque, almost. Then, thoughtfully, he began to masturbate. It was with a peculiar sense of guilt, as if he shouldn't when he was seeing someone. As if it was a betrayal, this slow, practised ease with himself. He squashed that thought and with long, perfect strokes and an occasional sip of neat gin, he made himself come.

ANOTHER POLICE CAR ARRIVED IN THEIR STREET. JANE AND PENNY watched its blue light give a brief flicker of interest. Something was up, but nothing huge. Jane sighed wearily. "I can't cope with this now."

Two burly policemen went into Fran's house. It seemed to be the centre of operations.

"I'll have to pick the bairns up from playschool."

Penny realised for the first time that the kitchen and dining room were still strewn with the wreckage of last night's entertainment. What's going on? she thought. Order has collapsed, there are pasta twirls swimming in orange grease in our sink. Jane told her, "Keep an eye out here. Let me know when I get back...if they've found a body or anything. I don't want to know yet."

A body. Penny didn't know Nesta, but she would certainly have a body. A body that could be found, dead, and have an impact on everyone here. Even those who hadn't known her. She might be disliked but she could still be murdered and mourned.

Fran caught Jane before she could reach the garden gate. Her slippers slapped on the wet tarmac and she carried a tea towel.

"They're starting up a body hunt, down the Burn. We need everyone's help. Get your coats on."

"I'm just off to fetch the kids," Jane began. "I've got to get their dinners on."

Fran looked at her with sympathy. It sounded so simple. She was jealous of Jane's evasion. "Hurry up and get them. We have to help."

Shit, Penny thought. I don't even know the woman.

Fran was looking at Penny. "Will you come over to help?"

"Sure," Penny said, sounding surer than she was.

"I'm going to go round the other doors," Fran said. "See who else is about."

Jane made her apologies again and was gone. Fran rolled her eyes.

HE WALKED THE LONG WAY ROUND THE TOWN, DOWN THE BURN, through the blustery morning. He thought he would go see Penny since, of all the people he'd talked to lately, she'd been the most sensible. His dad was out in the car, looking for things at B&Q. He'd asked if Vince wanted to come too, to look out for some tools for doing up the garage. He never usually asked him to come. But Vince had demurred anyway, making some tea, feeling woozy from the gin. On the way to Penny's, crossing the Redhouses, he decided to stop off for some cans. Might as well make a day of it. He wondered what Penny's mam might think, her daughter's teacher turning up with booze at lunchtime.

In the shop the woman serving had hair like Gary Glitter: thinning, teased up, hard with lacquer. The radio was playing Status Quo and, under it, she was talking with the women in the queue, their voices low and intent. There was a woman in a smart suit and clunky gold earrings, a very fat woman in a mustard-coloured cardigan and a short, thin woman who looked about ninety. They were all talking about Nesta Dixon, who had disappeared.

"They're reckoning they'll have to comb the Burn," the fat lady was saying. This was Big Sue. "And all the surrounding countryside."

"So they think she's dead then?" said the old woman. She was wearing a cape and a dashing hat with a feather in it.

The woman behind the counter in her blue gingham pinafore said, "They aren't going to rule out foul play, that's what I heard."

"I'm not going traipsing about looking for bodies," said the smart woman. "I can't be arsed. I've got work to do." With that she prompted Judith (her badge read 'May I help? I'm Judith!') for her change and was gone.

"Isn't she short with people?" asked the old woman.

"I've not got much time for her." Judith sighed. "She's the one that left her husband for a copper."

"Her husband with all the tattoos?" asked the old woman.

"Now they reckon he's with a feller."

"Never."

"It's true," pitched in Big Sue, who knew everyone because she ran the Christian café and craft shop in the precinct. "They live together in the flats were the bus driver lives."

"That lovely-looking bus driver?" asked Judith. "He's a smashing lad."

"Well, I'm off down to see what's going on with Nesta," Big Sue decided. "I'll go and see Fran. I won't shirk my public responsibility." Big Sue was, in her own way, fond of Nesta, even though she was always coming round after bread in the mornings. She picked her bags up off the counter. "Will I see you later then, Judith? Charlotte?"

"Aye, reckon so," said Judith, taking Vince's eight cans of Red Stripe for him and ringing them in the till. He was looking at the spirits and wondered if a little shop like this would have tequila.

ROSE HAD A MARVELLOUS IDEA.

"Jane rattles around in that empty house of hers like a maniac. She has two spare bedrooms. One's for Peter when he's old enough to sleep by himself..."

Ethan eyed her narrowly. He felt married all of a sudden. She went on, "You look a nice enough lad, Andrew. I'm sure if I introduced you properly to our Jane..." Not like this morning, she thought. Poor Jane, virtually chucked out of her own mother's house. Rose was thinking of ways to make amends. Bring two families together. "Jane could do with a few extra bob."

"I'm not sure –"

"How urgently do you need to move?"

"I don't want to go back to that bloody shop. Not now that I have to go anyway. It's like a morgue. I'm staying with a friend at the moment. Vince. Who you met."

"Then there's not a moment to lose. Ethan, grab your coat and brolly. We're going to Jane's."

She gun-barrelled the two of them into a fresh rainstorm, sure that somewhere in it their problems might be resolved.

They would arrive in time to find everyone heading for Fran's kitchen, already soaked to the skin, kids whingeing in the confusion, and receiving deliberate instructions from the impressive Detective Inspector Collins.

FRAN WAS PROUD OF HERSELF. SHE HAD CORRALLED MOST OF PHOENIX COURT and a few people she knew from nearby streets. She'd even bumped into Jane's mam and roped her in. Only one or two had refused to come out, or even answer the door. They were the people you'd expect not to want to help. The snobby lot from Sid Chaplin and that Gary. They could do without their help anyway.

Soon she was dealing with a whole kitchen full of familiar faces. At first, with everyone arriving and talking loudly and steamy condensation running down the paintwork in the kitchen and hall from the press of so many damp people and coats, it was like a party. Like the clothes parties and toy parties they used to have, or New Year's Eve. Sure enough, there was Frank in the corner by the fridge, being Mein Host and drinking a can. He had given one away, which surprised Fran. That Mark Kelly was standing there, drinking a can with him, his tattoos sinister in the gloom.

While they waited for the Inspector to arrive with her notes and instructions, Fran was mentally ticking off her list. Suddenly she was taking this all very seriously. For Nesta's sake, and also as a kind of charm, warding off fear. If she could get everyone together, here, then it might be all right. The door clattered open and Jane came in with Peter and Vicki. She looked startled to see the room heaving. Almost as if this was her own kitchen. "Shall I put the kettle on?" she mouthed. Fran nodded.

"Have you seen Liz?" Fran asked.

Jane shook her head, with her lips pursed as she went to hunt out enough cups. She looked as if it was only to be expected. As if she'd always been right in thinking that Liz was flaky.

"Here," Big Sue weighed in. "Let me help."

Fran counted round the room:

There's me and Frank and our four bairns and Nesta's two bairns

and Tony looking daft, head in his hands

and Jane and her bairn

and her mam and the old bloke with one leg and his...nephew, did he say?

and Big Sue and Charlotte from the bungalow

And Mark with tattoos and the bloke he's got lodging

and he's got his quiet little bairn here

her grandma Peggy and her baby, which Big Sue reckons she had when she was sixty

and Liz's lass Penny and a friend of hers

and dirty Sheila and Simon but I shouldn't call them that

their bairns little Ian and Claire who hasn't gone to school for two years because of nerves

Judith from the shop, she came straight from work, bless her, and her twins Andrew and Joanne

and who's left?

"I'VE BROUGHT DRINK," VINCE HAD GRINNED, HOLDING UP HIS CARRIERS.

"Great," Penny said, pulling her DMs on. "Bring it with you."

His head was spinning. "Where are we going?"

"Just over the way. We've got to pitch in."

"Is this to do with this woman who's vanished?"

"Aye," she said grimly, locking the door behind her, laces still undone.

Vince followed her over the grass, wondering what he was getting into. He felt stupid, carrying his booze along with him.

When Fran let them in it was to a whole roomful, adults and bairns perched on the tables, on benches, sitting on the carpet. They had to fight for a space. Coming right up behind them were the three women from the shop Vince had seen. They recognised him but he was too busy noticing Andy, sitting beside the taxidermist in the hall doorway.

Fran shouted from the kitchen door. "The Inspector's coming in again. She's ready now."

"If you find anything – anything at all – do not, I repeat, do not touch it. Call to the nearest policeman and he will investigate. We will start at the place the locket was discovered and gradually move the search outwards. Look for anything. Anything suspicious. You all know the missing woman better than I do. Good luck!"

No we don't, Penny thought. We didn't know her at all. She steals milk. What's that to go on? All we've got is the ability to recognise another body when we see one. It's pathetic. But I suppose – she looked round at everyone – we have to do our best.

Tony was still sitting with his head in his hands next to the fridge. The locket's chain was tangled up in his fingers.

'WHAT ARE WE SHOPPING FOR?' LIZ LAUGHED AS THE GREAT AUTOMATIC doors swished open and the warm, perfumed Metro Centre air pulled them in. Music was playing, 'Yesterday Once More' by the Carpenters. There were mirrors everywhere, fountains with money in, glass elevators and names that were meant to look written, belligerently neon.

"Holiday clothes and suitcases," Cliff hissed and dragged her up an escalator. "We are both getting out of it. Come on."

FOURTEEN

Go on then. Bring on the firing squad. We're ready for you.

Penny dangled her arms over the bridge's railing. She looked down at the toes of her shoes poking out underneath the bars. Below her, twenty feet down, the brown stream swished and gurgled.

We look ridiculous, in a line like this.

She had an aerial view of a policeman, his head a black circle, a single silver point in its centre. He came out from under the bridge and gazed up at them all.

Vince realised that both he and Penny were tapping their ash carelessly into the breeze. It was drifting down on the coppers. They would think they were doing it on purpose. Next to Penny and Vince was Jane, clutching Peter and gripping Vicki's hand like a dog's lead. Vicki had no interest in what was going on below, the fifteen policemen standing with their shoulders touching, ploughing through the water, turning stones over with their heavy-duty rubber gloves. Vicki was watching traffic go by, rumbling over the bridge.

Drawn into the tragedy now, Rose stood on tiptoe to see. Ethan was

there out of a sense of duty, his stump chafing from standing too long. Fran
and Frank stood with their four kids and a fifth, Nesta's baby, wrapped in
blankets and Fran's arms so that she was three times her natural size. Andy
strolled up and down the footpath behind everyone, unsure of his place.
He had spoken only briefly to Vince. "You two know each other?" Rose
exclaimed. "What a small world this is!"

Vince made a start on his cans of lager. To keep me warm, he thought.
It tasted of petrol. Why isn't Andy talking to me more? he thought. He
kept his eyes averted from the tattooed man who, it turned out, lived on
Penny's street. He was involved in his own intense, private debate with
his mother-in-law, standing a little way down the kerb. There are troubles
everywhere, Vince thought.

Tony huddled into his anorak a little way apart, also watching cars.

So we're all here, thought Penny. The Charge of the bloody Light
Brigade.

The policeman looking up at them from the footpath below was
joined by another, resigned and wiping his black gloves on his jacket.
He shook his head. The line of fifteen gradually emerged from under
the bridge. Everyone craned their necks to see them come out into the
light, switching their torches off, cricking their backs unbent. From the
spectators' vantage they looked like an optical illusion, a thick black line
through which the filthy water still flowed.

Nothing. Nothing suspicious down there.

Detective Inspector Collins strode briskly out of the tunnel, looked
up at the onlookers' gallery and addressed them. I notice she didn't get
into the Burn, thought Jane, who had taken a dislike to the woman.

"We're moving the area of the search outwards. You've all agreed to
help and as long as the rain holds off, we'll be glad of everyone here. If the
weather takes a nasty turn, or it starts to get dark, please would you take
your children home? The police force will not be liable for any accidents or
damages. It you come down here I will assign you your areas."

With Penny leading, they negotiated the gap in the wooden fence
and, clutching branches and damp clumps of grass, they slithered one by
down the bank to the footpath.

THERE WAS A PLACE IN THE METRO CENTRE WHERE LIZ PARTICULARLY
wanted to eat. They took an escalator right through Marks and Spencer
without even getting off, cutting right through the cloying air, smiling at
the pristine fresh foods, nodding politely at the uptight dummies and store
detectives.

Imperiously Liz led the way through the Roman Emporium with its
plaster statues of gods, its marble shop fronts. Eventually they came to
the mock open-air restaurant which offered food from every corner of
the globe, each corner having a special counter, the counters ranged like
market stalls around the screwed-down tables. The place was seething and
they had to fight to find a seat in the very middle.

Above them wheeled cranelike arms flung up from the outdoor
funfair. Screams of joy, fear and laughter played like music. But there was
no one on the big wheel, no one whizzing about in the chairs or hovering
in the hot-air balloons (on wires). It was a schoolday and the screaming
was recorded.

"What are we having to eat?" Cliff asked, leafing through a sheaf of
menus. "Italian? Chinese?"

"Oh, a little bit of everything, I think." Liz left him with her bags – she
had already bought a new frock – and headed off for the queues. "Excuse
me barging in like this –" she charmed her way through – "but I don't
want an *entirely* Portuguese meal, just a little something... You wouldn't
mind me pushing in for a single morsel, would you?"

And: "I need a few garlic mushrooms. A little wine. Thank you, dear."

And: "*Nachos*. With *jalapeño* chillis and green olives. I want the
biggest plate you've got."

Mouth open and starving, Cliff watched her and shifted round in
his seat, peering through the crowd as Liz made her way from corner to
corner of the globe.

The manager caught up with her at the centre of the restaurant.
He was about twenty-four, wearing a suit much too big for him, his hair
plastered wetly back.

"What do you think you're doing?"

"Taking advantage, dear." She beamed.

"You what?"

"Of the world's every nook and cranny. That, I take it, is the point?"

"I've watched you barge your way to the front of every –"

"You must excuse me, but my food's going cold."

The manager marvelled briefly at the way this woman could hold simultaneously two laden trays and an argument. "It isn't the done thing," he glowered, "that's all."

"Isn't it? People should be more adventurous with what they eat, shouldn't they? You make it so easy for them." She could see Cliff bobbing anxiously on his plastic seat, worrying about her and not wanting to leave their table. "Would you mind?" she asked the manager and passed him a tray to carry to her table.

As he followed he seemed to shrink even further into his suit, blushing furiously. The pensioners at nearby tables who were there mostly for the central heating, spinning out solitary cappuccinos, looked on with interest as Liz made him wait wile she rummaged in her purse for a tip.

Walking away with his ten-pence piece, the manager seemed smaller than ever. Small enough to crawl and hide inside Liz's Top Shop carrier.

I'M NOT SCARED OF THE DOG MAN. IT'S HIM WHO'S SCARED OF ME. BUT people won't see that.

He does things for me. He's good like that. When he likes, he can be a good dog. When he likes.

Ever since I was at school I wanted to have someone like the Dog Man. I don't know why. At first I wanted a dog. But my stepmother wouldn't. She never liked dogs. She and my stepdad wanted things clean. Everything was tidy. Dogs weren't clean.

So when I got a house and a husband, I wanted a dog. We got puppies, one after the other. People said my house wasn't clean. They said my daughter was neglected. I got so that I felt down.

My husband wasn't anything really. He wasn't like a dog; I couldn't boss him about, lead him around by his collar. Not because he was big and tough. He wasn't big and tough. He wasn't weak, either. He wasn't anything. He wouldn't do as I said, he wouldn't tell me what to do. He wouldn't do anything. The only good times we had was getting the giro, buying Woodpecker on a Thursday night. Give the kids Coke. We'd buy three great big bottles the same time as the Woodpecker. Coke makes kids pissed like cider does grown-ups, makes them dizzy, their eyes shine. We used to laugh.

But my husband wasn't anything. I couldn't do anything with him.

And the puppies died. We couldn't afford the injections. I'd get impatient to take them out for walks. They told me little germs got into the soft pads of the puppies' feet when I took them out when they were too little. And they died. But in the olden days we didn't have dog injections, did we? And the dogs didn't die from walking then. We didn't even have injections for people. And they tell me if the baby doesn't have all her injections, then she will die as well. But I forget what she's had. I forget about *her* sometimes, too. Some days she comes as a shock, when I go upstairs for a lie-down and I see her on the bed. She's asleep a lot of the time.

What difference is there? I'm still stuck in the house. I can't really go out, can I? But the Dog Man brings me what I need. He's going to bring me a disguise so we can go out together. That'll be fun.

I'll go back to see the women, dressed up in my disguise. And they won't know me. I'll be like Meg off *Crossroads*, Elsie off *Coronation Street*, going back to where they used to live. Looking around and then going back to where they are now. Somewhere better. In disguise.

I love the Dog Man. He has no one else to love now and so he loves me. He says I'm strong. Strong like Meg and strong like Elsie. His own wife, he said, wasn't very strong. And so he loves me.

I'm waiting for him now. He's at work. He says he has a surprise for me. I hope it has something to do with my disguise. That would make everything perfect.

THEY HAD BEEN GIVEN THE THICKEST PART OF THE FOREST. THE CLOSELY packed soil of the natural paths had been sliced and crosshatched into slush by rain and bicycle wheels. Penny trod heedlessly through puddles brown as coffee. She led Vince and Andy through the trees, pushing against bark and kicking through the undergrowth, her jeans soaked to the knees already. They were looking for a suitable starting point for their search. Vince had the feeling they had left it behind, left stones unturned. They were already failing in their mission. They were simply fannying about in a forest. And it was getting dark.

"Aren't you talking to me?" he snapped at Andy, who was content to lag along behind. He hadn't said anything since mildly remarking on the coincidence of their both being on the same body-hunt. "What's the matter with you?"

"I'm a bit freaked by all this. It's a bit morbid, isn't it?" Andy hugged himself inside his leather jacket. "We might find anything."

"It's a body-hunt. What do you want to find?"

Some distance ahead Penny had stopped short. She was at the mouth of a great natural bowl in the earth. She called them to come and see.

The last, gentle, well-laundered light of the day was playing through a canopy of leaves. Cloud shapes of brightness shivered on damp earth. The ash tree in the dell's dead centre shone a resonant blue, ringed by grasses and cramped roots, looking like a traffic island, hemmed in by BMX tracks. Everything else was turning black.

"What?" Vince asked.

"When I was little, I always had places like this," Penny began. "I think this is a magical place."

"I've had enough of this," Vince said.

"I always thought certain bits of countryside were like magic," she whispered. "I must have been mad. There's nothing special here. It smells like shite."

"No." Andy nudged forwards and started to trip down the slope into the bowl, finding the footholds that tree roots had woven into the soil. "There *is* something about this place." He padded down the incline and stood in one of the patches of blue light. "I think we should start the search here. Good vibes."

Vince muttered, "It still smells like shite," as he went slipping on dead leaves.

ROSE AND ETHAN HAD TAKEN THE GRAVEL PATH AT THE SIDE OF THE stream. They walked very slowly, talking all the while. Ethan had found himself a long branch, stripped it of twigs and leaves, and was trailing it through the dark water. Rose thought he looked like a dodgem car, crackling along on static electricity. She wasn't sure what good that branch would do. If there was a body in the stream, he said, the branch would snag. But every few feet the branch snagged on rocks or weeds and each time he pulled it unstuck without a single glance. He wouldn't know a body if one fell on him, she thought. Still, they were doing their bit.

"Andrew is who I had in mind for best man." He was still thinking about the wedding. Good.

"He seems a nice enough lad. Remind me to catch up with our Jane before we go home tonight. Don't let me forget. I could really see him in her spare room. And she could do with some rent money, helping her along."

"I think she's got other things on her mind at the moment, Rose."

"Yes." Rose considered. "Don't you think that Andrew is...well, about having Andrew as best man..."

"Hm?"

"What I'm thinking is that – don't take offence or anything, dear – but perhaps he isn't...well, impressive enough to be best man."

"Impressive?"

"He's a bit soft, isn't me? I mean, let's face it. If he wasn't an orphan I'm sure he'd be a mummy's boy."

"He's a queer, if that's what you're getting at."

Rose stopped in her tracks. Ethan's branch tangled itself up in water weeds. "He's a what?"

"That lad I was telling you about, the one with the poems in Germany, he was one too, as I remember."

Rose stared. "And you stood there and let me make plans to have him move in with our Jane? And our Peter? You let me ramble on like an old fool when you knew it was impossible? What were you thinking of?"

Ethan considered. "Actually, I was thinking about dead bodies. The one we're looking for. All the animals back at my shop in Darlington. I have to get rid of them. I think I've decided what to do."

"What have your bloody animals got to do with anything? With anything at all, Ethan Nesbit?" Rose was furious. She abandoned her part in the search and started stomping off the way they had come. "I'm talking about perversion and all you can think about is your bloody stuffing."

"It isn't really feasible, you know." Liz smiled fondly at him, not wanting to disappoint. It was late in the afternoon and they were in an empty bar. It was done up to seem as if it was in Manhattan, leather, glass, faked seaminess, the Carpenters: 'On Top of the World'.

"It isn't?" He was making cow eyes across the table's shiny surface. She suddenly felt like kicking him.

"No."

All afternoon Cliff had been flashing his credit cards around. Their plastic bags littered the floor in their corner of the bar, like things that didn't really belong to them. Nicely patterned shirts for Cliff, fabulous frocks for Liz, lingerie for both (he had succumbed; the pair of them ensconced in a cubicle in Ms Selfridge's, Liz in a giggling fit, Cliff in apricot), all of it spilling from the bags on to the carpet.

And then, in the Body Shop, he had confessed his shopaholicism. It was true, he was different here. Garrulous and almost feverish. "It's my feminine side coming out," he tried to explain. Liz was about to take issue that then when he went on to say that he was alone because he couldn't stop spending. But, he reckoned, he had disposable income and he didn't give a fuck. He was glad he had Liz to spend on. He suggested something that would cost a lot of money. A big trip away for the two of them. Liz looked uncomfortable. It wasn't on.

"Why not?" he asked. He looked like a child whose game had been thus far indulged by a fond aunt or uncle. There comes the point when the adult puts their foot down. Liz's stiletto heel was ground into the hood of his new heavy-weather anorak.

"I can't just leave. I can't just up and off. It's avoiding the issue. I've only just moved into a new house and a new life."

"Exactly." His eyes were as glassy as the table. "New lives. They aren't set yet. They can still be what we want."

"Reinvention." Liz smiled sadly. "But there's no point in reinvention if you don't stop for a bit to take stock. Handle your responsibilities. Enjoy what you've become."

He gave a short, barking laugh. "So you won't run away with me?" She had let him buy suitcases, even urged him to buy ones to match whichever outfit she would travel in.

"I'm not ready to leave yet. I have to see Penny gone first."

"Couldn't we take her with us?"

"It's very sweet of you to ask, but Penny has her own travelling to do."

THIS WALK TONIGHT PUT PENNY IN MIND OF WHERE SHE AND HER FATHER had walked in Durham. Forests by the river, winding through hilly, ageless countryside. On nights when their pretend laundry seemed dull or the car outside too claustrophobic, they took torches and explored the misty, squelching woods. Not for nature rambles. Neither of them were into nature. In the dark you could see nothing anyway. They went for the atmosphere and the magic. She was never afraid of the dark places with her father there. She grew up with a high tolerance of fear. Tonight Andy was jumpy. Vince was stroppy, quiet and drinking. Penny wandered along, quite at home.

In the forest when she was little there were particular magical places. Her father gave these names for her, some of them based around books she had read. Once, when she said a leafy gap led to Narnia, he pulled a face. He said she should watch out for people with a subtext. He thought Narnia was too much like godbothering. Penny didn't really know what he meant. It was just magical to her. She didn't see why it had to be exclusively Christian, middle-class or elitist, even if her father did.

She could see him here tonight, her father, standing in the blue light at the foot of the ash tree. Andy was crouching there, staring at the moon. Her father was in his intermediary stage, very thin and skeleton pale. It was as if he was waiting to put on new flesh, new clothes.

But aren't you off up the motorway with the bus driver? she wanted to ask. Here heshe was, making herself apparent.

Do you know who you're like? she thought, gazing at Liz's blue and gold smear of light in the glade. You're like Alec Guinness in *Return of the Jedi*, coming back as a know-it-all ghost. Shimmering and edifying and explaining the past. Use the force, Luke. Or you're like Marlon Brando and Suzannah York in *Superman: the Movie*. When they made holograms of themselves for their son when he grew up to be Superman. All around them Krypton is burning and Marlon and Suzannah are emptying crystals of knowledge and advice into the baby's crib. That's what you're like, Dad, Mam, Liz.

Liz was saying, "This light is from the moon, Penny. Sometimes the moon is said to be entirely feminine. This is wrong. This kind of light is the harshest to be under; it is the light women are often under. In this sense it is feminine. It is the light that forces you to reflect upon yourself, as the sun reflects upon it, as the day reflects upon night. Where we are now, we might as well be on the moon. When you were born, I told you you would go there, didn't I?"

She looked at her blackened, lightning-struck finger-ends. Did she still believe a single word he said? Oh, but his tone was seductive. She would listen to anything he said.

And here I am, in moonlight once more. Andy here, Vince here. Andy was scrutinising the bark of the ash. "There are so many things living in a tree," he said. His voice was harsh. His face was wet with tears. She had seen before, as they walked through the woods, that he was upset. She hadn't known what to say to him at all. Something was going on between him and Vince. Vince didn't seem to care. This reminded her that she hadn't seen him for a few minutes.

Penny followed a familiar hissing noise across the glade and through the rough, sticky grass. There was an enclosure, accessible by a narrow gulley through the trees. Here she found Vince, the hissing sound petering out, standing nonchalant at the mouth of this hidden province.

Penny pushed him aside. "Vince! You've been pissing on Narnia!"

He tucked himself back in with an amused laugh. "Yeah, right." He walked off to see what Andy was doing.

Andy was staring at the insects lining the bark. In the moonlight they were glowing, globular bodies invested with a radiance of their own. They ran up his wrists, into his jacket. He didn't try to stop them. Four-legged insects with antlers, black eyes, in primary colours.

"I'm going back to my roots," he breathed.

"Typical. I have a piss, you have an epiphany." Vince walked away from him. "You were always seeing things I wasn't."

Only Penny was listening to him as he tramped away, back out of the dell.

IT WAS A WONDERFUL SURPRISE. NOT REALLY A SURPRISE, BUT WONDERFUL. The Dog Man did what he said he was going to do. I love him more than ever. He brought our disguises in from work with him. I have just tried mine on and I look terrific.

Now I'm waiting for him to show me his.

FUCKING FUCKING FUCKING FUCKING FUCKING BLOODY HELL!

It was backbreaking work. Jane had to pull herself across the slanting landscape like a bear on all fours. Her tights were in shreds, she had leaves in her hair, and she was swearing like a bastard. It felt good to have a good swear. When you've got kids you can't swear. You have to pretend that it's only kids who swear.

Fucking fucking fucking nothing! Not a sausage. Not a single scrap of evidence that Nesta hadn't simply shot off to Barbados or somewhere for a while like that Shirley Valentine in the film. Jane had liked that video. She'd watched it with Fran and a couple of bottles of Country Manor one Sunday afternoon. They both thought that whoever wrote it must have known a lot about women and what they have to put up with.

"Don't you wish you could just piss off to Greece then, Fran?"

"I haven't got the guts to do that. Who has?"

Jane got up to wind the tape back. She knocked on the window to stop the kids kicking their ball against the wall. They'd hit the glass three times during the film. You can't watch anything in peace. "But someone must have. That must have been drawn from real-life experience, mustn't it? It looked just like real life."

"I suppose someone must have done it, some time."

Now it looked like Nesta had gone and done it. Maybe Shirley bloody Valentine wasn't all that real after all. It didn't show all her family and friends – even the ones who never liked her much – searching the countryside, rummaging in the bins for her. On the film she had written a letter, she had been clever. Nesta could barely write her name. And everyone knows, film actors and actresses are posh in real life. They pretend to be stupid and common.

"Shirley!" Jane yelled out. "I mean – Nesta!" She sighed out loud. She was so pissed off now that she didn't care any more. From behind some nearby bushes a policeman shushed her.

Oh. Right. They were doing important work, remember. Wanker! Bending up double again, she went on looking, even though it was dark and she wasn't sure what the object was. In a minute I'll look for Fran, offer to take the kids home.

The policeman had sidled over. "Hello," he said.

Fuck off, she mouthed.

"How's it going?" he asked.

"Oh, you know. Nothing as yet, but we've got to keep going, haven't we?" She cursed herself for simpering. She took a good look at the policeman. She didn't like men in uniforms. She'd gone right off bus drivers. And as for that wanker in the camouflage pants next door, playing kids' games... Still, this one didn't look so bad. About thirty-five, pudgy, a nice beard and friendly, squinty eyes.

"When...um..."

"Yes?"

His single *um* prevented any further simpering; it put her straight in pole position. He was obviously being coy. Jane straightened up. God, don't let him be a pervert dressed up as a copper.

"I was thinking, when this is all over, would you fancy coming out for a quiet drink somewhere?"

"With you?" She started looking for the nearest streetlamp. "Oh, right. OK, as soon as we find the dismembered corpse of my best friend in the whole world, then we'll fill in a few forms, get her carted off, and pop off for a quick half and a shag."

She stalked off towards the footpath, the chalky streetlights. He called after her, "I didn't mean it like that!"

"It didn't sound like it." She carried on. People like him just came out with stuff. It was as if they had nothing to cover up. It really narked her. They didn't care how it came out or what effect it had. There were people like that and people who hid the things they wanted. They kept them closer to their hearts because they were scared. Only occasionally were those things, or the ghosts of those desires, brought out for people to see. It was these people who seemed to have the worst time of all. Jane knew.

She saw that Fran and Frank were standing under a streetlamp some way along the path. They had all seven children with them. All of them were crying or shouting or whingeing. Fran and Frank were arguing, sealed against the darkness in their envelope of light; they couldn't see Jane as she approached.

Turning back to the policeman, Jane said, "I want your name, your serial number and your address."

"Why?"

"I'm not sure yet." They stood thirty yards apart, shouting to be heard above the kids' increasing racket. "Write it down and pass me it before I catch up with my friends and my children."

He became cagey and did as he was told. I only asked her out, for Christ's sake. Children, for Christ's sake. No, that's cool. I can deal with someone having kids. "What's this for?" he asked worriedly, squelching down the hill to hand her the note. Jane took it with a smile, looked at it and started walking away again.

She said, "I'm not sure yet whether I'll report you or fuck you. Anyhow, Bob, I'll be in touch."

She picked her way determinedly towards the sodium umbrella of light to rejoin Fran and Frank and Peter and Vicki and Jeff and Lyndsey and Tracey and Kerry and the baby who, Fran was finding, needed changing again.

"LIZ, DON'T MAKE ME BEG YOU."

Cliff was trying to grab her attention from the pinpricks of light on the black ceiling. She ignored him, surveying the fake night sky over the fake Greek fishing village. They were standing on a fibreglass humpbacked bridge, a shallow pool before them.

Clustered around were tavernas bulging with custom, shoppers sucking on bottles of Newcastle Brown. The shops, disguised as peasants' hovels, were closing down for the night: the toy-train specialist, the Egyptian jewellery specialist, and the perfumed pic-n-mix confectioners with the inflatable pink lips stuck in the window.

"I won't make you beg me."

"Good." He relaxed. He looks good in a Greek fishing village, she thought. Even an indoors one. Dead Mediterranean.

"Because I won't give you an opportunity to."

Cliff paused a beat. Suddenly the hollow bridge seemed a long way up. He was looking down on the dusty tavernas from a great height. The family groups, the thirsty pensioners, the lads starting out on a night on the piss – everyone craned their necks, staring at his predicament.

"What does that mean?" He was carrying all their shopping bags. "Yes or no? Will you run away with me or not?"

Liz had decided on a one-syllable reply. She stopped looking at the underbright stars and gave him a brilliant smile.

PETER FLEW INTO JANE'S ARMS AS SOON AS SHE STEPPED INTO THE LIGHT. He was a sensitive child, not used to the racket the others were making. "I don't believe you!" Fran was yelling. "I sent you to buy sweets for the bairns and you came back with bloody Strongbow!"

Frank was very nearly coherent. "I thought it would be useful if we found Nesta. It's what she drinks, isn't it? We could sort of...revive her."

Jane broke in, "She drank Woodpecker anyway..."

"Can we go home now, Mam?" Peter asked at the side of her neck, where his face was pressed. "I've had enough of this now."

"We've all had enough," she said and tried again to intercede but Frank was getting annoyed. "Look, I've put myself right on the line for you and your stupid bloody friend today –"

"She's not my bloody friend –"

"Getting me out of work early an' that. Don't say I don't do owt, 'cause I came straight home when you asked me to."

Fran conceded the point, tried to come back, as did Jane, but Frank continued.

"Gary didn't leave work. That slimy sod didn't offer to help. He'll be buggering up all my good work."

Fran had stopped dead with her mouth open. Frank hammered the point home.

"Yeah, maybe you'd rather be married to someone like that Gary. Someone who doesn't give a shit. But his wife left him, didn't she? Took the kid and left him. So what would you –" He stopped, noticing her expression. "What's the matter now?"

Even the kids had fallen quiet, looking at Fran, who was staring at Jane. At last she said, "Gary. Gary didn't come on the search party."

"Yeah? So?" Frank asked. "He's a wanker."

Fran blinked, looking down as if she had something in her eye. Jane felt she knew something Fran knew, and couldn't figure it out.

"Nothing," said Fran with a brief smile. She took little Jeff's hand. "It's getting really late. Let's all go and find out whether this search is any nearer being called off."

THIS IS SO MUCH BETTER THAN MY WILDEST DREAMS. WE'RE GOING OUT tonight in our disguises.

Then we'll wear our disguises all night, all tomorrow and the day after. By then we'll have forgotten who we used to be. We'll be our new people.

It's going outside that'll do this to us. Inside we could be anyone, anywhere. When there's just the two of us to see. It could just be a pack of lies. We could both be mad, even, and not like real people at all. But not when we go out. When we go out in our disguises, then people will see us.

The Dog Man said, "This will fix our new identities." He means being seen by people outside will make us into what they see us as. I like that. It's all people outside are good for.

That and for giving you bottles of milk. But you have to beg off them. I hate that. I would like to give. It must make you feel great.

Tonight I gave the Dog Man his milk. I put it in a saucer on the top landing. He came to get it and I kicked it away from him. It flew down the stairs, milk all over the carpet. He went away for a bit to be angry.

When he came back he was calm again. He knows he has to be calm. It's in our rules. Then he said, "Let's put our disguises on," and I could see he was excited.

So I said, "All right."

"COMPROMISE, COMPROMISE, COMPROMISE."

"But we always have to compromise." Liz didn't want to argue about it. She slung their shopping into the bag compartment and Cliff, still muttering, eased himself back into the driver's seat. It was dark outside.

Other buses with their blue fridge lights were moving in and out of the station.

People were drifting towards their stand.

"Close the doors," Liz instructed, sitting down. She crossed her legs. The doors shut with a pneumatic hiss. The people heading towards them with their carriers from Burtons, House of Fraser, St Michael and their soggy parcels from McDonald's, frowned in puzzlement. They pressed in closer to see.

"I'm going to be in deep fucking shit over this," Cliff said.

It was the first time she had really heard him swear. He must be under stress, under duress. Bless him. He should try being under a dress.

"We'll ditch the bus in Kendal. On the way."

He looked around, shoulders hunched at the wheel. Someone banged on the doors with a brolly and was ignored. 'But the Lake District, though... we could escape to anywhere...'

Liz had seen his bank statement from the cash machine. He was right but she was firm. "I want to be able to return when I want to. It's escape enough for me."

"But the adventure –"

"Stealing a double-decker bus should be sufficiently adventurous for any man, Cliff."

Muffled shouting could be heard through the glass. 'Are you going to...'

"Now, come on. Let's take off. Or whatever it is you do."

Cliff mumbled something and started the engine.

The queue of pensioners at the bus stop, laden down with their shopping, gaped in disbelief as their bus pulled away and roared off, too fast and in the wrong direction.

"That woman's got a whole bus to herself!" someone cried out. "Who does she think she is?"

Liz gave them all a regal wave.

DETECTIVE INSPECTOR COLLINS MET THEM ALL ON THE BRIDGE. THEY clustered around her, wet, scratched, bruised and depleted in numbers as if she was their teacher on a school nature ramble. She was trying to shake

Tony off. He had been following her around for hours. She called one of her coppers over. 'Take him home and make him some tea.'

"Distraught, is he?" asked the young copper.

"He's getting on my tits." Collins raised her voice. "Everyone. Thanks for all your help. We've got a few more leads to go on, but no real success as yet. We're carrying on through the night and widening the search. I suggest you all go home and get some rest. The TV people and the papers will be round tomorrow to take your pictures and have a word. Thanks again."

"Right," Jane said. "Let's go and buy some more cider."

ANDY WAS LIKE A LOST PUPPY STANDING BY HER GATE.

"Penny?"

She knew what he was about to ask.

They were back in Phoenix Court. All around the dark cul-de-sac there were garden gates slamming shut. The neighbours were calling good night to everyone. Their voices were going out to each other in a way they rarely did. They were checking on each other. This search had got to people. Big Sue had been the first to leave, worn out and emotional. Charlotte from the bungalow said she was going through a crisis of faith and she helped her home. Everyone, in fact, was looking slightly shaken as they made their way back from the Burn.

"I can't go back with Vince tonight," Andy said.

"No..."

Something deadening and awful had been happening to those two down in the woods, too. It was as if they had worn each other down, just in the few days they had been together. Once Vince had left them alone, Andy muttered a few things to her about him. He sounded as if he didn't even like Vince. And me, Penny thought, I don't know Andy at all. He could be anyone. She felt burdened with him.

Up at Phoenix Court the searchers were going in and turning on their lights, their kettles, their tellies. Pressing their doors and windows closed against the night. The sky was an inky blue, a brush dropped in a jar of water. Penny shivered. She was tingling despite herself. That didn't bode well.

Andy asked, "Is there any chance of staying at yours?"

"Sure," she said. She led the way up the path, feeling in her bag for the key.

Andy felt awful about this. Penny didn't know him from Adam.

Penny was saying, "About these creatures you said you saw coming out of the tree..."

There were no lights on. Strange.

He sounded defensive. "What about them?"

Penny stepped inside. "Mam?" The kitchen was dark and bleak, full of scraps and used crockery from the night before.

"I see those animals, too," Penny told him absently. It was something they had in common, so she thought she would tell him. She put the lights on.

"It's all right." Penny smiled, shrugging her coat off. "Do you want coffee?"

"I want a proper drink."

"I wish Vince had passed his booze around out there. He was really hogging it." She went to the dresser and fetched the brandy.

"He can be a piss-head when he likes." Andy snorted. "I can't believe he just stomped off like that."

"Was he really pissed off?"

"Oh, he gets these black moods. Acts like a bastard. When he can't see the good of anything. It's when he thinks he's losing out on something."

Penny was pouring out the brandy. It was only when she saw Andy's eyes had gone wide she realised she'd poured it by magic. "No hands!" she said, with an embarrassed laugh, and passed him his glass. "What does he think he's losing?"

"Me...probably. I dunno. He shouldn't. I'm here when he wants me. I always was."

"So tell me!"

"But he doesn't want me, Penny. Not really. He's just tried to convince himself of that."

She showed him somewhere comfortable to sit. "I think he's in a bad way," she said thoughtfully.

Andy tutted. "That makes me feel a whole lot better!"

"Ring him!"

"Nah."

"Maybe you should."

"I'll see him tomorrow. He'll still be arsey tonight. There's no talking to him."

Penny fingered the stem of her glass, frowning. Her fingernails tingled and buzzed like crazy.

SO THE SKY WAS A VERY DEEP BLUE. A LIGHT NIGHT. LIGHT ENOUGH FOR us to see. We ventured out about midnight. Ventured. That's not my word. Can't you tell? Ventured is the Dog Man's word. We ventured outside, dressed up. The only thing missing was my locket. Elsie and Meg, give me strength – wherever you are.

I'm cold now. But that will pass. Disguises are not for warmth, they're for show. No one has seen us yet. We walk proud, waiting for attention. He rubs his body against me as we walk. He is friendly. Happy. I'm giving happiness to him, just walking like this.

Across the road a woman comes out with her empty milk bottles. Big Sue. I can sense her straining her eyes to see us. We pass by the bus shelter. She slams her kitchen door and the light goes out.

We go for quite a long walk. There's a full moon. I'm on the top of the world, the world moves beneath me. I'm in a film and music plays about me, my smile on the screen. This is how I live now. And forever.

I will go out walking, the Dog Man by my side.

Life is wonderful.

FRANK PUT THE KIDS TO BED. FRAN WAS DRINKING HERSELF DRUNK. PAST midnight he came down to see her and she was staring at the gerbils. 'Are you OK?' he asked, wary of her lashing out. When he saw her like this he wanted to take her up to bed. He wanted her gripping him the way she did, fierce and almost cruel. She burned, deep down. Whenever he reached to touch her cunt it was the hottest he'd ever known. It surprised him every time.

"I've remembered something," she said, and Frank realised that she wasn't of a mind for going up to bed.

"I thought you were going to say that you've killed Nesta yourself, the way you're going at that bottle. What have you remembered?"

"I've given the police wrong information."

"On purpose?"

"I'd forgotten the last time that I really saw Nesta. It wasn't when I chucked her out of the house. It was later on. When we went on our night out. When me and Jane and Liz got on the bus."

Frank took hold of her shoulders, not sure why. "Where?"

"She was in the bus shelter. Just after nine o'clock."

"Catching a bus?"

"No. She was talking to your mate. The army man. Gary."

Frank's grip slipped. "He's not my mate."

"Whatever he is, Frank, it's him. It's got to be him."

"It's got to be him who did what? You're not making sense, Fran."

Now she was on her feet, none too steady in her slippers, her face grey suddenly. "He's taken her away. He's taken her away."

"Fran, Gary couldn't hurt anyone. He's pathetic, you've seen." Frank was almost pleading with her now.

"He said he was going to punch you that time!"

"That was bullshit!"

"His wife left him. Took the bairn." Fran looked stricken. "He was violent with her."

"They gave as good as they got. The pair of them."

"Frank," she took a deep breath. "We never saw his wife and bairn leave. What if he –"

"Stop this, Fran! Just stop."

"I won't stop. What if he's killed them? What if they're dead?"

"Don't be stupid –"

She squeezed her eyes shut and shouted, "I'm not being fucking stupid! Don't tell me that!" She glared at him.

Very quietly he said, "You can't stand me any more, can you?"

"Sometimes," she said through gritted teeth, "no, I can't."

"Right."

"Right now, I want to get this sorted out. Gary's got her, Frank. He's got Nesta. God knows what he's playing at."

"You saw her talking to him. What does that mean? Maybe he's shagging her."

"I hate that. I hate that phrase."

"Aye, well. Probably you can't remember what it means."

"You're a selfish little git, Frank." She headed for the door. "I'm phoning the coppers."

He said, in a tone that sounded almost warning, "Give it a rest, Fran. Come to bed. You're shattered."

"Are you covering up for him?"

"What?"

"Are you covering something up for Gary? You men are always doing that."

"No! I can't stick him!"

She looked at him long and hard. "I'm phoning that policewoman. Then I'll come to bed."

"She'll just say you're daft."

"Maybe. Go and put the leccy blanket on."

PENNY AND ANDY SAT UP LATE TALKING. THEY LEFT THE TV OFF AND RE-arranged the lamps so it was more atmospheric.

"It can't be easy, knowing that you're second best," Penny said, glancing at her watch. She winced at herself. God, that was tactful, Pen. "I mean, knowing that Vince is pretending he wants to be with you –"

Luckily Andy laughed. "God, you make it sound terrible!"

"I don't mean to. You know what I mean."

"Yeah. I'm not what he wants. I'm too fickle. And I'm not clever enough."

"Does that matter?"

"Sometimes it does. Vince needs someone to talk to. I'm not as good at that."

"We're managing to talk."

"Yeah. Well."

'So what are you after, Andy?'

He smiled. "Just something else. Something I haven't considered yet. Some new circumstances to live in. Maybe a new city. I don't know."

"Sounds good."

"What about Scotland? Edinburgh?" He smiled. "A different country.

A short train ride. Big queer scene."

"Smart."

"Perhaps I need to get away. Vince has been and done that. And come back. I don't feel...stretched yet."

The phone rang. Penny was straight on it, as if she'd been waiting.

"Mam?"

"Ehm, yes, dear. It's me. I'm –"

"Where are you?"

"I'm staying away for a little while. It's an impulse thing."

"Right."

"You can look after yourself, can't you?"

"Yes, but where are you?"

"I'm in Kendal at the moment, with Cliff. We're staying here tonight and then we're off to the Lakes for a while. We've got some things to sort out. Don't worry, he's got plenty of money. My cards are in the dresser drawer. Use what you need, dear. You understand, don't you?"

Penny wasn't sure. "Of course I do. Just come back with a tan."

Liz laughed. "It's piddling down in Kendal."

"Give Cliff my love."

"I will. I'll see you...soon. I'm not sure when, exactly."

"Thanks for phoning."

"Bye."

HE SLUNG THE EMPTY BOTTLE OF TEQUILA ACROSS THE DAMP SCHOOL field as he crossed. Where was the worm in the bottom? Before he threw it he looked down the neck as if it was a kaleidoscope and there was no worm. Neither were there glowing tiny animals romping about in the dregs. There were only dregs.

His dad was in front of the gas fire in his chair. It hissed and he hissed and, even smashed out of his mind, Vince thought about his dad expiring in carbon monoxide. He switched the heater off and left him there.

In his room he jammed the door shut behind him and left the light off. Moonlight washed in from above the field and the low, flat school buildings where he was meant to be working. He remembered the gin in his cupboard.

As he started to drink again he peeled off his clothes. He sat on the mattress, naked, shivering, and felt dirty from going all over the Burn. He was scratched and bruised. His shoulders shook.

Disney songs were going through his head. Songs he had on a record when he was little. He could only remember bits of them, all mixed up, and they went round and round.

> I've got no strings...
> You can fly you can fly
> To hold me down...
> it's mother nature's recipe
> you can fly
> you can fly
> as lucky as can be
> can fly can be
> can strings
> I've got no strings to hold me down...

In through his window came the gold and blue figure he had wished for. She was kindly and a bit smug-looking.

"Are you the Blue Fairy?" he asked.

"Aye, pet." She smiled, reaching forward to take the gin off him.

He frowned and tried to focus on her face. At first she looked like Penny's mam. He was holding her close and they were dancing on his mattress, slowly as they had in the nightclub. And then she didn't look like Penny's mam at all. It was his dad. He was dancing with his own dad. But only for a split second. They recoiled from each other.

Lastly the Blue Fairy was Andy's Nanna Jean. Burly and competent.

"I always wanted you to be my nanna," he said.

"I know, pet." She went to his cupboard and fetched down the bottle he had nicked from the taxidermist's. "Here, get this down you."

"What is it?"

"Do you want to be a real boy or not?"

"Yes! More than anything!"

She held out the bottle.

FIFTEEN

SOMETIMES I GET THE IMPRESSION THAT I'VE MISSED SOMETHING. Something has passed me by. For a while I was right on the edge, with the world at my feet. I was on a motorbike, the breeze in my Brylcreem, speeding on the wild side. Some mornings I wake up and I can't believe it isn't 1959 any more.

Vince's dad was spending his morning off in the garage, applying Turtle Wax to his already gleaming Triumph Herald and thinking out his life.

But I've missed something. Something in particular that happened yesterday. Vince came in late last night. He thought I was asleep, but he woke me. I watched him looking at me, turning off the fire. Where was his friend, that Andy bloke? The night before last he was happy enough to see him. Oh, he tried to hide it, but I could tell. I'm not his dad for nowt.

Cliff Richard on the wireless, the tang of wax in the air. It was brilliantly sunny outside, drying everything out. He was in a cheerful mood. Cheerful enough to ponder.

Will I ask him what's up? He'll bite my head off. He can be snappy when he likes. But I should show willing. I saw he had that poster up. I was right after all. But I'm glad.

I wonder what they were up to yesterday. His shoes were left kicked across the kitchen floor, and they were thick with mud. Like he'd been down the Burn. He'll have pneumonia. I *will* ask.

Gone were the days of not asking questions. That was the sure-fire way of letting things pass you by. That was how his wife had gone. When he thought back, it was to very few memories of her. Apart from those in the late Fifties, early Sixties, when she dressed as a Ted to be with him. Once she had stopped being with him and stayed at home, he had taken less notice.

One memory: she smashed all his records before leaving, in 1977. He was left to throw the pieces out. Thick records, heavy as smashed china. He pinned the empty sleeves to the walls. He felt allowed to do that, with the house suddenly his and his alone.

I'll ask Vince what the matter is. Openness and all that. I've missed too much, I think.

ROSE STEPPED OUT INTO THE SUNSHINE, DOLLED UP AND READY FOR THE cameras. It was like the postcard business all over again. She was ready for her public. "This appalling affair...such a nice girl...my daughter knew her very well..." Ethan was waiting at the corner of the street.

"Hello," he said, tottering towards her. "Am I allowed to speak to you?"

Rose was a vision in pink, her personal space scented with Poison. Ethan was damp and filthy. He had spent much of the night hobbling the streets. He sneezed.

"You stupid old bastard!" she cried, seizing his arm. "Where did you go last night?" She wheeled him around, marching him firmly back to her house. The news people would have to wait.

"I slept on the bench by the boating lake. Our favourite spot, Rose."

"It might well be. But I don't want you pegging out on it." She bundled him indoors and started to strip him off in the kitchen. "I'll run a nice hot bath."

"Will you still marry me?"

With a fastidious expression, she picked at his cardigan buttons. "We'll just have to see about that."

Ethan nodded glumly.

FRAN WAS WAITING ANXIOUSLY FOR DINNERTIME. JANE CAME ROUND and surprised her with a Battenburg. But her appetite was gone. Phoning the police with her new information had knocked Fran sick. She could just imagine that Detective Inspector Collins's face; her nasty puckered expression as she was told.

At ten past twelve Frank came back on his lunch break.

"Well?" asked Fran. Jane looked up, mouth full of cake.

"He never came in for work this morning," Frank said. "There's no sign."

"Right." Fran went to the phone.

"What's going on?" Jane asked. The kids were complaining. They weren't allowed to play out today.

"VINCE?"

No reply. Vince's dad knocked on the door again.

Well, if his little friend hadn't come back, there couldn't be an embarrassing scene to walk into, could there? He gritted his teeth against what that last thought meant and what his next action might bring.

He pushed the door open and saw Vince sprawled naked on the mattress, fast asleep. He was lying on his back with his mouth open. The room was brilliant with light.

How can he still be sleeping on a day like this?

With a kind of morbid fascination his father stared at the prone body. Finding out what Vince was had made him different. He wasn't just a son anymore. He was, in a sense, the enemy; they were no longer on the same side. For a second or two, a part of the older man's mind was weighing up the enemy.

His body is like his mother's, was the thought that emerged. Long-limbed, pale-skinned; a light dusting of auburn hair. His penis was large, nestling against one leg, different to his dad's. He doesn't take after me at all. He's bigger that me, even there. I'd never noticed. How could I? So private. So different.

"Vince," he said. "Vince!" He became irritated, went to shake him.

The flesh was cool. Pale and cool, too much like marble. His dad froze, noticing the bottle by the mattress. Not pills, that would be too corny for

Vince. But it happens. Vince's dad remembered Marilyn; where he was and what he was doing when the news came through. He looked at the bottle's label, scared to read. It was handwritten.

"Ethan Nesbit's Special Embalming Fluid."

Pulling his son into a sitting position, he tried to force his fingers into his mouth. The body remained still, but a sickly groan, a belch, fought past his fingers. The heart was still beating. "Vince, what was that stuff? Is it fatal? What?"

The eyes opened and looked at him coldly. "Hospital?" Vince asked and passed out again.

His dad picked him up in an expert fireman's lift and struggled with the suddenly massively heavy body. Vince's soft hair brushed into his face, starting his tears off. He became a man and I never noticed. Who cares what he does with that big cock of his. So long as he's still here.

Vince's dad shouldered him downstairs, outside, towards the garage. The sun struck white flesh, making him gleam.

ANDY WOKE UP IN LIZ'S ROOM AND, AS HE DRESSED, SURVEYED THE contents of her wardrobe in respectful awe. He was trying on a sequinned frock when Penny walked in. Her mouth dropped.

"Quite a woman, your mam," he breathed. "I've only seen her briefly, and not to talk to."

"You mightn't get the chance to now." Penny had brought coffee and cigarettes for breakfast. "I'm surrounded by cross-dressers!"

"Oh, I'm not," he said. "I was just trying it on..." He looked at himself in the mirror. "Looks all right on me, doesn't it?"

She sat on the bed and lit a cigarette. It seemed almost sacrilege to smoke in Liz's tasteful boudoir, but Penny didn't care. There was time for the air to clear. "Yeah. It hangs off you just right."

"Hm." He looked thoughtful. "Would your mam mind if I tried on some more things?"

She shrugged. "Probably. But she's not here, is she?"

Andy asked, "So what happens now?"

"You're welcome to stay while she's gone. It might be a while."

"That would be wonderful. We'd be company for each other."

"Yeah."

"You're really pissed off with her, aren't you?"

"I don't know, Andy. It would serve her right if I filled this house with all the waifs and strays of Aycliffe."

He went mock-indignant. "'So I'm a waif and a stray!'"

"I want to turn the house into a squat," she said. "I'd love that. A big shared house."

"Will she be away that long?"

"Who can tell?" She watched Andy wriggle back out of the blue dress. He was unabashed, standing there in his pants and looking at the rest of the clothes. "Listen," she said. "If you're going to live here a while, I want you to make your peace with Vince."

He sighed. "It wasn't even a proper argument. He was just cross. There was us two, on about bloody Narnia and those little creatures and everything...and Vince couldn't really give a shit. He's not that sort of a person." Now Andy had found the hats and the wigs. "Vince is a realist."

"Get him to come round here." Penny lay back on bedclothes rumpled overnight by Andy. She felt quite comfortable with him now. "We'll throw a party. Yeah, a house-warming. This is going to be my house for a while. I could levitate some objects for everyone's entertainment...and we could invite those creature things round to perform a miniature circus and prove that they exist. I really want to throw a party."

THERE WERE TWO POLICEMEN BY HIS GATE. THREE NEXT DOOR IN JANE'S garden. Two by the phone box. There were two marksmen, two dogs across the road, hiding behind the rosehip bushes.

"Shit!" Fran hissed through her blinds. "I hope I haven't made a horrible mistake."

Jane came to join her. "Better to be safe..."

Behind them Detective Inspector Collins was on her walkie-talkie. She switched it off. "They're all set up. There's no sign of life inside. I'm going to go and knock on the door myself."

Fran nodded. Hand on the doorknob, she glanced around the kitchen at her familiar accoutrements, in these circumstances all of them banal. Frank had a can on the go, slurping worriedly. "Right," she said, and opened the door.

VINCE'S DAD STRAPPED HIM INTO THE PASSENGER SEAT. AS HE DROVE them through town he noticed that the people out in the sunshine were watching. So he put a road atlas over his son to cover him up.

They drove over the Burn, across the big bridge, through the wet, healthy trees, then into the council estates. It was the fastest way on the main road to Darlington, to the hospital. Now he wished he'd phoned an ambulance. He was wobbling all over the road.

Vince was coming to, groaning. His head tipped forward and he vomited on the road atlas. It splashed with a stench of animal. His dad put his foot down.

Down the main road. Down here.

NO ANSWER. DETECTIVE INSPECTOR COLLINS GAVE THE NOD AND STEPPED away from the door. Big John Burns, the biggest copper in the town, came forward. He took a long look at Gary's door, though it was the same as any other council house's door. Everyone held their breath as he gathered his concentration in.

Big John Burns took a few steps down the path and launched himself at the door. The lock cracked.

John followed the door as it crashed inwards, into the dark hallway. Collins found herself dropping backwards, startled, as a huge shape lumbered past Burns. She looked up from the garden path to see a great soundless dog bounding past her. Even the marksmen and the police Alsatians were silent in awe as it burst out of the garden and bolted for freedom.

Detective Inspector Collins stood up and was joined by Big John Burns. "What the fuck was that?" she cried and tore out of the garden to see.

The marksmen followed her, ripping through the rosehip bushes, falling over themselves as they hurried out of patrol cars, coming at last to stand by the main road.

The unnaturally bulky dog was halfway across the road. He was also in the path of a screaming, gleaming Triumph Herald. Before screams could be exchanged, the dog was underneath and the Triumph skidding sideways to a halt.

Everybody froze.

The dog's head had rolled into a gutter. Its other head, its real head, was still on the body, but the body was mangled. The real head was Gary's, the army man's, knocked senseless on the front bumper.

Collins heard sharp footsteps behind, running towards her. A fat woman in a black PVC mac, bleached hair, fishnets and suspenders, furious.

"You've killed him! You've killed the Dog Man!"

Nesta stood clutching a leash.

And behind her: Fran at a run, her family and neighbours running with her. The kids all coming to see the accident, see all the blood.

"Mam!" one of them screamed at Nesta, seeing through her disguise.

SIXTEEN

IT WAS THE WRONG TIME OF YEAR FOR A HOLIDAY. BUT IT WAS A beautiful time of year. It was nearly Christmas.

A fine mist was rising in the valley, forming a wreath sprinkled by the fairy lights of the village. Getting dark, frost setting in.

Liz was standing at the very top, gazing up and then down. She was proud of having conquered vertigo. She wore a heavy anorak, thick trousers, hiking boots. Her toes were cold.

She heard Cliff scrabbling behind her. He thought she must be in a mood. "What did Penny have to say?" he called.

"We missed a good wedding, apparently. We were invited, as a couple, even though we've never met the bride or the groom." She watched her breath crystallise. Cliff came to join her at the top. "God, I feel like Heathcliff," she said.

"But where is he when you want him?" asked Cliff. By now he knew nearly all her jokes.

"The council let them use the two boating lakes in the park. Can you believe that? They used the park in November for the reception. Penny said the bride sat in a yellow canoe to throw her bouquet ashore. She said it was a scream; two pensioners in bridal dress paddling round and round the lake while everyone clapped. We should have been there."

"We should get married."

"Now, Cliff," she admonished, smiling. "You know we can't."

"You," he grinned, "can fool anyone."

"I think we should be getting back."

He was shivering. "You're right. Before it gets pitch black."

"No. I mean home."

"Oh."

"Although it sounds as if everyone's moved in with Penny. That Andy and Vince and God knows who else. Oh, well." She turned to see the way they had walked up. Cliff persisted.

"I was serious. About us getting married. It's all in the eye of the beholder."

"Like that dog thing. Mm. They'd all think I was a woman till I was knocked down in the street and they saw up my dress. Why can't we just stay sinful?"

"So long as we do."

"Fuck the beholder, dear. Look at me. What am I?"

"Wonderful."

"We know that, love. I mean, look at me now. Am I a man or a woman?"

Cliff opened his mouth to speak. Liz was dressed for hiking, in his clothes. The hood was over her face, over her hair. She nodded.

"Imagine I'm by myself. This isn't our town. With no one here to see me I'm neither a man nor a woman. Up this mountain nothing is imposed on me. I like it like that. I get to choose. I get to choose when there's no one else here."

She stepped off the pinnacle and led the way back to the rocky path. "I'm an exhibitionist. I'm a tart. I need to be looked at. But I needed to be here, to be *not* looked at, too."

"But I'm looking at you," Cliff said.

"So you are." They walked on down the hill in silence. "But I'm still not marrying you."

SEVENTEEN

On Christmas Eve the council sends a van round every street in town. The back is twined in fairy lights, daubed in red paint and stuck with cotton wool. One of the bin men is dressed up and seated on the top and he is driven around to say Merry Christmas to all the kids. The kids are let out in their dressing gowns to tell him what they want the next morning.

Vince and Andy and Penny remember this ritual. From Penny's window they watch the kids in their street being taken out. Fran and Frank with their lot, Jane and Peter, Nesta and Tony with Vicki and the baby. Vince and Andy and Penny will never have kids.

Just afterwards, another van pulls up. This is their van. A furniture removal van. They rush out, locking the door behind them.

Ethan is seated in the cab, married now for less than a month, happy to see them, glad of their help. They sit with him in the cab and laugh at themselves. They are off on an adventure.

Ethan parks on the wasteground near the Burn. Near, Penny slyly points out, Narnia. They have a lot of work ahead of them. They realise this when Ethan opens the back of the van and they peer inside by moonlight.

The van is crammed. They take a deep breath and start work. It still takes till after midnight.

When the van is empty and it starts to snow, they all troop down to the magical dell and, with secret, shared smiles, discover their completed handiwork.

The magical dell is full of animals, little and not so little. They are dusted off and, in the brightness of the moon, scabby no longer. No longer shopsoiled and rotting. And all of them are facing away from Narnia. Vince starts to laugh and the others follow.

Ethan, poised on the brink of the dell, ushers them all down. They wander through the maze of little creatures, laughing. Real little creatures are coming out to see the display, glaring wonderingly at the owls, the squirrels, the leopard and snakes. These are false. They shouldn't be here. But they are immovable.

The animals will stay here. The snow that is falling gives them a certain grace; meant to be here. Daubed by the same brush, painted into the same scene.

And the ash tree in the centre of the glade is growing apples. Perversely they grow in threes.

Vince and Andy and Penny start to pick apples, laughing and crunching at the crisp flesh.

NUDE ON
THE MOON

LIZ WAS THE PERFECT PASSENGER. SHE NEVER DROVE, THOUGH ONCE SHE could. She left it all to Cliff and made no suggestions, no criticisms. When he passed her the map, the day they came to the mountains, she looked at it and it was a different language. He was expecting her to tease out their route, but she looked blank. Liz didn't care.

Just go, she said, drive north.

This was two months after leaving home. They still had no aim but getting away. Liz concentrated on not looking back, passing the mints, lighting the cigarettes, and turning the tape over. Forty-one, she thought, and still running away from home.

In a car park between mountains she took advantage of the pause to touch up her make-up. Dabbing grey on to her eyelids in the rearview mirror, she caught sight of the valley they had driven through. It was like she could see all the way back to Avcliffe, the yellow council house and the teenage daughter she had left behind.

She saw her lover Cliff at the edge of the car park, pitching stones into a crevasse. His black hair whipping about in the wind, his shirt sleeves rolled. She hoped no one was down there. Sometimes he was heedless. It was he who had begged her to come away like this. Over dinner in the Around-the-world restaurant under the translucent dome of the Metro Centre. she had at first laughed in his face. "I can't run away with a bus driver!"

"Why not?"

"I have a child to look after!"

"She's seventeen. She'll look after herself." He reached across the table and grasped her hands in his. She felt his legs nudging aside the heaped carrier bags under the table. His knees pressed into hers. "I need you to come away with me," said the bus driver earnestly, and he was so ridiculous Liz had to give in. She was tempted to see if she really could just walk away from her life. And here she was. Up a mountain in January with mist all around the same dove grey as her eyelashes.

But look at Cliff there. He had stolen a bus for her. The bus he usually drove in pointless, intricate loops around Aycliffe and Darlington. One day in November he'd shook both himself and his lover free.

I DIDN'T ASK HIM IF THIS WAS THE HIGHEST WE'D BEEN UP. I THOUGHT IT must have been. He pointed out the moon, how we could see it coming up in the east and I said this was the blackest I had ever seen the sky. Look at the lochs, he said. We'd driven this long way especially to see them and now it was too dark. They had even smaller islands afloat on them, just tussocks of grass clumped in their middles. I said they look like bowls of stew and dumplings, that's what they look like in the night. Cliff didn't laugh. I think he's a real country boy at heart. He comes from Yorkshire and takes nature very seriously. Me and nature...I can take it or leave it. Coming over the glens I just wanted to sleep. You can only look at the yellow moon for so long.

Beside a black cut-out of a perfectly triangular mountain we found a hotel. Cliff had been here before, when he skied. He's sporty, too. I can't. abide anything sporty. This would do us for the night, he said. We could have a proper dinner in the bar. I pulled a face, knowing this meant scampi in a basket with the locals. Probably karaoke. We could take the bridal suite, he added, as we got out of the car. It's right above the bar and quite sumptuous. Bridal suite indeed. As we hurried into the porch of the hotel, I said, don't push it, sunshine.

But I like him sorting things out like this. Though I feel old enough to be his mother, Cliff's taken charge of everything, this trip, my life. Funny I let him.

The foyer was empty and smelled musty. Stuffed Otters. They had those glass cases on the walls, the ones everyone's got up these days, full of dried flowers, fruit and shells. They do them in Ikea. Before I ran away I was thinking of getting some for our hallway, and putting things in them.

DINNER LAST NIGHT WAS IN THE CAR, WATCHING MIST COME OVER THE sea, or a loch or something. I don't know what it was, or how open to the sea we were. I've lost all sense of direction.

We got ourselves a takeaway from the only Indian in Oban. Cliff's been flash with his money. "I'll get this," he always says. Buying this old car in Kendal for cash. And we're eating out every night. This place wasn't cheap. A restaurant with two tables. Two very young couples having an anniversary. "This must be a busy night," Cliff whispered.

Waiting for our food we crossed the main street and walked into the waterlogged grass that fronted the town and met the sea. I was in my heels and soon I was sinking. Mud smarmed between my toes. Cliff laughed at me and I was yelling. I only had about three pairs of tights with me. Back on the road, three or four lads were laughing too, as we traipsed back from the quagmire. That must be all the youth round here had to do, I thought. Stand along the roadside, looking for strangers. It was worse than Aycliffe. "What are you lot staring at?" I cackled as we went back to the Indian. They looked at each other like I was foreign.

I was so hungry by then, I didn't care about mucky feet. I'd make Cliff clean my shoes later. It was his fault.

We got the food and drove off to a picturesque spot across the bay, as twilight came on. We're always seeing sights in the dark.

I used his book of maps as a table mat. That caused a row later. It was too dim in the car to tell, but the brown grease from my Rogan Josh was spilling slowly over a lip in the tin foil tray. It bled into maps, page after page, orange and blotting out the north worst of all. But it was a tricky business eating with a plastic spoon and still managing to appreciate the view. The tinsel of the towns across the bay. Lit-up bed and breakfasts. It was like I had to admire everything Cliff stopped the car to look at. He had his camera with him. He would always say, come on, Liz. Let's get you in, standing next to this view. As if when he had a whole film with me on, it proved we were together. When he finished a roll he went to the first Boots we saw and got it printed in an hour. Me after me after me, in breathtaking locations.

"But I'm not dressed," I would say each time, unklunking and un-clicking my seatbelt.

"Oh, you are," he'd assure me, testing the light.

And of course I *was* dressed for my photo. I always am.

SO THEY LOOK TAKEN ABACK WHEN I WALK IN THE HOTEL BAR ON THE moors. I make an entrance; gold head to foot and shining. That's when I'm at my happiest, when I'm at my least reluctant to face the public. Roped in theatrical jewellery, with golden-heeled slippers and I'm...sheathed, I suppose is the word for it, throat to ankle in gold lamé. Out to dinner in a dress I shouldn't be able to sit down in.

I perch half-on, half-off a red barstool. I light black Sobranies for Cliff and myself as he orders our vodkas. The regulars go back to their darts, the other barman to his cable and satellite magazine.

Cliff tells me it's all right; they don't just do meals in a basket. We can go through and have dinner properly. Sometimes he talks to me like I'm Princess Anne.

IN THE BRIDAL SUITE ABOVE THE HOTEL BARROOM. BURGUNDY FLOCK wallpaper and a baby chandelier. "Like being in a western,' said Liz, twisting her back so he could find the zipper. "Like *Destry Rides Again*." She imagined herself all corseted up with a feather boa laid across her shoulders.

He lifted strands of hair away from her neck. Nowadays Cliff didn't say much when they went to bed. At first he had been chatty, almost hearty, and Liz wondered if that was because he thought she liked that. He was naturally quieter than her. In the car he didn't mind if the conversation died down. He could absorb himself in driving, which he loved. She became aware of how he changed gears, how he popped on different lights in the dark. Everything with great deliberation. Nothing was erratic about Cliff.

Down came her zip with a purr, unsealing the hard shiny fabric of her dress. She tried not to say anything else. Cliff's easy quiet made her tire of the sound of her own voice. That was a new thing for her. Now all she said was, "Here," and turned to undo his shirt. She felt the dark hair on the back of her hand and she grew hard just from that.

He kissed at her neck and then her mouth with hard, bunched, silly kisses. Again and again, like eating soft fruit. He made her laugh and tell him to stop. "Kiss me properly!"

"This *is* proper!" he said and started pecking at her again. "You're making me all self-conscious now."

"*You* self-conscious!" she smiled, because he was the most easy-going man she knew. At garages when he went to pay for petrol, he'd go loping in, holding the door open for anyone who wanted past. She would watch him talking with the girl serving, laughing about nothing. He behaved as if he didn't mind about giving himself away.

When he came back out to the car with Coke and mints and a tub of Häagen Dazs from the garage freezer, he'd still have a cigarette clamped between his teeth. No one told him to put it out. It was as if, because he wasn't concerned, no one else was.

"You worry too much," he told her. "You'll get ulcers."

"Ulcers!" she said. Then she thought about her stomach lined with pale white dots. Like sequins on the inside for a change.

LET'S SEE WHERE THIS GOES. WHY IS IT SOME PEOPLE GET ALL EXCITED? They see a turn-off like this and away they go. Ferreting off into the wide blue yonder.

Liz couldn't give a bugger. She was never much of an explorer. Stick me on the straight and narrow, she says, and I'll not wander far. I like to know what's what. A simple, prosaic soul; that's what she wants to be. Straight up and down.

"Oh, don't be sarcastic."

"I'm not," laughs Cliff, and he isn't. He thinks it's funny Liz like to think herself so normal. It tickles him.

He sees this turn-off which seems to lead nowhere. He wants them to chase up this road into a valley full of 'sharp crests and blind summits'.

"Sums up my bloody life," Liz tuts as they set off, with Cliff peeping his horn when they come upon each blind summit. It's an eerie punctuation to their ride. Eleven miles into the middle of nowhere and then the road simply stops, as if the planner's ink ran out, beside a lake the colour of old pennies.

As they get out of the car, Cliff says, "That mountain looks like two buttocks." He's always seeing shapes in things. Liz puts it down to him growing up on the Yorkshire moors, starved of diversions, bless him. She looks at this mountain.

"Honestly, you're arse-mad, you are," and she snorts with laughter. He thinks she looks like a horse. She looks round and sees only a dilapidated boat house right at the water's edge. "This is what you've brought me all these miles to see? A burned out little house?"

"I thought there might have been more here," he says, and tramps off through the broken shale and granite, looking for somewhere to pee. "You never know what's there if you don't look."

To Liz the boat house looks like where a maniac would drive with a transit van full of prisoners. His victims would be found butchered up months later. It's a landscape made for maniacs, this.

ALL THE PLACES GET TO BE THE SAME IN THE END. ONE NIGHT, WHEN they had set themselves a hundred miles to travel before they slept. Liz said, "Look for a phone." She wanted to call her daughter. Sometimes she would get impulsive like that.

They stopped in a village and Liz bundled out, into the phone box. Cliff sat watching her as she talked in that column of light. She was squinting at the houselights opposite, the pub lights, the closed shops. Liz was thinking: people live here; a place I might never come to again. These are people I will never meet. It made her feel perplexed, that she could dash through like this and use their phone, even if it was a public box.

In bed last night a similar thought had struck her. She mulled over all the beds where she'd fucked with Cliff just once. It seemed cavalier of them. It made her feel they were she trying very hard to keep the novelty up, under bedspread after bedspread and never the same one twice.

On the phone that night Liz's daughter sounded non-plussed. Nothing had changed at home. "She can be ever so surly," Liz sighed as they drove and left the village behind.

Cliff knew better than to add anything. He twizzled the radio on to a station with a request show for ninety-year-olds. Organ music from the 1920s. 'The Sun Has Got His Hat On'. After a while they sang along.

IT WAS ONE MORNING WHEN THEY LEFT ANOTHER OF THEIR BREAKFASTS that Liz said you could soon sicken of not having your own place.

"You can't exactly rest your bones in someone else's house. Not properly. I'm always on my guard."

Cliff was manoeuvring the car down the sharp zigzag back to the main road. He snapped, "When are you *not* on your guard?"

She pursed her lips, deciding not to tell him about this morning. He thought it was odd that the woman from the B&B let them see themselves out. When she told them to just leave the cheque on the breakfast table he marvelled at her trust.

The B&B woman had said, "I must dash. I've got a dress-making class starting at ten. I'm so silly I forgot!" She hurried out in a flap and Liz and Cliff listened to her engine revving in the driveway. They stared at the table. Cliff said, "I hope I haven't blocked her in the driveway." But he hadn't, and they watched her car hare across the bay.

Who has a dress-making class at ten o'clock in the morning? Liz thought. But she didn't say anything.

They had found the bungalow in the dark last night. It had a fine, wide picture window overlooking the bay, and they could see the woman sitting at her desk, under a green-shaded lamp. She was doing her accounts in a houndstooth jacket and a white blouse with ruffled collar. All the bungalows here did B&B, Cliff said. When summer came they cleaned up with passing trade. That's what we are, thought Liz gloomily, just passing trade.

SEVERAL YEARS BACK CLIFF HAD LIVED ON THIS PENINSULA, DOING manual work on somebody's estate. "It's such a close-knit community, with everyone looking out for each other. I wonder if they recognize me still!"

So far no one had. It amazed Liz that he wanted so much to be recognized here: in the petrol station, the post office and by this B&B woman. When at home, in Aycliffe, everyone knew Cliff by sight, because of his being on the buses. He had gained the easy appreciation of all the women Liz knew. She bet they still talked about him even now. What was so special about the people here?

When this woman let them into her bungalow — and it wasn't *that* special inside — Liz felt condescended to. Her hackles went straight up. The B&B woman looked her up and down, as if she thought she was too dressed up for a car journey. Liz felt like a mad woman, or someone kidnapped.

"I've a double room, or a room with twin beds."

"Double," said Cliff with a smile as Liz made her way to the door marked 'bathroom'. The B&B woman called after her: "We turn the 'occupied' sign over on the door when we use the bathroom. That way we *know*. And when we leave we open the window for the condensation. All right?"

Liz smiled and slammed the door after her.

Cliff put all their bags in the double room. The bed was very high up. He was sitting on it when Liz came back. "All right?"

She rolled her eyes. He went into the living room, to be sociable.

Liz looked at a shelf of books by the bed. Everything Dick Francis had ever written and seven years of the *Reader's Digest*. She picked one out and sat down on the two laid-out towels, pink and blue. *On Top of a Glacier*. She should be getting out her night things. She could hear Cliff mumbling away, asking about people here. The B&B woman recognized him at last. She said how last year had been bad for deaths. The weather came in and picked the oldies off. Someone's twins had been in a road accident. The roads were atrocious. One of the twins had died and Cliff said that's the one he'd been friendly with.

Liz changed into a black dress. Nothing too showy. She went through.

"Will you have some tea or whisky before you go?"

Cliff was saying they'd go for a drink down in the village, so he could show Liz where he'd hung out for a year. The B&B woman added, "I don't always drink whisky by myself, you know." She tilted her wine glass, full to the brim with gold. "Only when I'm doing my accounts." She chuckled.

"Ha!" laughed Cliff, over-eager, and Liz shot him a glance.

In the car Cliff said, "She didn't remember me at all." He waved vaguely at the picture window.

"Should she?"

"She used to come and cook for the old bag I was working for. I remember being in the kitchen once and she was being made to cook lobster 'the correct way'. She was bullied into it."

They got on to the main road. Liz didn't want to go for a drink, but anything to get out of the B&B. "What was the correct way?"

"Cut it in half lengthways, while it's still alive. Rubber bands around its pincers, or it have your fingers off. Then shove the two halves under the grill while it's still twitching. The old bag insisted and her from the B&B did it."

All the way to the village in the dark — another pub I'll never go to! Someone else's local — Liz thought about Cliff watching the B&B woman gritting her teeth and splitting a lobster into neat halves, the knife grinding down on the wet shell.

SHE SLEPT BADLY, EVEN THOUGH THE AIR WAS SO HEALTHY. EVEN THOUGH everyone round here said how it was gloriously peaceful. She lay awake and watched Cliff, who always went off like a light. Liz didn't even have anything to read.

They hadn't made love tonight. She didn't know which room the B&B woman slept in or how close within hearing range it was. Liz knew she and Cliff were noisy. "What does it matter?" he complained. "We're paying her thirty quid!"

Liz tutted. In the middle of the night she had to go to the loo. Cliff stirred. "You know me," she said. "My bladder holds as much as a dessert spoon." When she climbed off the too-high bed she couldn't be bothered searching in the bags for her kimono, or anything else to cover herself. Let the dark be enough. So she crept into the hallway in a pair of pants.

She stood a moment, readjusting to the moonlight. There was a noticeboard with a map of the whole area, plastic pockets full of leaflets to do with walks and nature. Fancy someone putting all this stuff up in their own house. It was to be helpful but Liz thought it was weird. Like playing at schools. A thermometer thing on a card was pinned to the map; a universal scale reader, whatever that was. You were meant to take it out of the plastic, read your scales, and put it back. Everything on the noticeboard looked like it had rules attached.

Liz opened the bathroom door.

There sat the B&B woman, on the toilet, in her slippers with her nightie pulled up round her midriff. She was holding the *Reader's Digest* at arm's length.

Liz jumped back, shocked. But the B&B woman looked more shocked. She stared.

Liz without her wig. And in nothing but her pants.

At first the B&B woman simply didn't recognize her house-guest. She saw a nude intruder. A skinny little man in black clingy pants. Not a stitch of hair on his pale body.

Then their eyes locked and the B&B woman knew she was looking at Liz.

They both heard the distinct plop as the B&B woman finished her nocturnal business. Liz slammed the door and hurried back to the room, her heart playing merry hell. As she flung herself under the heavy duvet, all she could think was: that woman didn't keep by her own rules. The 'occupied' sign wasn't turned round.

SO THE NEXT DAY THE B&B WOMAN RAN OFF TO HER DRESS-MAKING class. She couldn't face me, Liz thought, with a peculiar satisfaction.

She made herself up carefully at the old-fashioned dressing table. Crocheted antimacassars stood under everything, protecting the wood.

When she sat down to breakfast everything was out and ready. Liz ate some new kind of bran. Hard little brown balls. She ate sausages with mustard from Arran. Cliff had black pudding and she imagined kissing him later, pretending he hadn't had sticky pig's blood on his teeth. She kept eating, suddenly hungry.

"Get your money's worth," said Cliff, smiling.

Everything was laid out properly. Milk in a jug, even salt in a dish, with a tiny silver spoon. "What's this?"

He sighed. "I can't believe you've never seen a salt spoon before."

"A salt spoon," she muttered derisively and popped it into her pocket. "I want to go now," she said and stood up. She looked around. "Fancy sharing your home with strangers."

The B&B woman had explained she'd take just about anyone in. She wasn't prejudiced, though she'd had some bother with Italians. They shouted from room to room and the walls here were paper thin.

Liz said, "The next time I live somewhere that's my own, I won't let any strangers in. It'll just be for me and who I want."

"What's the matter with you?" Cliff said.

Liz shrugged. "Sometimes I feel like private property."

IT WAS WHERE THEY HAD THEIR FIRST PROPER ROW; SOME SORT OF National Park, crammed with wonders. It wasn't quite in public, but close enough. There were other couples wandering around the shaded, composty paths, and they all looked National Trusty, nature-loving couples, all in walking boots with leaflets open and pointing at things. Liz was embarrassed to be heard shouting by them.

"We didn't pay the two pound to get in," was how it started, Liz looking back at the people on the trail behind them. They were slotting coins into a perspex box on the gate.

Cliff tutted. "I'm not paying to walk round some old garden."

"It's a done-up garden," said Liz, sounding sullen even to herself. Small ponds were cut into the lawn, kidney-shaped and swarming with livid orange, shoe-sized fish. "You'd complain if someone climbed on your bus and didn't pay."

"That's different."

"I don't see why."

He grunted and they headed for the trees. "Anyway," he said. "Scotland's different. In Scotland you have the right to walk anywhere. It's not the same as England. No one can tell you to get off their land."

"I didn't know that."

"They think it should all be public."

"Well," said Liz.

In the woods it smelled damp. It smelled like something left in a fridge to go off. They left the path — oh, foolishly! Liz warned herself, thinking of Red Riding Hood — and Cliff went striding ahead. The mossy ground, springy and treacherous, made Liz's heart sink as, once more, her shoes got filthied up. "You keep dragging me out to terrible places!" she muttered. She watched his back as he wove and ducked through the trees. His beautiful back incensed her. "I mean, what are we doing here? Looking at trees!"

"I like looking at trees," he said.

They came to the edge of the woods, where the ground dropped away and there was the sea, suddenly. Cliff was kicking at the vast, upturned roots of a fallen tree. They were ripped apart, as if in a terrible storm. Broken shards of bark and blackened wood stood up in nasty spikes. "This looks like lightning," said Liz with a shudder.

He shook his head. "Just frost." He pointed to clearly cracked-open rocks tangled in roots thick as his arm. "Water in cracks in the rocks freezes and the whole thing bursts open."

"You always know everything," she said, turning away. "You can be too practical you know. It gets on people's nerves. I still say it was lightning."

"Well, you would."

She raised an eyebrow. There was a bench so you could watch the sea. Liz swished over to it, and Cliff followed.

"Didn't you tell me some story about you being struck by lightning once?" he asked.

Liz eyed him. "I remember," he said, sitting beside her. "You said you were holding your Penny at the time. She was a baby and you were outside—"

"In a car park," Liz prompted.

"—in a car park, and lightning struck you...and that's why you turned into a woman!" He sat back on the metal bench, stretching out his legs with a chuckle.

Liz had gone red, but her voice was very cold. "You're simplifying that just a bit."

Cliff laughed. "You make things sound so sensational. It's ridiculous." He shook his head. He realized what he thought Liz was like: a comic book superhero. Each superhero had an origin story that they flashbacked to, telling you how they ended up like that. The She Hulk was bathed in green radiation. Spider Woman was bitten by a radioactive spider. Liz got struck by lightning. What did she become? *Woman* Woman.

"What's ridiculous about it?" Liz was shrill suddenly.

He sighed. "Lightning can't give you ideas about a thing like that! You just made it up! You make everything up!" He stood up. "You know what I think?" He was baiting her now.

Liz saw one of the couples with proper leaflets and boots coming through the gap in the trees, and she shushed Cliff. The intruders looked mortified at disturbing the row and they backed carefully away.

"What do you think?" she asked through gritted teeth.

"You can't face the truth of any of it. You make up all these over the fact of your own decisions."

"Oh, really?"

"You can't face it, so you dress it up like fate, like everything changed in a flash of light."

"Cliff," she said "You understand nothing."

"I understand that you think you're the Queen of bloody Sheba, and the laws of the universe run different for you."

They both fell quiet at this. Liz was shocked by his bitterness.

"Have I been getting on your nerves?" she asked.

Cliff glowered. "All you go on about is leaving Newton Aycliffe behind, about how I've taken you away from everything that's yours." He sighed. "You make me feel like I've dragged you off and made you a rubbish bargain."

"Cliff," she said. "It's been wonderful, this trip. I've loved it. It's just not..."

"It's not real life, is it?"

When they walked back through the park they started to notice the brighter flowers that hung from some of the trees, looking tagged on like Christmas decorations. Amazing this far north, this time of year. Obviously a well-cared-for garden. Liz dropped some change in the box as they left.

In the car Cliff said, "Do you want me to take you home?"

She stared at the windscreen as it started to rain. "Don't know, Cliff." She pulled a face into her mirror. "I don't think so."

I TRIED TO TELL HIM I NEEDED A ROUTINE. IT DOES ME NO GOOD NOT knowing what's coming next. That sense that you are free to do anything depresses me. Because in the end anything that free has to be boring. Life made up minute-by-minute makes me sad. It's like being old or mad or with nothing to do. Cliff never agreed. Cliff with nothing to do was like a child.

My Aycliffe routines. I loved them even though I didn't know it. How's about that for a sad, small life? But it's only when I'm stranded in the mountains, looking at bigger skies than I've ever seen, that I start to appreciate...I don't know. Getting the Road Ranger to the town centre. The tantalizing Cliff taking my money, punching my ticket. Belting round the supermarket, filling a trolley. Fresh bread and sausage roils from the bakers. Picking up shiny magazines in Stevens. Sitting in the Copper Kettle and gassing with whoever I see there. Swanking through the precinct and knowing that I — more than anyone there — am looking drop dead.

Here there's no one to see me but Cliff and is it awful to say this? He looks less tantalizing driving a car than his bus, when it was scandalous to talk too much with him. The sign by his head warned his passengers not to address him when he was driving. So we stared at the sunburned nape of his neck, his dark curls sweated down on the skin.

I've got him and don't know what to do with him.

HE POINTED OUT THAT IT COULD BE THE COUNTRYSIDE THAT WAS GETTING her down. "You're not one for open spaces."

He took them to Glasgow, where the rain kept up and the turn-offs into town confounded them. The middle of the city was like being in canyons. They parked and hunted the car boot for an umbrella.

"Full of holes," Cliff muttered and chucked it. They went by the town hail. Elkie Brooks was on posters outside.

"Pearl's a singer..." said Liz reflectively.

"We could go and see her if you liked," Cliff said.

They found a bar instead.

WHENEVER CLIFF COMES CITY HE WANTS TO KNOW ABOUT THE GAY scene. It's funny but I can never be bothered, really. It's the same old thing wherever you god. Smell of poppers, dance music, old fellas sitting round.

It's not something I'm used to but Cliff likes it and so I go.

This bar we're in, Friday teatime, is like a barn and filling up already. I'm forty-one and sitting in a bar where the only words in the song they're playing that I can make out are, 'Tie me up'. If I wasn't in a frock, would I look like the other, older men here?

Cliff has a theory about me and gay bars. If he believed in it, he wouldn't bring me to another one, but he does anyway. He says they are the places I look less real. Is it because of strobe lighting? My make-up looks put on with a shovel. Once he said I had this mask on. When he said it my face could barely move. My eyes felt like holes cut into an egg shell. My clothes feel over-dressy, but that's not me trying to look smart, me trying to outshine. It's me sending up the idea of wearing women's clothes. That's what it looks like when you put me here. That's what, I think, Cliff's trying to say. Here, everyone can tell I'm a man.

No one has to look twice. Of course I'm going to hate a place like that. The scene unwomans me.

THE ROOM THIS TIME IS SMALL. WHEN THEY OPEN THE WINDOW FOR more air the noise of the rain is too fierce. It bounces off the glass and soaks into the golden, velvety curtains.

Liz lies her slimmer, paler body over her lover's and wriggles herself as if into him. His cool knees press against her sides and how secure she feels. Her palms rest flat on his stomach. So hard, like a carapace, like the red, cooked shell of a lobster. Imagine sliding your lover under the grill.

And what else did he say — that expert — about cooking a lobster?

She stirs, wondering what to do with him next. Their eyes lock over his body and they pause. Seconds creep by.

He said you have to keep their claws still with elastic bands, or they'll cut you to ribbons. They'll nip your vitals off. And here is Cliff, flat on the mattress, trussed up with the belts from both their dressing gowns. His wrists are bound and lashed to the door handle of the en suite bathroom. How he loves to be beyond control like this.

Liz looks him over, gives the smooth, rosy skin of his rib cage a cautious lick. She savours the bouquet of their mingled smells and pulls both their cocks together in one hand.

She's almost delirious with tiredness because once again they've been awake most of the night. In hotel rooms and B&Bs they've taken to watching late movies, one after another. Tonight in this fuggy Glasgow hotel room they've seen *Queen Christina*. Garbo dressing in a velvet Robin Hood suit in snowy old Russia, being a pretend boy to woo a Spanish nobleman. Playing Cesario to his perplexed — until he sees her breasts — Orsino.

As they make love Liz thinks about the film. She looks far away. Cliff has noticed that this is what she's like, in the seconds before she comes. When she does, her sperm shoots past him, falls on the pillow case with a loud crackle in his ear. Cliff comes at the exact same moment she does. He always does. Somehow, like spies, they've managed to get themselves synchronized.

He lies quiet and waits for Liz either to untie him or wipe him off. He feels covered, as if someone has painted him with the stuff. Jackson Poilocked, he rests with Liz's slight weight keeping him down. He stares at her thin chest and torso. The plump nipples and the odd swelling of her pectorals, almost like an adolescent girl. As if Liz's gender is changing course through sheer force of will. He knows she is off the hormone treatment. Liz stares down at him, with one fingertip smearing sperm into his hairy stomach, like Nivea.

I DREAM SOMETIMES WHEN I HAVE SEX, SHE THINKS. THAT'S NOT TO SAY I get bored and make things up to pass the time. Nor does it mean I've fallen asleep and these are real dreams. And I don't exactly mean those all-too-brief flashes of utopian insight you might get on the way to coming with someone. I don't exactly mean that, but it's similar. It's just funny, what goes round your head when you're making love.

I saw Cliff in red and gold soldier's braid, in a horrid woodland, banging on a tree under which he knew a witch lived. She had a home tiled in black and white, well below the stinking forest floor, its roof tangled in tree roots. She showed Cliff the three dogs guarding the three pots of treasure — gold, silver and copper. And the dogs had eyes in ascending sizes; eyes the size of dinner plates, of cartwheels, of round towers. I thought, how does she fit such vastly-eyed hounds in her underground home?

As Cliff thought about stealing the treasure and winding up with the beautiful princess — which was me, of course - I was coming to the realization that it was *The Tinder Box*, the story I was thinking of.

Cliff took both of us in his hands to make us come; seeding up, making the red tender flesh inside the skin appear, then disappear. Now you see it, now you don't.

I saw the nude princess strapped to the back of the dog with the biggest eyes. Baying at the yellow moon, he pelted through the streets of the city; obeying the soldier, his new master. And no one from the princess's family ever saw her, or could find her again.

That was the dream I was going over.

Cliff says that, during sex, all he ever thinks about is whether he's doing it right. He says he can't stop it. And there's me supposing he's all easy and unselfconscious. He tells me how he thinks over what we're doing. Afterwards he narrates it all back to me. I think it's just an excuse to talk dirty to me.

Bless him.

IT RAINED THE WHOLE TIME THEY WERE IN GLASGOW.

They went to the Versace shop and made each other try things on. Liz always found herself marvelling at Cliffs perfect shape. She liked to show off for him. She marched him into their poky, minimalist dressing rooms, and out again, in a variety of improbable outfits. Clothes just hang off him, she thought. He looks so nonplussed.

A display dummy fell and almost crushed somebody's child while they were there. The mother was off chatting to her friend and, before she knew it, the kid had pulled this metal thing down on himself. Liz managed to pull him away just in time.

The woman looked a bit spacey as she thanked Liz, then Cliff, then Liz again, and she pulled her toddler to her. Cliff dragged Liz out into the street before she gave the woman a piece of her mind.

"Careless people like that," Liz ranted, "shouldn't be allowed to have kids."

He looked glum. "I'm careless."

IN ANOTHER GAY BAR FOR LUNCH — CLIFF WAS FINDING THEM EVERYWHERE — they were playing Karen Carpenter's long-lost solo LP.

"She should have sung a song with Elvis," Cliff said.

"That would have been something." Liz looked round. The bar was dark and full of flashing games machines. Karen Carpenter's voice made Liz feel sad, and vaguely guilty for being hungry and looking through the menu. She was pleased Karen managed a year away from her drippy brother for her own music. At least she had that time away.

"Just think," said Cliff. "As Elvis was getting fatter and fatter, Karen Carpenter was getting thinner and thinner."

"Maybe he was eating her."

"That's horrible!"

"I wish I hadn't thought of that." She shook her head to clear it. "Look, can we go to a *normal* bar one in a while?"

"What's wrong with this?"

She sighed. "It's like the Cantina scene in *Star Wars before* they farted it up."

"I thought we were escaping from the straight world."

"Well, that's ridiculous. That's like saying we're into the universe of anti-matter. Life's not like that."

He had *BOYZ* magazine open on the table. it showed a map dotted with all the queer hotspots. It was an alternative Britain. When they re-entered England tomorrow, as they planned to, it would be according to this map. Heading down the west coast; to Blackpool, then across to Manchester. You could plan your life and never go near the straight world again. Suddenly Liz felt queasy.

"Everything's about having a good time," she said thoughtfully.

"Yeah?"

"I mean, it's what we used to call the nite life. Everything on this map is about the nite life."

"Don't sound so disapproving," he said. "*We* met in a seedy nightclub, remember."

"I know, and I wouldn't be without it, but...you can't you do at night!" She burst out with this too loudly and the people at the next table looked up.

Then their food came and the next thing was that Liz had a headache because of the dim lights. It could have been any time of the day or night in lighting like that, which is flattering to the over-forties, but it always killed Liz's eyes.

THEY SET OFF THE NEXT MORNING. THE WEATHER WAS LIFTING.

Cliff said, "Anyway, when we get back to England it won't all be fun and games. We need money. I'll have to get some work."

"Doing what?"

"Some kind of labouring thing, I suppose."

She watched the countryside flash by. They were heading to some gay B&B in Penrith he'd read about.

"I don't know where all the money's gone," he said. "We've just been chucking it away."

"Yes," she said. Talk of money always filled Liz with dread. Being asked what she did with money was like being asked what she did with time. They both just vanished. That's how life went by. Best not keep count. She'd never balanced a cheque book or kept a diary in her life.

"You're very quiet," Cliff said.

"I was just thinking, I never have anything to show for what I spend."

He laughed. "That just means you've had a good time. You've blown it all."

She smiled. "People are jealous of people like you," he added. "You don't worry about blowing it."

"Everything vanishes," she said.

WHEN WE LEAVE SCOTLAND, MORE PICTURES AT THE BORDER.

A twelve-foot column of rock on a hill marks the change, with the names of the countries it divides chiselled either side. Cliff wants to photo me pointing at the names. This is where we've been.

A woman with an accent you can't pin down is boiling hot dogs and pouring cups of tea in a caravan. She's got a plastic headscarf on, keeping down her wispy hair, because the wind manages to reach right into her van.

We are about to be served when from behind us a little old man shouts out that he wants two bacon sandwiches, but he's ot queueing in the cold. He'll wait in his car with his little old wife. Then he sees he's pushed in on us.

"Sorry, honey," he shouts to me across the car park. "Ladies first."

BARGAINS FOR CHARLOTTE

EACH STREET ON OUR ESTATE OF YELLOW BOX HOUSES HAS A SMALLER box somewhere in it and these are bungalows for old people. They never look happy. In the street just down from us a car tore through the wall of their bungalow because it was right on the main road and they go mad on that corner. The car screamed through the itchyback bushes and bang: killed the old bloke inside on the spot. He'd been sitting watching daytime TV. Those walls must be held up with nothing.

Do the pensioners inside know the sort of danger they inhabit daily? Is their irksomeness excused by that knowledge of the threat of sudden, arbitrary demolishment?

Charlotte lives at the end of the row and she has nothing to complain about. Her bungalow is nowhere near the main road and her garden is smashing, nothing like the poky bits of concrete we've all got. You get all the perks if you're old. They put you on the phone for nothing. She had lovely flowers out all the year round, it seemed. She used to get a man in to do that, but now her garden arrangements have changed. Her garden is, if anything, even more sumptuous.

We always reckoned she must have quite a bit stashed away. Her husband had been someone, they said, and she still had an accent. Not posh but a bit southern, which marked her out. She played hell when the bairns went near her windows.

Think of a tortoise with white, flaccid skin and its shell crowbarred off. Charlotte to a T. You'd see her silhouetted in her french window of a night in her orthopaedic chair that swivelled round and we used to say she'd put herself back in for the night. She had one of those dowager's humps and we'd think it was wet and adhesive beneath her cardigan, fresh from the shell, lobster pink.

She never had tortoise hands — those are like elephants', aren't they? Though her fingers were oddly short, as if she'd worn them to the bone, working. Old, she still worked, in the Spastics Society shop down the precinct. Those short fingers had crossed my palm with copper once, when I was about ten — Hallowe'en 1980. We were running from door to door wearing bin bags and asking for money. Charlotte made a big show of looking for her purse in all her kitchen drawer, asking me about my family. She seemed genuinely concerned about them, making me worry whether I wasn't concerned enough. Her questions placed them in peril, I felt. She hoped, she said, that my mummy and daddy would sort out their problems soon and that it wouldn't affect me too deeply.

Back home, later, I counted up my carrier of coppers and told my mam this in an offhand manner. She went up in blue light. My dad and she were living in different places, he at one end of the estate and she, with us, at the other on a social fiddle. The council had given him a single person's flat by the shop and the Chinky. We went over to hoover and dust every Saturday morning. His shared front door faced the grass at the back of the Chinky and I found heaps of discarded pink shrimps. For a while I thought they'd been rained, the way they said things got rained in *The Unexplained*, that magazine.

Mam said Charlotte was a nosy bitch.

Charlotte has worked down the Spastics shop for years. In there it always smells of washing powder and sweat. They arrange second-hand clothes on chrome stands in order of colour. In spring everything to the front of the shop is yellow. They fill the window with chickens made out of woolly pompoms. These are made by Charlotte, all winter long. Sits in her orthopaedic shell through the devastating cold days, when she lets the younger volunteer lasses do the earlier shifts, and she runs up furry lemon chickens. I bet it's a lonely thing being old on our estate. Even if they do put your phone line in free.

They're all pensioners who work in the Spastics shop down our town. Is this because they have more hours to fill in? When you are old, life has shrunk horribly to nothing and its warp and weft can't be pulled back to a decent size, no matter how much you tug. Surely in those circumstances you want to wring the best you can out of what's left? How can giving it all to charity constitute the best? An overflow, if anything, a by-product of pleasure: you can give leftovers to charity, but the main action?

I'd ask Charlotte if she was as selfless as this. Why does she put on that red nylon pinny in the morning to stand behind her counter doling out bargains, oddments, other people's discarded crap?

Would she admit 'I get first dibs on the decent stuff'?

My goodness, the bargains!

The things people do away with!

They don't know when they're well off. I tend to be in there quite often. I like to look at books because they get quite a good, eclectic selection. There's always somebody literary dying in Aycliffe and their goodies wash up here. I became addicted to checking out the Spastics shop after finding *Anna Karenina* for fifty pence. But on every stiffened yellow page, can I inhale someone else's last gasp? It's a wonder if I can't. Intellectuals always smoke and these books are preserved with a laminate of nicotine. I think, Was this the book dropped from a dying grasp? This, the last sentence read? Look: I've read on further!

I'm educating myself to leave.

You really have to poke about, between Cartlands and Macleans, to find the good stuff. But it's there. *Jane Eyre* - thirty pence.

I heard Charlotte speak quite sensitively to Ashley, a seven-foot-tall transsexual who models her hair on Liz Taylor in *Cleopatra*. She'd been hanging on to some special heels for her. They were a kind of present for after Ashley's op. I was in the day Charlotte produced them from under the counter; but they were lime green. Ashley's face just dropped and she left the shop without buying anything at all. Charlotte was furious and took a perverse delight in telling the rest of queue behind that the woman who'd just left had once been a man.

She collected handbags for one daft old wife, Sonja, who always wore a wig, though hers was for cancer, a beehive ever on a tilt. Sonja said, "It's forty-seven now! Forty-eight with this one, ta very much, Charlotte! And every one a different colour. I'd have a different bag to go with every outfit I could ever have!" Daft Sonja looked up at Charlotte again and Charlotte blinked those steady, judgemental eyes. "Thank you, Charlotte. Would you keep a watch out for one in baby pink?"

Charlotte nodded tersely, regal arbiter of justice for cast-offs.

Expert, she sat each morning in the back room of the shop with her pot of tea and barrel of digestives (in the shape of Dougall, the dog from *The Magic Roundabout*) and for an hour or more she would go through the bags newly hauled in for redistribution. In the dusky half-light she would gut the plastic bin bags. They'd spill and strew like a trawler's nets. Turning stuff over in her hands, she'd inspect it, unfold and refold garments, giving them a good, careful sniffing. She counted the pieces in jigsaws and, in case one or two were missing, kept a spare, useless one to the side of her to make up the numbers. It all went with her job and her perk was first refusal and the chance to set a price on whatever she didn't care to offer the public.

She found an earthenware pot of gold coins. At first it looked like somebody's urn of ashes. Somebody, perhaps, whose treasured books were stacked in boxes close by. But the pot jangled inside and she heaved and grunted at the stuck lid until it popped free and the gold poured out on her lap.

"How much is here?" Charlotte cried, although she wasn't a greedy woman. She was careful and always had been. Her widow's pension went on the extravagant food she had delivered from Marks and Spencer of a weekend. Their white and green van pulled up beside her bungalow on Saturday mornings and Charlotte laid out a banquet for no one but herself. Seen in silhouette by the rest of our street. All of it would be out, uneaten, in the bottom of her wheely bin by Sunday morning. Sometimes we'd sneak a look: check. Miss Havisham. (*Great Expectations* - forty-five pence.)

Her needs were met. They weren't always outrageous. But a whole pot of gold! Who'd turn their nose up at that?

"But what is it worth?" asked Charlotte of the bags and boxes of detritus, the heaps of semisoiled clothing, the single stuffed rocking donkey. "What's the going rate for gold?"

And she saw, sitting astride the donkey, a human skeleton, bracing its frail weight on the felt saddle, gazing at her with terrible blank sockets. Its skull was disproportionately large. This was a baby's remains, rocking steadily on the donkey.

"I don't know what they give for gold," said the child. "These days." Charlotte blinked, for now it was a fully fleshed child, chubby and brown, its head full of tangled curls. "But think, Charlotte: if you bought this pot and took it home, wouldn't you lie awake and worry?"

She never worried. It was a point of honour with her. Her face clouded. "Worry about what?"

"Even though your garden is wonderful, your bungalow is still ever so delicate. How easy for somebody to huff and puff and blow it in! How easy to take away your crock of gold! They leave rainbows behind, you know, for thieves to follow."

Lips pursed, Charlotte was writing out a tiny label for the pot, '20p', and sticking it to the lid, which she had replaced. Really, it was an ugly thing. Ethnic-looking. No pattern on it or anything, no flowers. She shrugged, not to be put off.

"I'm not one of these silly old women who keep money and valuables vulnerable in the home and get murdered in their beds for it. My mattress isn't stuffed with fivers. I'd get these gold coins down to the bank at the first opportunity."

The child had small wings flapping, but these were featherless and thin: dead sycamore leaves. "You might lose the gold coins on your way to the bank." The child smiled. "Wouldn't you fret that the gold shone through your pocket or your bag and everyone would know what you were carrying? Wouldn't you feel exposed?"

Charlotte was quick. She'd been a junior-school teacher once. She knew something about answering children back. "Then I'd carry my gold in the urn. You can't see it shine through the urn, can you?"

She held up the nondescript pot in the meagre light of the room's flyblown lamp. The child squinted. "I can," he said. "And what if the bank tricks you, gives you only half the gold's worth?"

"I can check the exchange rate," said the old woman vaguely.

"Did you look at the coins? Aren't they strange and old? Perhaps, for all they may look like gold, they are useless here and now? Mightn't they excite suspicion and cause the bank people to point their fingers at you and jab at their alarm buttons?"

Charlotte had heard enough. She left the storeroom clutching her new pot and paid for it down in the shop, wrapping it and putting it away in her bag before anyone could inspect it.

But that night she walked home nervously across the Burn. She imagined that every stranger she passed could see through her shopping bag and knew about her treasure.

The next day was Saturday; there was no going to the bank. She had her usual banquet and the only person she saw all day was the cheery delivery boy from Marksies in his green and white van. He came up the garden path with her usual boxes of luxury items. Charlotte startled him this time with a tip. He careered off in the van a little wildly, she thought, dangerously.

She sat down to her feast with a heavy heart. The pot was in pride of place like a centrepiece at Christmas dinner, surrounded by cakes and dips and asparagus tips, flans and chicken drumsticks and salads busy with colour, stiff with dressings. The urn of gold seemed to exert its own dull pressure on her spirits. "Get rid of me," it urged tonelessly; "I'll bring you nothing but ill fortune. Why didn't my last owner cash me in? Have you thought about that?"

"That's a point," the infant clucked, fleshly again and sitting across the table from Charlotte. "One simply doesn't get lucky like this. Gold coins! It doesn't happen! Not to people like us!"

"Why are you going on at me like this? What do you want?" She was a touch distraught.

The child looked solemn. "Allow me to do your garden. I'd like that."

Overcome, Charlotte stood shakily and went to embrace the child, but she tripped on the rug beneath the table, fell and hit her head.

She came to, feeling dreadful, quite early on Sunday morning. With a throbbing headache she emptied the ruined party food into her wheely bin. While out there she took in her garden. It was looking unkempt by now. Her little man hadn't been round in a while.

She went to bed for the rest of the day, leaving Classic FM playing on the Teasmade by her bed. She mulled over the course her life was taking.

All Sunday she dreamed listlessly of when she was married, to a soldier and taught children and had a garden with roses in the south.

Monday morning she was late in at the Spastics shop. She'd stopped down the Burn on her way and, in a little ceremony, on the wooden bridge, dropped the pot in the water. It hit with a ker-plunk. The water looked exactly like morning sun coming through her full cafetiere. She went to work.

Monday morning meant a good deal of new belongings in the back room. Charlotte put on her rubber gloves. This Monday was a little below par, she thought. Or maybe she was disgruntled, throwing a fortune away. She almost wished she was religious; couldn't she have felt virtuous,

She struggled with the clasp of a battered blue suitcase. Picturing the gold scattered on the rocks in the Burn. Those stunted fish nosing at the abandoned coins. There was definitely something inside the case; she had to check.

Not many books this week. Not many bargains for me, she was afraid. (Though she was wrong, I found *Lady Chatterley* - twenty pence. But it was my own copy, donated out of spite by my sister.) And inside the case: heaps of crumbling newspaper. It came onto her fingers like grey pollen and went up her nose. The pages were dated 1933 and a heavy stench came out after all that time: rotten fish and chips. The papers were bundled around some light, solid object and she worked into this parcel, soon discovering the child's skeleton.

SILHOUETTED THAT EVENING IN THE MATTE BLUE WINDOW OF HER yellow brick of a bungalow we could see Charlotte slumped in her swivelling tortoise shell. She watched, rapt, while the child sat up at the smallest of her nest of tables and ravenously ate a meal she had cooked him. His bones were faintly yellowed, slick with plaque.

At last the child finished his first supper for many years, belched, and began:

"I was a child who menaced an old man who lived down our lane. He worked in his garden and I would stand in his gateway, aping his every action in order to annoy him. Cutting grass, pruning hedges, pressing saplings into the earth. I'd take him off for badness' sake. I was only a child. Only learning. And one day he must have had enough because he brought out a sharp knife and I thought, This is it! I've pushed my luck!

"Yet he came nowhere near me. He simply mimed, for my benefit, slashing his own throat, there and then in his garden. Then he went in for his tea, still furious, leaving the knife on the lawn.

"When he returned for a last go at his beds, there he found me, white and slashed in a gleaming pool on his garden path."

"There, there," Charlotte consoled him.

AN EMACIATED CUPID, A STRIPELESS BUZZING BUMBLEBEE HAS SUPPLANTED Charlotte's young man in the garden. You can see the skeletal child hovering about her shrubs in the very middle of the night, if you're coming in late, sneaking round the houses. The child will have secateurs in hand, being businesslike, wearing its ineluctable maniac's grin. But the child is glad of the work. He's handy, too, because his spiritual powers and know-how ward off disasters. So Charlotte hopes she'll never get a van or a lorry through her front-room wall, like that old bloke did. She exists within an enchanted circle of the child's deceit and sups contentedly alone still, on Saturday nights.

PAUL MAGRS
_____

1997

ABOUT THE AUTHOR

Paul Magrs lives and writes in Manchester. In a twenty-odd year writing career he has published novels in every genre from Literary to Gothic Mystery to Science Fiction. His most recent books are *The Heart of Mars* (Firefly Press) and *Fellowship of Ink* (Snowbooks.) He has taught Creative Writing at both the University of East Anglia and Manchester Metropolitan University, and now writes full time.

  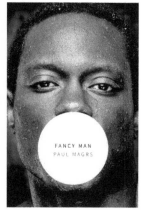

MARKED FOR LIFE

Meet: Mark Kelly – a man tattooed with glorious designs over every inch of his body. He's married to the slightly unhinged Sam and has a young daughter who's about to be kidnapped at Christmas by an escaped convict and old flame of our hero's. Over one snowy festive season the whole family sets off in perilous pursuit... accompanied by Sam's mother, who's become a nudist lesbian and her girlfriend, who claims to be a time-transcending novelist known as Iris Wildthyme...

COULD IT BE MAGIC?

Meet: Andy, a young gay man who finds himself quite unexpectedly pregnant. Andy runs away to Edinburgh to sample the delights of the wicked city and to give birth to a child of his own: one covered in golden leopard fur...

*

FANCY MAN

The never-before-published 'lost' novel that continues in the same inimitable style of Phoenix Court.

Meet: Wendy, who grows up the youngest of three brash sisters in Blackpool and who leaves home when her mother dies. She moves to Edinburgh under the wing of her vulgar Aunty Anne – whose sights are set on the millions her ex-husband has recently won on the lottery. Wendy spends a happy summer finding herself amongst her new family – Uncle Pat, frail cousin Colin, Captain Simon and Belinda, who believes herself to be an alien abductee.

Lightning Source UK Ltd.
Milton Keynes UK
UKHW01f2004270518

323284UK00001B/23/P